CLOCKWORK ANGELS

CLOCKWORK ANGELS

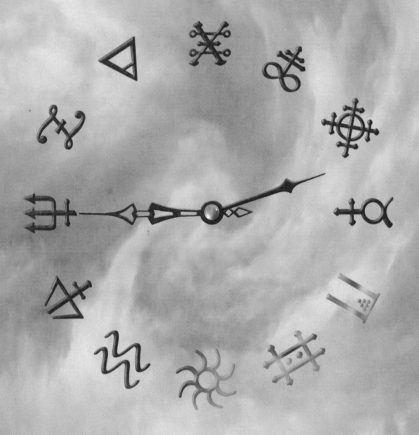

KEVIN J. ANDERSON

FROM A STORY AND LYRICS BY NEIL PEART

Illustrations by Hugh Syme

ECW PRESS

Published by ECW Press
2120 Queen Street East, Suite 200, Toronto, Ontario, Canada M4E 1E2
416-694-3348 / info@ecwpress.com

This is a work of fiction. Names, characters, places, and incidents either are the product of
the author's imagination or are used fictitiously, and any resemblance to actual persons, living or dead,
business establishments, events, or locales is entirely coincidental.

Library and Archives Canada Cataloguing in Publication

Anderson, Kevin J., 1962-

Clockwork angels : the novel / Kevin J. Anderson
from a story and lyrics by Neil Peart.

ISBN 978-1-77041-121-0

I. Peart, Neil II. Title.

PS3551.N373C56 2012   813'.54   C2012-902771-5

Editor for the press: Jennifer Knoch
Cover Design: Hugh Syme
Cover and interior images: Hugh Syme
Text design: Tania Craan
Production and typesetting: Rachel Ironstone
Printing: Friesens 1 2 3 4 5

We acknowledge the financial support of the Government of Canada
through the Canada Book Fund for our publishing activities.

Canadä

Printed and bound in Canada

To Olivia and to Harrison,
who are just beginning all the journeys of a great adventure

Time is still the infinite jest

It seems like a lifetime ago—which, of course, it was . . . all that and more. A good life, too, though it didn't always feel that way.

From the very start, I had stability, measurable happiness, a perfect life. Everything had its place, and every place had its thing. I knew my role in the world. What more could anyone want? For a certain sort of person, that question can never be answered; it was a question I had to answer for myself in my own way.

Now that I look back along the years, I can measure my life and compare the happiness that should have been, according to the Watchmaker, with the happiness that actually *was*.

Though I am now old and full of days, I wish that I could live it all again.

Yes, I've remembered it all and told it all so many times. The events are as vivid as they were the first time, maybe even more vivid . . . maybe even a bit exaggerated.

The grandchildren listen dutifully as I drone on about my adventures. I can tell they find the old man's stories boring—some of them anyway. (Some of the grandchildren, I mean . . . and some of the stories, too, I suppose.)

When tending a vast and beautiful garden, you have to plant many seeds, never knowing ahead of time which ones will germinate, which will produce the most glorious flowers, which will bear the sweetest fruit. A good gardener plants them all, tends and nurtures them, and wishes them well.

Optimism is the best fertilizer.

Under the sunny blue sky on my family estate in the hills, I look up at the white clouds, fancying that I see shapes there as I always have. I used to point out the shapes to others, but in so many cases that effort was wasted; now the imaginings are only for special people. Everyone has to see his own shapes in the clouds, and some people don't see any at all. That's just how it is.

In the groves that crown the hills, olive trees grow wherever they will. From a distance, the rows of grapevines look like straight lines, but each row has its own character, some bit of disorder in the gnarled vines, the freedom to be unruly. I say it makes the wine taste better; visitors may dismiss the idea as just another of my stories. But they always stay for a second glass.

The bright practice pavilions swell in the gathering breeze, the dyed fabric puffing out. That same gentle wind carries the sounds of laughing children, the chug of equipment being tested, the moan and wail of a calliope being tuned.

While preparing for the next season, my family and friends love every moment—isn't that the best gauge of a profession? My own contentment lies here at home. I content myself with morning walks along the seashore to see what surprises the tide has left for me. After lunch and an obligatory nap, I dabble in my vegetable garden (which has grown much too large for me, and I don't mind a bit). Planting seeds, pulling weeds, hilling potatoes, digging potatoes, and harvesting whatever else has seen fit to ripen that week.

Right now, it is squash that demands my attention, and four of my young grandchildren help me out. Three of them work beside me because their parents assigned them the chores, and curly haired Alain is there because he wants to hear his grandfather tell stories.

The exuberant squash plant has grown into a jungled hillock of dark leaves with myriad hair-fine needles that cause the grandchildren no small amount of consternation. Nevertheless, they go to war with the thicket and return triumphant with armloads of long green zucchinis, which they dump into the waiting baskets. Bees buzz around, looking for blossoms, but they don't bother the children.

Alain braves the deepest wilderness of vines and emerges with three perfect squash. "We almost missed these! By the next picking, they would have been too big."

The boy doesn't even like squash, but he loves seeing my proud smile and, like me, takes satisfaction in doing something that would have gone undone by less dedicated people. He feels he has earned a reward. "Tonight could I look at your book, Grandpa Owen? I want to see the chronotypes of Crown City." After a pause, Alain adds, "And the Clockwork Angels."

This is not the same book that I kept when I was a young man in a small humdrum village, but Alain does have the same imagination and the same dreams as I had. I worry about the boy, and also envy him. "We can look at it together," I say. "Afterward, I'll tell you the stories."

The other three grandchildren are not quite tactful enough to stifle their groans. My stories aren't for everyone—they were never meant to be—but Alain might be that one perfect seed. What more reason do I need to tend my garden?

"The rest of you don't have to listen this time," I relent, "provided you help scrub the pots after dinner."

They accept the alternative and stop complaining. How can this be the best of all possible worlds when doing the dishes seems preferable to hearing tales of grand adventures? Of bombs and pirates, lost cities and storms at sea? But Alain is so excited he can barely wait.

Adventuring is for the young.

Ah, how I wish I were young again. . . .

CHAPTER I

In a world where I feel so small
I can't stop thinking big

The best place to start an adventure is with a quiet, perfect life
. . . and someone who realizes that it can't possibly be enough.

On the green orchard hill above a sinuous curve of the Winding
Pinion River, Owen Hardy leaned against the trunk of an apple
tree and stared into the distance. From here, he could see—or at
least imagine—all of Albion. Crown City, the Watchmaker's capital, was far away (impossibly distant, as far as he was concerned).
He doubted anyone else in the village of Barrel Arbor bothered to
think about the distance, since only a few had ever made the journey to the city, and Owen was certainly not one of them.

"We should get going," said Lavinia, his true love and perfect
match. She stood up and brushed her skirts. "Don't you need to get
these apples to the cider house?" He would turn seventeen in a few
weeks, but he was already the assistant manager of the orchard; even
so, Lavinia was usually the one to remind him of his responsibility.

Still leaning against the apple tree, he fumbled out his pocketwatch, flipped open the lid. "It won't be long now. Eleven more

minutes." He looked at the silver rails that threaded the gentle river valley below.

Lavinia had such an endearing pout. "Do we have to watch the steamliners go by every day?"

"Every day, like clockwork." Owen thumbed shut the pocket-watch, knowing she didn't feel the same excitement as he did. "Don't you find it comforting that everything is as it should be?" That, at least, was a reason she would understand.

"Yes. Thanks to our loving Watchmaker." She paused a moment in reverent silence, and Owen thought of the wise, dapper old man who governed the whole country from his tower in Crown City.

Lavinia had a rounded nose, gray eyes, and a saucy splash of freckles across her face. Sometimes Owen imagined he could hear music in her soft voice, though he had never heard her sing. When he thought of her hair, he compared it to the color of warm hickory wood, or fresh-pressed coffee with just a dollop of cream. Once, he had asked Lavinia what color she called her hair. She answered, "Brown," and he had laughed. Lavinia's pithy simplicity was adorable.

"We have to get back early today," she pointed out. "The almanac lists a rainstorm at 3:11."

"We have time."

"We'll have to run . . ."

"It'll be exciting."

He pointed up at the fluffy clouds that would soon turn into thunderheads, for the Watchmaker's weather alchemists were never wrong. "That one looks like a sheep."

"Which one?" She squinted at the sky.

He stood close, extended his arm. "Follow where I'm pointing . . . that one there, next to the long, flat one."

"No, I mean which one of the *sheep* does it look like?"

He blinked. "Any sheep."

"I don't think sheep all look the same."

"And that one looks like a dragon, if you think of the left part as its wings and that skinny extension its neck."

"I've never seen a dragon. I don't think they exist." Lavinia frowned at his crestfallen expression. "Why do you always see shapes in the clouds?"

He wondered just as much why she *didn't* see them. "Because there's so much out there to imagine. The whole world! And if I can't see everything for myself, then I have to imagine it all."

"But why not just think about your day? There's enough to do here in Barrel Arbor."

"That's too small. I can't stop thinking big."

In the distance, he heard the rhythmic clang of the passage bell, and he emerged from under the apple tree, shading his eyes, looking down to where the bright and razor-straight path of the steamliner track beckoned. The alchemically energized road led straight to the central jewel of Crown City. He caught his breath and fought back the impulse to wave, since the steamliner was too far away for anyone aboard to see him.

The line of floating dirigible cars came down from the sky and aligned with the rails—large gray sacks tethered to the energy of the path below. There were heavy, low-riding cargo cars full of iron and copper from the mountain mines or stacked lumber from the northern forests, as well as ornate passenger gondolas. Linked together, the steamliner cars lumbered along like a fantastical, bloated caravan.

Cruising above the rugged terrain, the linked airships descended at the distant end of the valley, touched the rails with a light kiss, and, upon contact, the steel wheels completed the circuit. Coldfire energy charged their steam boilers, which kept the motive pistons pumping.

Owen stared as the line of cars rolled by, carrying treasures and mysteries from near and far. How could it not fire the imagination? He longed to go with the caravan. Just once.

Was it too ambitious to want to see the whole world? To try everything, experience the sights, sounds, smells . . . to meet the Watchmaker, maybe work in his clocktower, hear the Angels, wave at ships steaming off across the Western Sea toward mysterious Atlantis, maybe even go *aboard* one of those ships and see those lands with his own eyes . . . ?

"Owen, you're daydreaming again." Lavinia picked up her basket of apples. "We have to go now or we'll get soaked."

Watching the steamliners roll off into the distance, he gathered his apples and hurried after her.

They made it back to the village with fourteen minutes to spare. At the end, he and Lavinia were running, even laughing. The unexpected rush of adrenalin delighted him; Lavinia's laughter sounded nervous, not that a little rain would be a disaster, but she did not like to get wet. As they passed the stone angel statue at the edge of town, Owen checked his watch, seeing the minute hand creep toward the scheduled 3:11 downpour.

The clouds overhead turned gray and ominous on schedule as the two skidded to a halt at Barrel Arbor's newsgraph office, which Lavinia's parents operated. The station received daily reports from Crown City and words of wisdom from the Watchmaker; her parents, Mr. and Mrs. Paquette, disseminated all news to the villagers.

Owen relieved Lavinia of her basket of apples. "You'd better get inside before the rain comes."

She looked flushed from exertion as she reached the door to the office. Grateful to be back on schedule, she pulled open the door with another worried glance, directed toward the town's clocktower rather than the rainclouds themselves.

With his birthday and official adulthood approaching like a fast-moving steamliner, Owen felt as if he were standing on the precarious edge of utter stability. He had already received a personal card from the Watchmaker, printed by an official stationer in Crown City, that wished him well and congratulated him on a happy, contented life to come. A wife, home, family, everything a person could want.

From the point he became an adult, though, Owen knew exactly what his life would be—not that he was dissatisfied about being the assistant manager of the town's apple orchard, just wistful about the lost possibilities. Lavinia was only a few months younger than him; surely she felt the same constraints and would want to join him for the tiniest break from the routine.

Before she ducked into the newsgraph office, Owen had an idea and called for her to wait. "Tonight, let's do something special, something exciting." Her frown showed she was already skeptical, but he gave her his most charming smile. "Don't worry, it's nothing frightening—just a kiss." He looked at his watch: 3:05, still six more minutes.

"I've kissed you before," she said. Chastely, once a week, with promises of more after they were officially betrothed, because that was expected. Very soon, she would receive her own printed card from the Watchmaker, wishing her happiness, a husband, home, family.

"I know," he continued in a rush, "but this time, it'll be romantic, *special*. Meet me at midnight, under the stars, back up on orchard hill. I'll point out the constellations to you."

"I can look up constellations in a guidebook," she said.

He frowned. "And how is that the same?"

"They're the same constellations."

"I'll be out there at midnight." He quickly glanced at the clouds, then down at his pocketwatch. Five more minutes. "This will be our special secret, Lavinia. Please?"

Quick and noncommittal, she said, "All right," then retreated into the newsgraph office without a further goodbye.

Cheerful, he swung the apple baskets in his hands and headed toward the cider mill next to the small cottage where he and his father lived.

More thunderheads rolled in. The day was dark. With the impending rainstorm, the town streets were empty, the windows shuttered. Every person in Barrel Arbor studied the almanac every day and planned their lives accordingly.

As Owen hurried off, sure he would be drenched in the initial cloudburst, he encountered a strange figure on the main street, an old pedlar dressed in a dark cloak. He had a gray beard and long, twisted locks of graying hair that protruded from under his stove-pipe hat.

Clanging a handbell, the pedlar walked alongside a cart loaded with packets, trinkets, pots and pans, wind-up devices, and glass bubbles that glowed with pale blue coldfire. His steam-driven cart chugged along as well-oiled pistons pushed the wheels; alchemical fire heated a five-gallon boiler that looked barely adequate for the tiny engine.

The pedlar could not have picked a worse time to arrive. He walked through Barrel Arbor with his exotic wares for sale, but his potential customers were hiding inside their homes from the impending rain. He clanged his bell. No one came out to look at his wares.

As Owen hurried toward the cider house, he called out, "Sir, there's a thunderstorm at 3:11!" He wondered if the old man's pocketwatch failed to keep the proper time, or if he had lost his copy of the official weather almanac.

The stranger looked up, glad to see a potential customer. The pedlar's right eye was covered with a black patch, which Owen found disconcerting. In the Watchmaker's safe and benevolent Stability, people were rarely injured.

When the pedlar fixed him with his singular gaze, Owen felt as if the stranger had been looking for him all along. He stopped clanging the handbell. "Nothing to worry about, young man. All is for the best."

"All is for the best," Owen intoned. "But you're still going to get wet."

"I'm not concerned." The stranger halted his steam-engine cart and, without taking his gaze from Owen, fumbled with the packages and boxes, touching one then another, as if considering. "So, young man, what do you lack?"

The question startled Owen and made him forget about the impending downpour. He supposed pedlars commonly used such tempting phrases as they carried their wares from village to village. But still . . .

"What do I lack?" Owen had never considered this before. "That's an odd thing to ask."

"It is what I do." The pedlar's gaze was so intense it made up for his missing eye. "Think about it, young man. What do you lack? Or are you content?"

Owen sniffed. "I lack for nothing. The loving Watchmaker takes care of all our needs. We have food, we have homes, we have coldfire, and we have happiness. There's been no chaos in Albion in more than a century. What more could we want?"

The words tumbled out of his mouth before his dreams could get in the way. The answer felt automatic rather than heartfelt. His father had recited the same words again and again like an actor in a nightly play; Owen heard other people say the same words in the tavern, not having a conversation but simply reaffirming one another.

What do I lack?

Owen also knew that he was about to become a man, with commensurate responsibilities. He set down his apples, squared his shoulders, and said with all the conviction he could muster, "I lack for nothing, sir."

Owen got the strange impression that the pedlar was pleased rather than disappointed by his answer. "That is the best answer a person can make," said the old man. "Although such consistent prosperity certainly makes my profession a difficult one."

The old man rummaged in his packages, opened a flap, and paused. After turning to look at Owen, as if to be sure of his decision, he reached into a pouch and withdrew a book. "This is for you. You're an intelligent young man, someone who likes to think—I can tell."

Owen was surprised. "What do you mean?"

"It's in the eyes. Besides," he gestured to the empty village streets, "who else stayed out too long because he had more to do, other matters to think about?" He pushed the book into Owen's hands. "You're smart enough to understand the true gift of Stability and everything the Watchmaker has done for us. This book will help."

Owen looked at the volume, saw a honeybee imprinted on the spine, the Watchmaker's symbol. The book's title was printed in neat, even letters. *Before the Stability*. "Thank you, sir. I will read it."

The stranger turned a dial that increased the boiler's alchemical heat, and greater plumes of steam puffed out. The cart chugged forward, and the pedlar followed it out of town.

Owen was intrigued by the book, and he opened to the title page. He wanted to stand there in the middle of the street and read, but he glanced at his pocketwatch—3:13. He held out his hand, baffled that raindrops hadn't started falling. The rain was never two minutes late.

Nevertheless, he didn't want to risk letting the book get wet; he tucked it under his arm and rushed with his apples to the cider house. A few minutes later, when he reached the door of the cool fieldstone building where his father was working, he turned around to see that the old man and his automated cart had disappeared.

"You're late," his father called in a gruff voice.

Owen stood in the door's shadows, staring back down the village streets. "So is the rain"—a fact that he found far more troubling. A crack of thunder exploded across the sky and then, as if someone had torn open a waterskin, rain poured out of the clouds. Owen frowned and looked at the ticking clock just inside the cider house. 3:18 p.m.

Only later did he learn that the town's newsgraph office had received a special updated almanac page just that morning, which moved the scheduled downpour to precisely 3:18 p.m.

CHAPTER 2

We are only human
It's not ours to understand

Bushels of apples sat in the cool, shadowy interior of the cider house, patiently ripening to soft sweetness. Owen and his father were scheduled to press a fresh half-barrel that afternoon, which would require at least three bushels, depending on how juicy the apples were.

A flurry of ideas distracted Owen as he helped his father with the work, manning the press machinery, adjusting the coldfire to keep the steam pressure at its appropriate level. As assistant manager of the orchard, Owen had already learned every aspect of the apple business. While going about his rote tasks, he pondered the mysterious pedlar, and he longed to page through the book the man had given him. As if that wasn't enough to preoccupy his thoughts, he was even more distracted by the promise of a romantic midnight kiss from Lavinia while the stars looked down—it was like something out of an imaginary story.

His father, Anton Hardy, formed his own, entirely incorrect, explanations for Owen's daydreaming. Indicating the cider press, he said, "Nothing to worry about, son. I've trained you well. Very soon now, you'll be able to manage the orchards as well as I do, in case anything happens to me."

Owen took a moment to piece together where the comment had come from. "Oh, I'm not worried." He decided it was easier to accept his father's conclusion than to tell him the truth. "But nothing's going to happen to you. Nothing unpredictable ever happens." He glanced at the book he had set on top of a fragrant old barrel. "Thanks to the Stability."

"I wish that were so, son." A surprising sparkle of tears came to the older man's heavy eyes, and he turned away, pretending to concentrate on the hydraulics connected to the apple press. The comment must have reminded Anton Hardy of his wife; she had died of a fever when Owen was just a child.

He'd been so young that his memories were vague, but he remembered sitting on her lap, nestled in her skirts—in particular, he recalled a blue dress with a flower print. Together, she and Owen would look at picture books, and she'd tell him wondrous legends of faraway places. Though he was now grown, he still looked at those treasured books, and often, but Owen had to tell himself the stories now, for his father never did.

Anton Hardy preserved his memories of his beloved Hanneke like a flower pressed between the pages of a book: colorful and precious, yet too delicate ever to be taken out and handled. Even though Owen knew she was dead, in fanciful moments he preferred to imagine that she had merely faked her fever so she could leave the sleepy farming town and go off to explore the wide world. "On my way at last!" He imagined her adventuring even now, and one day she would come back from Crown City or distant Atlantis, filled with amazing stories and bringing exotic gifts. He could always hold out hope. . . .

His father sniffled, muttered, "All is for the best," then topped off the fresh-squeezed cider in the half-barrel. He hammered the lid into place with a mallet.

While Anton completed a few unnecessary tasks around the cider house, Owen seated himself near one of the small windows, which provided enough light to read. *Before the Stability* was a compact volume full of nightmares, and the young man grew more and more disturbed as he turned the pages.

The world had been a horrific place more than a century ago, before the Watchmaker came: villages were burned, brigands attacked unprotected families, children starved, women were raped. Thievery ran rampant, plagues wiped out whole populations, and isolated survivors degenerated into cannibals. He read the stark accounts with wide eyes, anxious to reach the end of the book, because he knew that Albion would be saved, since everyone was now happy and content.

He skipped ahead to the final page, relieved and reassured to read, "And Barrel Arbor is a perfect example of what the Stability has brought. The best village in the best of all possible worlds, where every person knows his place and is content." Owen smiled in wonderment, glad to know that, despite his daydreaming, his situation here could not be better.

His father didn't ask him about the book. They shared an early supper of crisp apples (naturally), cheese from the widow Loomis, bread and a slice of fresh apple pie from Mr. Oliveira, the baker. The Hardys provided him with all the apples he needed, and in return they received regular supplies of apple pie, apple tarts, apple muffins, apple strudel, and whatever else Mr. Oliveira could think of.

The two didn't have much to talk about—they rarely did. Attuned to each other and attuned to the day, Owen and his father looked at their pocketwatches at the same time. They had finished the scheduled work and were satisfied by their casual meal. Afterward, Anton Hardy had his evening routine, and Owen tagged along. They headed for the Tick Tock Tavern.

In a small village, the most efficient way to hear the news was to listen to gossip, and the best place to get gossip was in the tavern.

Anton Hardy sat back in his usual wooden chair, drinking a pint of hard cider, while Owen sat beside him with a mug of fresh cider. Others preferred intoxicating mead made from the Huangs' honey, harvested from the town apiary that followed the standard design distributed by the Watchmaker's own beekeepers.

When Owen turned seventeen, he would switch to drinking hard cider, because that was expected from an adult. (In truth, he had already sneaked a few tastes of hard cider, even though he wasn't supposed to. He suspected his father knew, but hadn't said anything.)

As the tavern customers settled in to their routine, Lavinia's father came in with his stack of typed reports and announcements, which were delivered by resonant alchemical signal to the news-graph office. Mr. Paquette—a man who took great pride in his lavish sideburns—held a yellowish sheet of pulp paper up to the lamp of coldfire light and squinted down at the uneven typewritten letters. Conversation quieted in the Tick Tock Tavern as Mr. Paquette drew out the suspense.

He adjusted his spectacles, cleared his throat, and spoke in a voice that carried great importance. "The weather alchemists announce that this afternoon's rainshower is to be delayed by seven minutes, in order for the moisture-distribution systems to run more efficiently." He shuffled his papers, seemed embarrassed. "Sorry, that came in this morning."

Picking up the next newsgraph printout, he read, "The Anarchist planted another bomb and ruined a portion of the northern line, disrupting steamliner traffic. Fortunately, the airship captain was able to lift his cars to safety just in time, and no one was hurt." The people grumbled and made scornful comments about the evil man who was singlehandedly trying to disrupt the Watchmaker's century-long Stability. Mr. Paquette continued, "The Regulators closed in on the perpetrator just after the explosion, but he escaped, no doubt to cause further destruction."

"The devil take him," Owen's father said.

"Hear, hear!" Others raised their pints in agreement.

Owen drank along with them, but asked, "Why would anyone want to ruin what the Watchmaker created? Doesn't he know how dangerous the world was before the Stability?" He had known that much even before reading the pedlar's book.

"He's a freedom extremist, boy. How does a disordered mind work?"

"It's not ours to understand," Mr. Oliveira said. "I doubt the monster understands it himself."

Mr. Paquette cleared his throat loudly to show that he had not yet finished reading the news. He picked up a third sheet of pulp paper and raised his eyebrows in impatience until the muttering had quieted. "The Watchmaker is also saddened by the loss of a cargo steamer fully loaded with precision jewels and valuable alchemical supplies from Poseidon City. The Wreckers are believed to be responsible."

More grumbling in the tavern. "That's the third one this year," said Mr. Huang.

Little was known about the Wreckers, the pirates and scavengers who preyed on cargo steamers that sailed across the Western Sea to the distant port city of Poseidon. These ships carried loads of rich alchemical elements and rare timekeeping gems mined from the mountains of Atlantis, all of which were vital for the services provided by the Watchmaker.

"I'll bet the Anarchist is in league with them," Owen said. "They all want to cause disruption."

"The Watchmaker will take care of it," said Mr. Paquette with great conviction, setting aside the sheets of paper to emphasize that he was stating his own opinion rather than reading a pronouncement from the Watchmaker. "They will get what they deserve."

"But how do you know that?" Owen said in a small voice.

His father nudged his arm. "Because we believe, son—and you were brought up to believe. Everything has its place, and every place has its thing." He looked around at the others, as if afraid they would think he was a failure as a father for letting his son doubt. "And I'll believe it myself to my final breath."

Everyone agreed, louder than was necessary, and toasted the Watchmaker.

As the evening wound down, he and his father spent a few quiet hours in their cottage. Anton Hardy sat by the fire with a sharpened pencil and his ledger, going over how many barrels of fresh cider were to be delivered, how many would remain in storage to ferment into hard cider, how many were reserved for vinegar, and how much the Watchmaker allowed him to charge for each. Every villager had a role to play, and all accounts balanced.

Finished, Owen's father set the ledger aside and began reading the Barrel Arbor newspaper, which was little more than a weekly compilation of newsgraph reports from Crown City, thought-provoking statements from the Clockwork Angels, and a few local-interest stories that Lavinia's parents wrote and appended to each edition.

The current issue had an early announcement of Owen's impending birthday, to which Mrs. Paquette had added a small comment, "And we hope to have more substantial news to report on this matter soon." By tradition, of course, his betrothal to Lavinia was more than likely.

Owen had already read the newspaper and was more interested in looking at the well-thumbed volumes he had taken down from the high shelf. Reading *Before the Stability* that afternoon had disturbed him, but these other publications were dear to his heart, the picture books he had loved as a child: beautiful hardbound volumes with tipped-in chronotypes, color plates specially treated with a reactive alchemical gloss that gave the reader a giddy feeling of looking *into* the image.

First, he paged through the picture book of Crown City, dwelling on the poignant chronotype of the Angels, the most famous symbol of the Watchmaker's ordered world. Four graceful female figures installed in Chronos Square, looming high above the crowds—symbolic, yet utterly perfect, divine machines who spread their wings to dispense grace on humanity. Though he could barely remember his mother, Owen was sure that each of the four Clockwork Angels must have been molded with her face.

The second volume was even more inspiring, though none of it was real. Legends of sea monsters and mythical beasts, centaurs, griffins, dragons, basilisks . . . and imaginary places far from Albion, including the wondrous Seven Cities of Gold, collectively called Cíbola. These volumes were so old that they had been printed before the Stability; after reading about the chaotic times in the pedlar's book, he considered it a wonder that any publication had survived that turmoil.

Owen was so intent on the book that he didn't notice his father standing behind him. Anton Hardy had never forbidden his son from looking at the books, but neither had he approved of the young man's fascination.

Startled, Owen tried to close the cover, but his father reached out to stop him. In the vivid chronotype on the page, sunlight gleamed through an exotic rock formation in the Redrock Desert. Together, the two stared down at the fanciful pristine towers of intricate stone, the amazing architecture of the Seven Cities of Gold.

"These were your mother's books. And I miss her, too." Anton Hardy held his hand on the page for a long moment, staring down, but no longer seeming to see the illustration. "I miss her, too," he said again in a faint voice, barely a whisper. "Ah, Hanneke . . ." Owen had never heard such emotion in his father's voice before.

The emotion was gone as quickly as it came. "Soon enough, it'll be time to put away these books for good, lock away that part of the past. The Watchmaker says we can't make time stand still. Don't look back, but take the time to look around you now."

"But it's all we have left of Mother—these books and our memories."

"You have to look forward," Anton said. "Once you become an adult, the Watchmaker has expectations. You must put all this foolishness behind you."

Owen closed the book but kept it on his lap. In his quiet, ordered world, he'd never been allowed any "foolishness" in the first place.

His father turned the coldfire lanterns down to a comforting glow. "Time to wind the clocks." Before getting ready for bed, the two went through their ritual. Owen turned the key in the mantle clock and wound the spring; his father did the same with the kitchen clock. Owen hung the counterweight and set the pendulum swinging in the main grandfather clock. They went from clock to clock, shelf to shelf, room to room. As a final check, Owen poked his head outside and looked at Barrel Arbor's main clocktower to verify that the time was accurate and every tick was right in the Watchmaker's world.

Each night, this was time he and his father spent together, but because they took such care to maintain the clocks, they didn't actually *spend* the time at all: they saved it. Not one second was allowed to slip away.

When they were done and his father was satisfied, he bade Owen goodnight. "I'll stay up just a little longer," Owen said. He usually did.

Saddened by the reminder of his lost wife, his father didn't object to letting Owen look at the picture books some more.

Sitting alone, Owen's pulse raced as he thought of his planned foolishness for midnight. Only two more hours before he would slip out and meet sweet Lavinia for a stolen kiss. Although he knew it would be over in a moment, the memory would last for a long time.

After he turned seventeen and the rest of the Watchmaker's safety net wrapped around him, he would have no further opportunity to be so impetuous. He intended to make the best of it.

CHAPTER 3

On my way at last

His father was quietly snoring by 10:06 p.m., but Owen wasn't sleepy at all. Even the synchronous ticking of the clocks in the house failed to lull him. Anticipation was a tightly wound spring inside.

The more he thought about it, the more surprised Owen was by his impulse. What had driven him to suggest it? In Barrel Arbor, decent people didn't sneak out at midnight. He and Lavinia were a comfortable pair who spent most days together doing their assigned tasks, compatible, clearly intended for each other in the scheme of things. None of the villagers gave a second thought to seeing him in the young woman's company, but the two were not yet betrothed, and Owen could imagine quite a scandal if anyone discovered that they were meeting in secret long after dark.

Which made the idea all the more exciting . . .

He hoped Lavinia was as captivated by the thought as he was. This daring little escapade would be something they'd both remember and pointedly *not* tell their children. As they grew older and settled in their lives, who would believe that reliable, predictable Owen and Lavinia Hardy had been reckless or impetuous in their youth? He laughed at the very idea that his own father might have done the same when he was young. But maybe his adventurous mother . . .

He daydreamed that Hanneke had gone off to see the world, that she had visited the Seven Cities of Gold, that she had ridden steamliners and found distant shores. Someday, maybe he and Lavinia would also run off, explore the enticing continent of Atlantis. The thought of his mother still miraculously alive, a queen of some lost country, brought a smile to his face; she would welcome her son and his beautiful wife as a prince and princess. They would feast on hundreds of types of fruit, instead of just apples!

He kept trying to imagine Lavinia traveling with him, but his thoughts wandered off. . . .

He woke with a start and saw by the ticking bedside clock that it was 11:28. Only half an hour before midnight—still plenty of time, but he felt rushed. He pulled on his trousers and gray homespun shirt, took a small sack with two apples, thinking that he and Lavinia might sit together for a while under the starlight. It would be nice if he recited poetry to her, but Owen didn't know any poems.

The door creaked as he pushed it open. He slipped outside, closing it quietly behind him so his father would never know anything was amiss. He made his way up the streets, past the dark cottages and their slumbering inhabitants, beyond the cold and silent racks of the Huang beehives that produced more honey than the village could possibly use. The town's angel statue appeared pale and ethereal under the stars. The night was bright as he climbed the path that led through the close rows of apple trees and reached the top of the orchard hill.

Lavinia wasn't there, although he had hoped she might come early. He checked his pocketwatch—ten minutes until midnight.

The Watchmaker claimed that punctuality was the surest demonstration of love.

While waiting, Owen looked up at the stars, tracing the constellations that he knew from books, but rarely saw for himself. Barrel Arbor villagers got up with the first light of dawn and spent little time outside late at night pondering star patterns. The study of such things, as well as the phases of the moon, the movements of planets, combinations of elements, and magic, was the province of expert alchemist-priests, not simple country folk. The Watchmaker understood the clockwork universe, and he told his people everything they needed to know.

To Owen, the assortment of bright lights in the sky looked distressingly random, so he decided to pick out his own patterns, drawing lines, connecting dots. Were his proposed constellations any less valid than the ones in official books? How did the stars know which patterns the Watchmaker imposed?

He became so engrossed in his own thoughts that he lost track of time. Still no sign of Lavinia. He glanced at his pocketwatch and saw it was five past midnight. With a sinking heart, he gazed through the shadowed orchard, trying to see the path leading down the hill. He heard no one approaching, no swish of skirts as she hurried toward him. Maybe she had overslept.

By 12:36, she still had not shown up. He feared that something bad had happened to her. Her house might have caught on fire! But he saw no flames down in the village. Maybe her parents had learned of her illicit plan and locked her inside. But how could they have known?

He waited another ten minutes, then ventured down the path calling her name in a heavy whisper, but there was no response. No one else was abroad at night. Could she have taken another path? He hurried back up to the top of the hill.

By 1:15 a.m., Owen knew that she wasn't going to come. She had let him down.

The real reason whispered around his ears, though he didn't want to hear it. Lavinia hadn't come simply because *she hadn't*. She had been afraid, or simply unwilling, to bend the rules and break her habits. Now that he thought about it, Owen realized she hadn't taken his bold suggestion seriously at all. Warm and content in her own bed, sleeping peacefully, she probably did not believe that he had been serious. A stolen kiss at midnight under the stars—what a silly idea.

You must put all this foolishness behind you.

In another few weeks, he was going to have to put his dreams away on a high shelf. It didn't seem fair. All his life he had followed the rules. He had done what was expected of him rather than what he wanted; every day mapped out, every event scheduled, every part of his existence moving along like a tiny gear in an infinite chain of other tiny gears, each one turning smoothly, but never going anywhere.

In the distance, he heard a clanging sound, that haunting far-off passage bell, and he turned to see the pillar of steam as a caravan of swollen steamliners chugged out of the mountains, drifting down out of the sky to the rails that followed the river in the valley below.

From the printed schedules, he knew that a steamliner rolled past Barrel Arbor at 1:27 a.m. each night, though he had never been awake to see or hear it. He caught his breath.

On impulse, just to prove that he could, Owen ran down from the top of orchard hill toward the valley, not looking for any path through the tall dewy grasses. Clutching his satchel of apples, he ran as fast as he could without tripping. He could go right to the rails and watch the magnificent caravan roll by, so close he could touch it.

Even though Lavinia hadn't joined him, he vowed to do *something* exciting this night. What if he never had the opportunity again? What if, when he became an adult, even the very ideas died within him? At least he would see a steamliner up close, and that would be something to remember.

The clanging bell and hiss of steam grew louder as he raced to the tracks. Upon landing on the glowing rails, the train transformed into a narrow stampede of mammoths, a long line of heavy cargo boxes and passenger gondolas lit with phosphorescent running lights, balanced by graceful balloon sacks. A geyser of exhaust bubbled out of the lead engine like the breath of a sleeping white dragon. Steel wheels rolled along the metal lines, and the engines huffed.

As Owen reached the tracks, the sound built like excitement and laughter, energy and applause rolled into one. He stared as the steamliner thundered past. It came from mysterious lands he had never seen, rolling across the landscape toward Crown City . . . which he had also never seen.

He stood transfixed, watching several cargo cars, then a dim passenger gondola filled with the silhouetted heads of sleeping passengers, then more cargo cars. He felt the breath of wind as it rolled past, smelled the steam and sparks and hot metal.

He wished Lavinia were there beside him but knew she would never be. She'd never even think of doing this. His father had shown no interest in watching the steamliners either; they were just a part of daily life, like the sunrise and sunset, coming and going on schedule. *All is for the best.*

Albion was vast, and Barrel Arbor was not. Would he ever see Crown City and the Clockwork Angels? Ever meet the Watchmaker in his tower? Ever sail the Western Sea? Soon he'd have to put away his mother's books, never again look at the pictures. It seemed impossibly sad to him.

As a battered old cargo car came toward him, he saw the shape of a man hanging out of the open door, the silhouette of a head peering out, a waving hand. Owen was startled as the man shouted over the noise of the steamliner, as if he *knew* Owen was there. "Hold out your hand, and I'll pull you up."

He froze. He could get aboard the steamliner! He could ride the rails into Crown City. He could see the Angels with his own eyes, before it was too late.

"I shouldn't," he yelled back.

"But do you *want* to?" the man called, hurtling closer.

The car was upon him, and Owen instinctively—impulsively—reached out to grab the man's hand. The stranger was strong and yanked him off the ground. Owen felt his feet lift away from the siding of the steamliner track, and before he knew it, as quickly as a sudden sneeze, he was pulled up and into the cargo car.

"You did it, young man," said the stranger. "I'm proud of you."

Owen looked back with a dazed feeling, watching as his village rolled away in the distance. The stranger gripped his shoulder to keep him steady.

He couldn't believe he had actually done it, even though he didn't yet grasp *what* he had done. Owen felt the brisk night breeze on his face, as he turned his gaze away from the receding view of Barrel Arbor to look forward, toward Crown City and the future.

"On my way at last," he said.

CHAPTER 4

I was brought up to believe

Listening to the humming thunder of the steel wheels on the tracks, Owen couldn't believe he was riding the rails that had always beckoned him. He laughed out loud—just one quick laugh of astonishment at where he was and what he had done.

Then he drew in a hitching breath, and an avalanche of realization hit him: what *had* he done? Owen's legs went weak, and he slumped to the side of the cargo car. The prickle of excited sweat sent an icy chill along his skin as it evaporated in the night breeze. His heart hammered, not from the danger of climbing aboard a moving steamliner, but from the danger of doing something he knew was wrong.

His father had always chided him that his head was so full of pointless dreams that he had no room left for brains. Yes, Owen had prayed just to get away, but that had been a fantasy, never meant to be made real, regardless of the strong grasp it had on his heart and his imagination. It was like those stories of mythical dragons and lost cities; he had never believed he would actually *do this*, had never made plans that were anything more than wistful imaginings.

And if he ever did go on an adventure, he had assumed Lavinia would be with him, that they would run off to exotic lands together. Instead, his companion was some stranger who had extended an arm out of the darkness, offering an invitation that Owen hadn't thought quickly enough to refuse. . . .

Panic set in. *What did I just do?*

As the steamliner pulled along, he peered out at the passing shadows and cast a longing glance at the silhouetted buildings, the Barrel Arbor clocktower he could barely see, the slumbering hulk of the orchard hill. His father was already so lonely with his wife gone . . . and now Anton Hardy would have to do the work in the orchard, press the cider, wind all the household clocks by himself. And Lavinia, who had expected to marry Owen (or so he assumed, once they both had their printed cards from the Watchmaker, wishing them happy, stable, contented lives), would be alone, too.

But Lavinia hadn't come to meet him at midnight as she'd promised. . . . *Had* she actually promised, or had that been his own assumption and hope?

So often, the assistant apple orchard manager had buoyed up his days with hope, while everyone else in Barrel Arbor simply had faith that the world was as it should be. *All is for the best.*

But Owen wondered if all *was* as it should be. His father had said he would put away the remarkable books on Owen's birthday. *Put all this foolishness behind you.* To the young man, that meant more than just cutting a fond, last connection with his lost mother—it would lock away his dreams. Owen had never stopped thinking big, and this was his chance, even if it was an accidental chance, to see the wide world. Perhaps *that* was for the best.

He slumped down and looked up through the tattered canvas hood that covered the cargo car, seeing a swatch of constellation-speckled sky through a gap. "On my way at last," he said again.

He remembered his companion—host? fellow traveler?—and blinked at the man, who had been waiting patiently for Owen to settle himself and catch his breath. The stranger had a lean face, a sharp nose, a razor-thin mustache, and a pointed goatee. His expressive brown eyes had a piercing intensity even in the shadows of the cargo car. The man had shrugged down his hood to reveal wavy, dark brown hair and eyebrows of some significance. His traveling clothes looked comfortable but impeccably tailored, much finer than the garb Owen would have expected from a man riding in a dirty cargo car.

"I wasn't planning to do that," Owen said. "I . . . I don't know what to say."

"You can say thank you, young man. Sooner or later you'll realize what I've done for you . . . or, more accurately, what you've done for yourself."

Owen extended a hand, suddenly remembering his manners. "I am Owen Hardy from Barrel Arbor, assistant apple orchard manager." He waited, and when the man didn't speak, he said, "And what's your name?"

The stranger shrugged. "Names are so confining. They put you in a box. I'm *me*, and you can see who I am. I may change later. Why would I want a name to lock me into somebody I once was?" Without asking, the man reached into the satchel Owen had brought aboard and took one of the apples. His left hand was puckered and scarred, the skin angry red in places and too white and waxy in others. The man shifted and hid the burned hand in his sleeve. "We're traveling companions—let's leave it at that. I saw you there, and I knew you wanted to come. So I invited you to join me."

"How could you possibly know I wanted to get away?"

"You were outside at the steamliner track after midnight."

"That doesn't mean—"

"Yes it does, my good friend. You should have been in bed,

ready to get up early in the morning for your everyday . . . *everydayness*. Because you were out where you wanted to be, I knew you were a seeker of freedom instead of an adherent to mundane rules. Maybe I know you better than you know yourself." He raised his impressive eyebrows.

Owen felt flustered. This was the strangest conversation he'd ever had. "I've never heard the Watchmaker's way called *mundane* before."

The stranger took a bite of the apple. "If you've listened only to the Watchmaker and no one else, then there are a great many things you've never heard. Good for you to escape the rules! Now you can go where you want, do whatever you decide to do. All people should be free like that."

Owen swallowed in a dry throat. "That's not what the Watchmaker says."

"This is your chance to break from the past. The devil take the Watchmaker!" said the man, and then laughed at his bravado.

Uneasy, Owen glanced around the cargo car. He realized that the sweet, resinous smell came from stacks of pine lumber harvested from the forests to the north—he had read about them in school, as nothing more than a list of the products and resources from across Albion, but Owen had never visited the dark, tall forests. Sawmills processed the logs into thick boards, and now the lumber was heading into Crown City, where it would be used to construct new homes, new businesses, new . . . everything.

As he settled against the stacked pinewood, looking for a comfortable position, the second half of the realization struck him—not only was he traveling away from the home he had never left before, but he was actually going toward Crown City, the glorious metropolis of his dreams, site of the Watchmaker's headquarters, where the Clockwork Angels graced Chronos Square and gave their magical blessings. The center of the world.

"You've been to Crown City before?" he asked the nameless stranger.

"As often as I like . . . or more often than I prefer."

"What takes you there?"

"Business."

Owen waited, but the man did not elaborate. "Tell me about the Clockwork Angels."

"Wind-up contraptions. Symbols of oppression."

"Oppression! But they're . . . the Clockwork Angels! They're beautiful."

The man took a moment to consider, then admitted reluctantly, "They have some aesthetic merit, and they function smoothly enough. But to worship them because the Watchmaker activates them and lets them deliver pre-printed announcements? People believe such nonsense."

Owen was no longer comfortable riding beside this odd, intense man. "But that's our loving Watchmaker!"

The man's voice dripped with scorn. "Yes. He loves us all to death."

"But . . . we've had more than two hundred years of peace and stability."

"Yes, the Stability. A statue has stability. A living creature requires freedom." The stranger finished his apple and hurled the core out through the open door of the cargo car. Owen had only one left.

He drew his knees to his chest and wrapped his arms around his legs, hugging himself. The adrenalin was wearing off now. He'd never had an intellectual argument with another person before. Even in school, he hadn't been taught how to debate. There was no need when everyone believed the same thing and the Watchmaker always provided the answers. What was there to debate?

As he knew from the pedlar's book, in times past, the world had been torn apart by chaos and unpredictability, warfare, famine, poverty, starvation, and disease. But the Watchmaker and his alchemist-priests had brought order to Crown City and the surrounding lands. He gave them a map, gave them Stability. Without the Watchmaker, anarchy would rule the land. No one would know his place. Lawlessness would abound.

Thinking about the frightening old tales, Owen gathered his courage. "That's not what I was brought up to believe."

"You were brought up to believe—how easy for you!" the man said with an edge to his voice that could have peeled an apple. "It's easy to *believe*. But now you should learn the truth. See Crown City for yourself."

Owen squared his shoulders. "That's exactly what I plan to do. I'll see what there is to see. I'll go where I want."

The steamliner rolled on for hours and Owen felt overwhelmed by the strangeness of it all, by his own inexplicable audacity and his companion's bizarre beliefs. Outside, the faint light of dawn seeped into the sky.

Back home in Barrel Arbor, the ticking alarm clocks would ring within the hour, rousing his father for another day's work. But the alarm clock in Owen's room would ring and ring. His father would think he had overslept, would come in to rouse him, would find the bed empty. . . .

People would be worried about him, but Owen couldn't regret it, not now. He would tell them everything once he came back home. He closed his eyes and pictured the buildings of Crown City from the chronotypes in his mother's book. Now that he thought about it, this was what he'd wanted most in his life. Certainly, it was for the best. Owen could jump aboard another steamliner and ride back to Barrel Arbor whenever he liked. But first he would have a grand adventure that he could one day tell Lavinia and eventually their children and grandchildren.

The steel wheels scraped on tracks that glowed faintly with alchemical residue. When the steamliner began to slow on its approach to the city, the nameless stranger stood and brushed himself off. "Are you prepared for what awaits you, young Owen Hardy? I see you didn't bring much."

"I have an apple . . ." he said, but realized that wouldn't be enough.

The stranger wasn't impressed. "Do you have money? Crown City operates on money."

Owen was flustered. "I'm sorry, sir. I'm poorly prepared."

"Sometimes it's best not to plan." The man reached for a leather pouch at his side and upended it into Owen's hands, giving him all the money he had—nine coins of various denominations, each embossed with the Watchmaker's honeybee. "Take this, my good friend. It gives you more freedom to do whatever you like."

Owen gratefully accepted the gift. "Thank you, sir. You're very generous."

The man gave him a smile that was not a smile and held on to the edge of the cargo car with his burn-scarred hand. "Generous, am I? Maybe I just like the idea that you'll owe me."

"Then I'll do my best to repay your kindness someday," Owen said.

The steamliner slowed toward its destination, and the first buildings flashed by, warehouses and factories sprawling on the fringes of the city. They rolled past streets crowded with row houses; some of the windows were brightly lit, while others remained dark as sleepers clung to their last few moments in bed.

"You'll want to get off the steamliner before it reaches the heart of the city." The man raised his significant eyebrows. "The Regulators don't like stowaways."

The cargo car rolled past a thick, bushy hedge. Without a glance at Owen, the stranger hopped off the steamliner as if levitating and vanished out the cargo door. With a yelp, Owen leaped to his feet, sure the man must be dead. But when he leaned out the cargo door and looked back down the line, he saw the man pick himself up from the hedge, brush himself off, and dart away.

Owen pocketed the coins the stranger had given him along with his remaining apple, and looked ahead at the buildings of Crown City. Above them rose the glorious, monolithic clocktower, the tallest in the land—no doubt in the whole world. He already knew many of the wonders to expect, but his mother's book was old and ragged. Surely Crown City had thousands more wonders for him to discover. The anticipation was almost unbearable.

The stranger had mentioned the Regulators, however—the Watchmaker's security force. These trusted watchers helped maintain the Stability and stopped anyone from breaking the rules. Owen had never considered them frightening before, but now he realized with a skip of a heartbeat that *he* was a rule-breaker.

Sparks showered up from the steel wheels as the brakes on the leading cars clamped down on the rails. Owen saw a transfer station coming up, the rail yards crowded with the business of offloading.

Having come this far, he didn't want his adventure cut short, not until he got a chance to explore Crown City, see the Clockwork Angels with his own eyes, perhaps even a glimpse of the Watchmaker himself, or the throbbing source of coldfire beneath Chronos Square. The steamliner had slowed significantly, and although the next hedge looked prickly and not at all welcoming, he braced himself and jumped out of the car with far less grace than the manner in which he had climbed aboard.

CHAPTER 5

Where a young man has a chance of making good

Each autumn in Barrel Arbor, Owen and his father would rake the fallen leaves from around their cottage into sweet-smelling heaps. On one such afternoon a few years ago, Owen had nearly finished raking when a gust of unexpected wind rushed past and caught up the yellow leaves, swirling them into the air. Laughing, he had run into the midst of the golden whirlwind, holding up his hands as the colors skirled around him.

Crown City was like that.

After the steamliner left him behind, he extricated himself from the hedge, brushed off his clothes, and trudged into the city. The path along the rails turned into a track, and the track became a street. In the space of an hour, he witnessed enough surprises to make his eyes ache, and Crown City engulfed him with its majesty. He wanted to see it all, experience everything. He couldn't believe he was actually here, whether by accident or determination.

Owen walked past individual warehouses, each of which rivaled the size of his village. Industries hummed with heavy pistons, hydraulic stamping presses, assembly lines—coldfire-driven machinery that manufactured the conveniences and necessities of daily life: efficient vehicles, harvesting machines, mining engines, household gadgets, and alchemical contraptions for the delight and comfort of all the Watchmaker's people.

Farther along, on tree-lined boulevards, he walked past the huddled and secretive buildings of the Watchmaker's university, where the next generation of engineers and mathematicians learned how they could contribute to the Stability. An image of a honeybee was carved into the keystone of the entrance arch.

In adjacent university buildings, thin smokestacks spewed colored smoke and fumes from various experiments conducted within reinforced laboratories. From his mother's book, Owen recognized the Alchemy College, where apprentices struggled against the elements to unlock the chemical secrets of the universe, expanding human knowledge beyond the simplicities of air, water, fire, and earth. Hoping to become members of the Watchmaker's elite cadre of alchemist-priests, the apprentices worked with metals, salts, acids, rare earths, and even rarer substances that had not yet been named.

Owen looked wistfully at the college buildings, imagining classrooms full of attentive students taught by philosopher-professors. If Owen had been born in a different place, set on a different path, maybe he could have been one of those students. Surely, he possessed the required intellect, or at least the imagination. But he was part of the Watchmaker's plan, and all was for the best. It wasn't for him to complain.

He continued to explore the city, greeting everyone he encountered because that was the polite thing to do. They responded in kind but did not pause for a relaxed chat, the way people did during quiet afternoons in Barrel Arbor or evenings in the Tick Tock Tavern. He envied the inhabitants of Crown City, to whom the capital's marvels were as commonplace as his apple orchards.

Thanks to his familiarity with his mother's book, he made his way toward Chronos Square, the center of the city, where the Watchmaker had his headquarters. That was where he would find the gigantic clocktower and the Clockwork Angels. Wide streets radiated outward from the square, crossing circular outer boulevards. Owen knew their names: Crown Wheel, Center Wheel, and Balance Wheel . . . a combination of straight paths and perfect circles, all part of a master plan that simple people like Owen could never comprehend.

The buildings grew taller, the streets crowded with people and adorned with awnings, shops, stands. Owen's neck hurt because he kept turning his head from side to side to absorb everything, like a playful kitten distracted by butterflies in the air. He didn't keep track of where he was supposed to be, swept along like those golden leaves in the gust of wind.

He strolled past fruit vendors, coffee shops, and market stalls with chalkboards announcing "special sale prices" (although the prices were Stability-set, and each vendor was required to charge exactly the same in order to remove the uncertainty of unnecessary competition).

Two workmen with long-handled bristle brushes, pump cans of smelly solvents, and buckets of soapy water stood at the mouth of an alley; the workers seemed embarrassed, rushed. One man squirted solvent on a crudely painted symbol on the brick wall. It was clearly visible from the main street—a large white "A" surrounded by a slapdash circle. After the application of the solvent, the paint began to run, melting the symbol—whatever it was. The second worker dunked his brush in the soapy water and furiously scrubbed and scoured, as if trying to take off the surface of the bricks along with the paint. The offending mark vanished under their toil.

Four straight-backed men in dark blue uniforms strode forward like windup soldiers. Each wore a crisp tricorn hat; their jackets were pressed, their silver buttons polished, their cuffs the epitome of what a rectangle should be. People moved aside to let them pass, and Owen tried desperately not to call any attention to himself, but he couldn't hide his stare.

The Watchmaker's Regulators were renowned enforcers of the Stability. Only the candidates with the most perfect rhythm and

THE
WATCHMAKER

Est. MMCXII

timing were accepted into the Blue Watch, who patrolled the streets on a rigid schedule. They walked a prescribed inspection route, eyes forward, seeing everything. They didn't command adherence to order so much as they demonstrated it.

The Blue Watch walked by, and as they passed, people seemed to stand straighter and go about their business with greater purpose. Owen felt an increased confidence that everything in his life, even this unexpected adventure, was part of an immense and intricate master plan.

Men and women bustled in and out of a large building carrying sheets of paper. The walls were studded with thick hexagonal windows, like a beehive, and a clattering din came from inside, where row after row of automated metal keys clacked on spools of pulp paper—a central newsgraph office, far grander than the Paquettes' small shop with its single newsgraph machine back in Barrel Arbor. Newsgraph workers ran out and posted the latest releases on public kiosks: service announcements, security alerts, weather reports, and even philosophical pronouncements that rattled into the machines from the Watchmaker's mind.

At a bookshop next door to the newsgraph office, Owen saw a table stacked high with *The Official Biography of the Watchmaker, Updated Edition*. Each book had a honeybee symbol stamped on the spine, just like the pedlar's book, *Before the Stability*. Owen flipped through a few pages of the thick volume, promising himself that someday he would sit down and read about the centuries of Stability and how the Watchmaker had made this the best of all possible worlds. An informative sign noted that the current edition "included events as recent as last week." By the time Owen got around to reading the book, he supposed it would be much thicker.

For now he had to see Crown City.

Ahead, a woman was trying on hats in front of a shop. The haberdasher hovered beside her. "It looks lovely on you, madam. Absolutely lovely." The woman cocked the hat one way then another, preening before a small mirror. "But perhaps you should try this blue one," he said. "It would look magnificent." The haberdasher extended a hat that was bright scarlet, not blue at all.

The woman took the scarlet hat. She made no comment about its actual color and tried it on. The man said, "Oh, yes, madam—blue is definitely the best fit for you."

The haberdasher was an old man with arthritic knuckles, a wispy beard, and a wrinkled face. His eyes were folded shut, the lids like soft, wadded suede, and Owen realized the man was blind.

Hesitating, the woman tried on the hat, unsure about its color. "Are you quite certain, sir?"

"Oh, yes, madam. The Watchmaker chose me for this profession. It is my particular skill. Trust me in this; you look beautiful," said the blind man.

"Very well, then. All is for the best." She paid the haberdasher and took her new scarlet hat, which did not match the rest of her outfit at all.

Though he was at first surprised, Owen also felt reassured that the Watchmaker's society was so ordered that even a blind man knew which hats to sell his customers. Trusting in the Stability, the people did exactly as they were expected to.

"And you, young man," the gruff haberdasher called out, turning his head in Owen's direction. "For you, a porkpie hat, I think."

"I . . . I do need a hat." Owen said. He hadn't even thought about it when he'd gone out after dark to meet Lavinia.

The haberdasher fumbled among his wares, settled on a gray tweed porkpie hat, felt the rim to check its size, and extended it in Owen's general direction. The young man placed the hat on his head and admitted that it did look good on him. "How did you know I needed a hat if you can't see?"

"Because I expected you to come," the haberdasher said. "How else could I do my business?"

Since Owen didn't know how much to pay for a hat, he extended a handful of the coins from the nameless stranger. The blind man fumbled among them, plucked a medium-sized coin, and dropped it in a small box on his hat-strewn table. Owen thanked him and continued on his way.

He ate his last apple, although he wanted something more substantial. But despite his growling stomach, he had too many things to see. He could eat later. Besides, he really had no idea how much a meal of roast mutton or a chicken pie might cost.

As he continued toward Chronos Square, astonished by the sheer size of Crown City, he found people gathered in a crowd of laughter and applause. Curious, he peered around shoulders and between arms, standing on tiptoe until he saw a red and gold mechanical marvel inside a glass case framed with varnished wood. The head was made of transparent crystal filled with swirling colored steam; the body was a cluster of spheres and generators, a central boiler brought up to pressure and connected to half a dozen hydraulic arms and curved piston legs. At the end of each copper articulated arm, a wooden drumstick was affixed to a socket; the bent legs were connected to pedals. The entire device was surrounded by drums of a variety of shapes and sizes.

A man with a small mustache and a bright red scarf around his neck stood to the side, beaming with pride at his invention. "I present to you Dr. Russell's Fabulous Clockwork Percussor! Let us make a joyful noise."

With a sudden release of steam, the arms began to move, at first randomly, then into an organized sequence of strikes at the array of drums and cymbals. Each limb stretched and moved in a graceful arc, and the whole assemblage created a rat-a-tat sound like some manic, percussive alarm clock.

Owen was dazzled by the intricate dance of copper limbs across rosewood drums and brass cymbals, each one rocking on its stand. More than that, the rhythmic power of the automated drumming seemed to affect his entire being. Each deep note from the bass drum sounded like a blow to his chest, making him catch his breath. The dry pop and rattle of the snare drum assaulted his skull with its rapid-fire volleys, and the primal beats of the tom-toms seemed to fire his blood until he felt feverish. The cymbals crashed like waves breaking against his skin, electrifying every nerve ending.

The Percussor continued its mechanized drumming with unbelievable speed and complexity until Owen felt giddy, exalted by the power of rhythm. The people around him cheered at the sheer spectacle, but Owen was deaf to all that.

Suddenly the spell was broken as one of the Percussor's drumsticks slipped out of its socket, striking the glass window of its case and cracking it from side to side. The unbalanced limb flailed in the air, and that one rogue motion upset the equilibrium of the entire hydraulic mechanism. The Percussor degenerated into a frightening chaos of uncontrolled motion and random noise.

Dr. Russell ran to open the door of the glass case, ducking and dodging the thrashing machinery, and released the steam pressure through a valve in the machine's core. Slowing, hissing, the articulated arms lowered, and the Percussor returned to rest.

Wiping his sweaty brow with the red scarf, Dr. Russell remembered to set out his hat, so that people could toss in donations for the performance. Seeing what was expected of him, Owen threw one of his coins into the hat without looking at the denomination.

As marvelous as the Percussor was, though, it could never hold a coldfire glow to his mental image of the Clockwork Angels.

It took him all afternoon to make his way through the distractions to the heart of the city. There, the buildings were more massive, more impressive, with columns and luminous clock faces on every main arch, the honeybee symbol chiseled into foundation stones.

Owen hoped he would be in time to see a performance of the Angels, but as he approached the mouth of the square, he saw a line of red-uniformed Regulators standing like forbidding statues.

The Red Watch served as anchors and guards at important land-
marks, stoic and unmovable.

Not to be deterred after his long journey, Owen presented
himself to the Watch captain at the barricade, smiling politely.
"Excuse me, sir, but I've come to see the Clockwork Angels."

The Regulator captain continued to stare forward like a bird of
prey intent on a distant hare; he did not look down at Owen. "Do
you have a ticket?"

"Not yet. How do I obtain one?"

"You should have been issued a ticket."

"Is there a way I can just have a look at the square?" Owen
asked.

"No, it's Tuesday."

"Should I come back tomorrow then?"

"No."

Owen felt his urgency growing. "Can you tell me how I get a
ticket? Please, sir?"

"I'm not allowed to say. You should have been issued a ticket."

Owen tried to peer around the man to glimpse the square, but
the Regulator captain puffed up his chest and closed ranks with
the other red-uniformed men.

Owen backed away, disappointed. Maybe this would take him
longer than he expected, but he would find a way.

CHAPTER 6

Spinning lights and faces
Demon music and gypsy queens

After dark, Owen had nowhere to go, nowhere to stay, nowhere to sleep. The Watchmaker might have a plan, but Owen didn't have much of one.

When he saw a sign for an inn, Owen inquired about lodgings and a meal, and the innkeeper was happy to take his money—most of it. The meal consisted of part of an unfortunately scrawny chicken and some overboiled turnips. His bed was hard, the sheets stiff and starched, but the room had its own alarm clock, and Owen was able to set the bell for just after sunrise. He was eager to see more of Crown City and didn't want to waste time sleeping.

Next morning, he left the inn with no regrets. On the street, he found a pie vendor, whose wares smelled delicious. Every golden pastry had been drizzled with honey. He paid with one of his small coins and reached for an apple tart out of habit, but stopped himself. Since he had already done so many unexpected things, he decided to try a *raspberry* tart. Why not take the risk? The flavor exploded in his mouth, sweet and rich, intensely juicy, full of tiny seeds. What a marvelous discovery! He wanted even more flavors for comparison, but he would work on that—one thing at a time. Everything had its place, and every place had its thing. And Crown City was filled with wondrous things.

As he munched the sweet pastry, he came upon a commotion on the street, where ten members of the Red Watch had gathered near a tall stone building. The guards set up barricades to prevent people from seeing the defaced wall, but their very presence served only to incite curiosity.

Owen was shocked when he read the scrawled letters. *Who made the Watchmaker?* And, *Do you know what time it* really *is?* Again, he saw the painted letter "A" circumscribed with a rough circle.

A wagon rolled up carrying a steel barrel connected to a coldfire-powered compressor. City workers tugged out a hose, activated the compressor, and sprayed a smothering blanket of gray paint on top of the offending words.

"But what does it mean?" Owen asked a balding man, mainly because he was standing nearby, not because the man was likely to possess any intimate knowledge.

"Damned Anarchist," the man grumbled. "Wants to mess up everything."

"Scribbling graffiti is better than blowing up bridges, you can say that much," commented another bystander. "At least this'll be fixed with a fresh coat of paint."

Unsettled, Owen made his way back toward Chronos Square, hoping for better luck today. He inquired of several people how he might obtain a ticket, hoping that the restrictions applied primarily on Tuesdays, as the Red Watch captain had explained. People kept telling him that he should have been issued a ticket, and when he persisted in his questions, they responded with skeptical looks. He decided not to point out that he didn't belong here.

By now, Barrel Arbor must be abuzz with news of his disappearance. He wondered what Lavinia thought about it; did she even remember that she had promised to meet him on the orchard hill at midnight? Would his neighbors fear something had happened to him? Owen missed his father, too, but remembered the older man's admonishment that he would have to give up his "foolishness" when he became an adult—so Owen decided that he had best make the most of his foolishness while possible. Though he was not yet ready to go home, he had already experienced enough amazing things to keep his mind busy for a lifetime. Anything could happen.

And then he saw the carnival.

The traveling show had set up in an open city park; an arched sign blazed in swirling phosphorescent letters, *César Magnusson's Carnival Extravaganza*. A Ferris wheel lifted passengers to a dizzying height, from which they could look out upon the city. The spokes of the Ferris wheel were adorned with a façade of painted metal sheets to make it look like a gigantic gear. On other rides, passengers shrieked as boxy cars whirled and spun on the ends of pneumatic arms, or steam engines chugged to lift padded seats high up a scaffolding and then let the riders rattle at high speed down an abrupt incline.

As if in a trance, Owen was drawn toward the carnival like an iron filing pulled to a magnet. People were passing through the ticket gate, handing over coins, and Owen did not try to resist as he was swept along. He didn't count his coins, didn't care how long they might last; he couldn't imagine anything more wonderful than this (except maybe the Clockwork Angels).

The plump, middle-aged woman selling carnival tickets had strawberry blond hair, a lavender dress, and a full beard that covered her cheeks and chin. Her facial locks were so long that she used lavender ribbons to tie ponytails along her jawline.

Owen couldn't help staring. He had never seen a bearded lady before, but she took no offense, merely chuckled. "I am the least of what you'll see inside there, young man! Gypsy queens, acrobats, fire-eaters, sword play, games of chance. The Magnusson Carnival Extravaganza has it all."

He looked down at the ticket in his hand, which advertised "Marvels to Thrill and Delight." He had no doubt the carnival would be true to its promise. "Do you . . . do you know where I'd get a ticket to see the Angels?" he asked. "You seem to have some knowledge of tickets."

"Not those tickets," she said. "Isn't our show enough?"

Afraid he had offended her, Owen hurried into the carnival grounds.

Inside, the noise and energy was like a symphony. He walked past game booths crowded with eager players. A wizened carny with a liver-spotted scalp hunched over three inverted bowls, under one of which he had placed a small ball. Though the old man looked doddering and feeble, he switched the bowls around, reshifting their positions while chattering and wheezing to distract the observers. "Big money," he said with a cackle. "Big money!" He always managed to trick the observers into guessing the wrong bowl, and he pocketed their bets.

In another game booth, a thin woman spun an upright clockwork wheel with colored segments; players tossed darts and tried to hit winning patches. At yet another game, young men threw balls and tried to knock down a surprisingly persistent pyramid of beakers.

He heard loud music and saw three clowns in colorful garb and painted with extravagant tattoos playing an off-key rendition of "The Anarchist's March." The clowns clashed cymbals with a foot pedal, banged the sides of a drum, and tooted on a horn in raucous demon music, which was appropriate for the villain who tried to disrupt the Stability of their lives. The crowd reacted with disturbed laughter.

A bronze-skinned strongman wearing only a loincloth flexed his biceps, each of which was larger than Owen's head. The strongman squatted down and amazed the crowd by lifting a barbell laden with weights the size of a steamliner's steel wheel. The strongman raised the weight over his head and stood, straining with the effort until it looked as if his muscles would burst free from his arms like severed fan belts. Exhausted, he dropped the weight with such a crash that it left divots in the ground. The strongman reeled, disoriented, and Owen was convinced his effort was not an act.

A handsome young man with dark hair and dark eyes pranced along with a dancer's gait; he removed a packet from his pantaloons, dumped a sparkling blue powder into his mouth, then pressed his lips together. His cheeks bulged, making him look like a misbehaving child holding his breath; his eyes widened and watered, and at last he coughed out a gout of blue-green flame. Afterward, he burped with just a little flash of fire, wiped his mouth, and stepped back with a grin for the astonished audience.

Owen had never heard so much laughter and hubbub in his life. Young couples walked arm in arm. Parents brought their children. He saw burnished copper, colored glass, painted metal; he heard the hiss of steam, saw a billow of smoke, all part of the sensory show.

As he walked along, buffeted by sights and sensations, a tinny voice caught his attention, "What does the future hold for you, young man?"

He turned to see a windowed booth painted the color of the ripest red apple; inside sat the clockwork figure of an old woman. The sign said, *Gypsy Fortune Teller*. She wore a patchwork dress, and her mechanical hands were covered with gloves, so as to seem more human; her head looked like a shriveled old crone's, a dried-apple doll with gray-blue hair tied back in a bun. In precisely the same voice—no doubt words recorded on an engraved metal sound spool—the clockwork contraption repeated, "What does the future hold for you, young man?"

He looked around but saw no one else nearby. She had to be talking to him. A small slot invited him to insert a coin; how could he not do so?

He gave her one of his coins, and the fortune-teller automaton did not complain, nor did she make change. He turned the metal key on the side of the booth, clicking and clicking until the spring was tight. As the key whirred and the gears turned, the fortune teller's hydraulic hands jerkily gathered cards from a thick tarot deck spread out there. She lifted the deck, shuffled the cards, fumbled them into place for her reading.

"Justice against the Hanged Man," she said, then placed two more cards opposite. "Knight of Wands against the Hour."

"What does it mean?" he asked.

Two more cards. "The Hermit against the Lovers."

Owen was so intent on watching the intricate movements of her clockwork hands that he was surprised when he glanced at her face. Her bird-bright eyes were blue and alert, and she blinked at him. "The Devil against the Fool." Her mouth puckered and drew back in a smile.

She was *alive*—or some part of her was!

Unsettled, he pulled away, not sure he wanted to learn his fortune. Still clicking, the turning key wound down and stopped. The fortune teller gathered the cards, then sat upright again and returned to rest. Owen mumbled his thanks and left, feeling both happy and confused.

In the center of the carnival ground, poles had been strung with ropes for a high-wire acrobatic act. The ringmaster—a man with such an imposing presence that Owen assumed it must be César Magnusson himself—stood wearing a top hat and sleek black tails, with a huge handlebar mustache that seemed a feat in itself. He shouted out above the noise of the crowd in a voice suited to command thunder. "On the wires, our most beautiful angel—Francesca! Watch her death-defying feats of poise and balance. Never before has danger looked so graceful."

A lissome young woman sprang forward and cartwheeled with the perfection of a smoothly turning gear. She wore a pearlescent white leotard and a decorative white skirt that did not impede her movement. Her flowing black hair looked like a swirling river of ink, tresses that captured the purity of the darkest moonless night. Francesca turned to smile at the audience, revealing that she held a long rose in her teeth. Owen had never seen anyone so beautiful in his entire life.

Like a cat climbing a tree, she ascended the pole on small pegs that were arranged like a ladder's rungs. Owen saw, and promptly forgot about, a flat pack strapped to her back, cleverly hidden by her hair.

She climbed to the first platform and looked across an imposing narrow rope that extended to the far pole. Higher up, Francesca unfastened a dangling trapeze. With casual, breathtaking skill, she wrapped one arm around the bar and swung herself out, gliding forward, then back, like the pendulum in a grandfather clock. She raised herself on strong, slender arms, twirled, and launched herself into the air where she caught the upper rope and used her momentum to swing her body around. She dropped back down and caught the trapeze bar in its arc as if it had been waiting there for her.

Francesca swung again, never once letting the rose fall from her mouth. Then, twenty feet above the hard ground, toes pointed straight forward, one foot in front of the other, she walked along the tightrope with as much ease as Owen walked down a street. She seemed to have wings on her heels.

During the performance, he worked his way to the front of the crowd and stood there, his entire world centered on her. He gaped at the sight with his eyes wide and his mouth open like a moonstruck cow. He could think of nothing else, could see nothing else, and when Francesca glanced down at the audience he was certain that she looked right into his eyes. His new porkpie hat fell off, and he scrambled to pick it up.

Raising her hands as if to stretch on a lazy morning, she grabbed the trapeze and swung high. As she came back down, she pushed her legs hard against the elastic tension of the tightrope and catapulted herself into the air. At the apex of her flight, she yanked a tiny string on the front of her costume, and the half-hidden pack on her shoulders burst open to reveal spring-loaded angel wings. They were fashioned from thin slats of aluminum and tin layered one upon the other like giant feathers, and they looked glorious in the light.

On angel wings, Francesca spread her arms and soared downward in ecstatic flight. The wings braked her descent enough that she alighted on the ground with barely a hair out of place. She landed in front of Owen, who could do nothing more than gasp while the rest of the crowd applauded.

With a flourish and a secretive smile, Francesca removed the rose from her mouth and extended it to him. He didn't know what to say. His hands trembled as he took it, and she rewarded him with a bright burst of laughter, then bounded off, leaving his whole world out of balance.

Owen was so stunned that he didn't notice the hush that rippled through the crowd. A troop of Regulators, twelve men with perfect tricorn hats and crisp blue uniforms, marched past the game booths, issuing orders to shut down the carnival.

The Blue Watch marched to where César Magnusson stood with his top hat and tails, straight-backed, not looking at all intimidated. "How may I help you gentlemen?" He stroked his long mustache.

"Irregularities were found in your permit," said the lead Regulator. "Your allotted performance date has expired. By decree of the Watchmaker, you must shut down these operations and remove all items by sundown. You may reapply for a proper performance permit in twenty-four hours." The Regulator reached into his buttoned jacket and withdrew a citation slip, which he presented to the ringmaster.

Magnusson accepted the paper without protest, took off his top hat, and bowed. "We shall do as the Watchmaker wishes. All is for the best."

The Watchmaker

While our loving Watchmaker
loves us all to death

The Watchmaker sat in the highest clocktower in the land of Albion and contemplated the universe.

His chalkboards were covered with equations; worktables held blueprints with precise drawings of how the world should be ordered. In more than two centuries of Stability (he no longer let the people know exactly how many years it had been), he had accomplished much, but so much more remained to be done. The world was such a large and chaotic place.

His adept engineers and physicists understood cause and effect, the epiphany of straight lines and perfect circles. His alchemist-priests, once considered magicians, understood the clockwork interaction of atoms and elements. But to him, the Watchmaker, fell the greatest responsibility: he was the prime mover, the gear that turned all gears, the precision spring that saved the scattered and inefficient populace of Albion from debilitating disorder.

Tick. Tock. Tick. Tock.

He pulled the chair close to his desk with its neatly stacked papers, his ruler and compass, his many-keyed adding engine.

From here, he could hear the relentless mechanism of the tower's huge timepiece, brute-force gears that beat time into submission. The loud ticking provided a rhythm as comforting as a heartbeat, and without variation. Though the Watchmaker's own pulse might quicken when he thought of a new idea or when he learned news of yet another disruption caused by the Anarchist, the tower's great clock maintained its perfect tempo. It helped him concentrate.

The Watchmaker was a clean-shaven man with a face full of years that even his own rejuvenation treatments could not erase; the barber came in at precisely 7:30 a.m. every day. His gray hair was cut to what he deemed to be the perfect length. His nails were clipped once a week, manicured exactly even.

At precisely 10:00 a.m., his assistant brought in a tray and poured him a cup of hot tea. The Watchmaker pressed a dipper into a honeycomb in a bowl beside the tea set, then dripped exactly the right amount of golden syrup into his tea. Two complete circle stirs with the silver spoon, and the cup was perfect.

He hated to disrupt the perfect hexagonal wax in the honeycomb, but it was a necessary bit of disorder. The angles, the interlocking chambers in the comb, a natural geometrical perfection rarely seen; it fascinated him. Bees innately understood order, the perfection of geometry. If only people could so instinctively learn the lesson of lowly insects.

And the honey: liquid gold just like the gold his alchemy created—but created through the alchemy of insects, an arcane transformation from nectar by the biological processes of bees. Not even his most brilliant alchemist-priests could reproduce it. The Watchmaker kept his own bees for recreation, for study. Little wonder that he had chosen the bee as his personal symbol, a reminder to all people of the sweet, perfect order of the Stability. . . .

He looked at the blueprints before him—an expanded wing for the Alchemy College; a new steamline spur line to bring in processed copper and molybdenum from the strike in the north-east; a modified design for cargo steamers so they could better weather the storms as they crossed the Western Sea from Atlantis, laden with vital alchemical supplies.

Tick. Tock. Tick. Tock.

At 10:30 a.m. the commander of the elite Black Watch marched in and presented his report. "All is well, sir," he said, as he did every day. "All is as it should be, and all is for the best."

He handed over a summary document, which the Watchmaker skimmed. It was the same as yesterday and the day before, neatly handwritten with close attention to detail. The Black Watch commander could have used a printing press to run off the document day after day, but the Watchmaker did not encourage complacency, especially with that mad dog, the Anarchist, trying to ruin perfection.

The man had so much potential, so much failure. . . .

The Watch commander departed at 10:45, and the Watchmaker remembered with a sad wistfulness that it was time to walk the dog, as he had done for years. Curled on the rug in his office near the window was his Dalmatian, Martin; a perfect dog, well trained, never a bother, with a white coat and a wonderful random-ness of spots (one had to allow for a certain amount of Nature's unpreventable disorder). The Dalmatian did not shed, was not dis-ruptively playful; he would sit when commanded to do so, and he heeled whenever the Watchmaker called him. Yes, a perfect dog. Martin looked so beautiful there on the rug.

Unfortunately, the clockwork of biology had run down; dog years were different from human years, although when viewed through human eyes, the loss still felt deep and painful to him. Martin had died four years ago. Not wanting to disrupt his daily routine, the Watchmaker had appointed Albion's best taxidermist to stuff and mount the dog so that he sat, curled up in his accustomed place all day long, a comforting bit of Stability for the Watchmaker himself. He had decided this solution was better than getting a new dog.

Fortunately, his sophistication with the subtleties of alchemy, biological hydraulics, and hair-fine clockwork mechanisms allowed the Watchmaker to overcome even the obstacle of Martin's death. Opening the locked drawer of his desk, he withdrew an eyedropper filled with an intensely luminous fluid, liquid electricity . . . distilled quintessence.

The dog wasn't his first experiment, and certainly not his best, but still very important to the Watchmaker. This was *Martin*. He petted the spotted fur on the dog's back, found the small access hatch that revealed the clockwork heart and hydraulic muscle motivators, and squeezed two drops of the shimmering fluid into the animation battery.

He just had time to seal the hidden access hatch again and replace the eyedropper in the drawer before Martin became active, rising up on his four legs, wagging his tail in a perfect metronome. The Watchmaker smiled. So much better than a real dog's regrettable messes or spontaneous behavior.

He caught himself pondering, listening to the heavy ticking of the huge clock. 10:55 a.m.—time to visit his alchemist-priests for the daily inspection. "Come on, Martin. Let's go for your walk."

Crown City was the heart of Albion, and Chronos Square was the heart of Crown City. In the catacombs beneath the great clocktower, the Watchmaker could see the actual alchemical heart of the world beating. His coldfire source.

Cleverly concealed conduits beneath the cobblestoned streets delivered energy throughout the city, charging steam boilers, illuminating street lamps, heating homes, powering hospitals. The alchemist-priests had created a great vaulted chamber in the catacombs, the nexus of all the coldfire that kept his Stability stable. The people lacked for nothing, and the machinery of society ran on well-oiled gears.

The Watchmaker walked purposefully, with the dog pacing beside him in a stiff, measured gait. He could hear the ticking of Martin's mechanisms, the movement of not-quite-smooth gears in his major joints. He believed even this semblance of the dog enjoyed the daily walk, however, and he himself was reassured that all was as it should be, and forever.

His chief alchemist-priests, ten of them—because that was a perfect round number—maintained the pulsing coldfire heart. They added the prescribed amount of sulfur and antimony, mercury, natrium, and their associated distillates, crystallizations, and powdered allotropes. They followed the reaction recipes as specified in great tomes filled with alchemical symbols.

The spells and rituals were the height of modern science. In a release of elemental empathy, a change of synergy, the blissful chemical reactions powered the city's underground turbines. A crackle left the air with the metallic scent of ozone after a thunderstorm. Several alchemist-priests covered their faces with scarves to ward off the chemical fumes, but to the Watchmaker, the aroma was a mixture of hope and potential, although not everyone could smell it. His eyes didn't even water.

More than two centuries ago, the city had been a riot of smokestacks and slums. People crowded together in squalid conditions. Murder, sickness, even plagues swept the underclasses. Countless industrial accidents, uncontrolled fires, horrendous mayhem—it was every man for himself in a lawless, sprawling "civilization" that proved to be anything but civilized.

Amidst that turmoil, the man who had become the Watchmaker had organized his research and gathered a team of adept alchemists to begin methodical investigations. And finally they found the Philosopher's Stone, which allowed him to turn common metals into gold.

For a simpler man, the dreams would have ended there. He would have made himself wealthy, built a palace, and relaxed in a fine life. For the Watchmaker, however, that was only the first step. He manufactured immense quantities of gold, built a stockpile greater than the greediest dragon's imaginary hoard, and swept into Crown City with wagonloads of riches. He simply purchased everything he needed, every building, every factory, in such a swift and methodical manner that he controlled the city before the economy collapsed under a blizzard of cheap gold.

Then his real work began. He was already the wealthiest man in the land, but even gold grew dull after a while, and he intended to pursue greater challenges. His alchemists discovered coldfire, which cleanly and cheaply powered the city, removing the necessity for dirty coal and inefficient industry. After that great shift, he set about changing the world.

He continued to make improvements, raised the standard of living, cleaned up the city, fed and clothed the people. And he imposed order, giving them a place, showing them straight lines, inviting them to follow the mystic rhythms of the timepiece of the universe.

Tick. Tock. Tick. Tock.

With Martin beside him, the Watchmaker stared at the swirling, hypnotic blue phosphorescence, a glorious sight that would have made even the core of the sun envious. He did not know how to create diamonds or the variety of gems that were vital for the many timepieces around the city, but his numerous alchemical discoveries, among other things, allowed airships to take flight, let steamliners continue their perfect commerce, and produced a quintessential tonic that had maintained the Watchmaker's vigor, despite his advancing age.

Wearing a tall white hat that held back his hair, the chief alchemist-priest presented his report. "A new shipment from Atlantis is due in port tomorrow, sir. Our stockpiles will last for two more months, and the next steamer will arrive much sooner than that. Even with the recent loss of a full cargo due to the Wreckers, our Stability is secure."

"Of course it is. Come, Martin." He nudged the clockwork dog, who followed him without complaint or deviation.

Two hundred years ago when he had imposed his Stability, giving the people the best of all possible lives, they had proclaimed him more than a king, more than a leader. He was the *Watchmaker*, which he considered the best title for himself, for he was, after all, a humble man.

The average person did not wish to, or need to, understand the inner workings of a machine. They went about their lives unaware of the circulatory system beneath Crown City; they never saw the numerous slight adjustments the Watchmaker made.

He had taken apart and reassembled all manner of clocks, pinions, wheels, escapements, springs, balance staffs, rollers, clicks, and crowns. He was intensely interested in the detailed functioning of his city, as well as the universe as a whole. He had written his own history for more decades than the people remembered, and by now they had all forgotten what the rest of reality was like.

Before the noon performance of the Clockwork Angels, he climbed his private metal staircase to the tower's gear room. Alone behind the machinery of the four surreal figures, he stood next to the enormous gears. The counterweight fell at a calculable rate, causing the pendulum to swing, the gear to move, the escapement to click upward then back into place, which advanced the second hand, one notch at a time.

Tick. Tock. Tick. Tock.

When the hour, minute, and second hands of the great clock aligned at noon, other gears began spinning, counter-wheels whirring. Brightening coldfire heated the steam, which powered pistons and drove special mechanisms in order to work the Angels.

Though he was inside the machinery looking out, the Watchmaker knew the people gathered in the square would be in awe, bowing down to worship, viewing the polished ethereal automatons as heavenly visitors who dispensed wisdom every day. Outside in front of the grand building, the Clockwork Angels awakened and spread their wings.

The Watchmaker stood inside the great machine, overwhelmed by the gears as well as the responsibility, but with his grand thoughts he could never feel small. . . .

After the Angels finished their programmed sequence and thrummed their benedictions, the Watchmaker climbed back down the spiraling metal staircase and returned to his office. All was right with the world, but he could not let himself grow content.

Some time ago, his destiny calculators had pinpointed one particular young man, no one of special talent or interest, just a representative. Someone who might cause trouble . . . or who might reaffirm everything. A single person in a perfect world was little more than an identical grain of sand or a tiny pebble alongside the road. What sort of effect could a young man like that have? And yet, if a grain of sand got into the eye, or a sharp pebble lodged in a shoe, it could cause tremendous problems. The Watchmaker would have to keep watch.

And he knew he wasn't the only one watching Owen Hardy of Barrel Arbor.

In his office, he went to his closet and found his old rough cloak, donned his false gray beard and the wig of twisted, gray locks. He adjusted the eye patch on his face, added the stovepipe hat, and, after petting the Dalmatian's head out of habit, slipped outside to walk among the people, watching and listening.

CHAPTER 7

Stars aglow like scattered sparks
Span the sky in clockwork arcs
Hint at more than we can see
Spiritual machinery

The Winding Pinion River was a gentle green waterway that flowed past Barrel Arbor. There, Owen had often gone swimming on hot summer days. Inside the Watchmaker's great metropolis, however, the river took on an entirely different character.

With his new porkpie hat in place, Owen followed the waterway down to the Crown City docks at its widening mouth, near the coast. Barges carrying passengers and goods from upriver tied up at the docks for unloading. Swarthy porters carried heavy crates on their backs, chanting rhythmic songs as they tugged on pulleys to swing cargo up and off the decks, while coldfire-driven cranes lifted the heavier items into place.

Grocers guiding steam-powered carts bought sacks of potatoes, bushels of grain, even apples fresh off the boat. Owen stopped to look at crates piled with knobby fruit larger than a melon, and when he asked one of the dockworkers about it, the man laughed. "It's a pineapple, boy!" He used a knife to hack off the top and slice a chunk of the dripping, golden fruit for Owen. He took a bite, and the pineapple tasted like sunshine and honey mixed with molten gold. He'd never experienced anything like it before.

He helped where he could, just because he liked talking with the workers. None of them imagined that their daily jobs were particularly interesting, but they were glad for the unexpected assistance. When Owen mentioned he was visiting from Barrel Arbor, nobody had ever heard of the place.

Gulls swooped about, snatching rotting scraps of food. No one minded when Owen ate his fill of bruised produce from the cargo ships as a makeshift lunch. The sheer bounty of it all made him giddy with the Watchmaker's benevolence.

As ships came and went from the port, accountants kept track of each vessel, maintaining ledgers of every cargo and every crew member. Owen thought the local boat traffic was impressive enough, but when he saw the arrival of a seafaring cargo steamer that billowed white smoke, he was even more amazed.

The big ship pulled up to a special dock, large enough to accommodate three normal barges. Crates marked with alchemical symbols were stacked high on the deck, some covered with tarpaulins to protect against the rain and sea spray; other boxes were open to the elements. One of the dockworkers told him that more valuable substances were locked in the hold behind steel bulkheads, where they were prevented from engaging in unauthorized chemical reactions, which were the sole province of the alchemist-priests. Nature could not be allowed to take an accidental course.

According to the newsgraph reports, wild pirates were responsible for sinking an increasing number of cargo ships that plied the waters to and from Poseidon City. The notorious Wreckers caused great mayhem, although Owen had to admit that they sounded exciting.

As the cargo steamer docked, he ran to the loading ramps to help. When he offered his strength to carry sacks of chemical powders down the gangplank, he marveled to think that he was touching something that came from another continent. Atlantis across the sea, Poseidon, and the fabled Seven Cities . . .

He couldn't believe his good fortune to experience such things. This was everything he had dreamed about in all those days on orchard hill. After nearly two days in Crown City, Owen's vocabulary failed him—and he hadn't even seen the Clockwork Angels yet, which had drawn him here in the first place.

He wished he had Lavinia there to share it with him. Or anybody who could see the marvels for what they were.

He found a building that contained the entire universe—the sun, the moon, the planets and stars. Originally built as an educational exhibit, the Orrery was a clockwork representation of the heavens, wheels within wheels in a spiral array. Radiating from a central globe that represented the world, long metal arms held the moon and the sun. Surrounding that construction, thin armillary spheres represented the diamond light of stars arcing over the heavenly vault.

Owen stood in the middle of the contraption, staring up until his neck hurt, unable to tear his eyes away; he had to hold his hat on his head. He'd always been fascinated by the constellations, both from his books and in the real night sky, and he remembered that last bright night on the orchard hill, while he waited in vain for Lavinia to join him.

Now, in this model, he tried to find the patterns he had made up himself.

The Orrery's astronomer-docent was glad to have a visitor. "How does it work, sir?" Owen asked. He had seen the large hydraulic engine in the back of the building, which drove it all. The celestial engine was now silent, and the planets hung in their places, the moon and sun frozen in position, although the real ones continued along their heavenly paths high overhead.

"How does the universe work?" the astronomer-docent said with a sniff. He was a bald man with a bland voice, entirely unsuited for the grandeur of his lecture. "Only the Watchmaker knows for certain, and we, in our imperfection, can only try to understand. This representation shows us not how the universe *is*, but how it should be."

"So, it is inaccurate?" Owen asked.

"The universe is inaccurate. We are trying to fix it."

"I'm not an astronomer. Just the assistant manager of an orchard."

"Then you have no need to understand, but I'm happy to have the company." The man's expression softened; he seemed lonely, even though he had the universe as his place of business.

Owen pointed up at the machinery. "Can I see it move?"

The astronomer-docent fluttered his fingers, as if he were trying to catch birds. "There is a nominal charge as imposed by the Watchmaker." Owen pulled out his remaining coins, and the docent snatched them all. "That will be nominal enough."

Owen hadn't expected to pay the rest of his money, but as he looked up at the Orrery, he realized how much he wanted to see it in operation. More important than coins, he still had the red rose Francesca had given him; it was tucked away in his homespun shirt, though wilted and worse for wear.

The bald man went over to the machine, dispensed the coins, and wound the mechanism. He twisted valves to increase the bright blue light of coldfire from the battery within. "The machine is cold. It hasn't been run for some days."

Owen waited as the pressure built up, the channels filled with frothy impetus, the hydraulic tubes thrummed. Overhead, with a clicking rattle, chains pulled, gears turned, and the planets, sun, moon, and stars began to revolve.

Owen saw the graceful swooping arcs as if he were in a time machine. The days, months, and years whirled by at dizzying speed.

He raised his voice. "If this is the perfect order of the celestial vault, how is it different from the real stars and planets?"

The astronomer-docent clicked his tongue against his teeth. "At first, we believed our observations were faulty, but records go back for many years, even before the Stability. The planets stray from their paths, like unruly dogs. Rather than traveling in perfect circles, they change their minds at times, looping back in retrograde orbits before getting on the correct path again. That's inexcusable! In a perfect universe, the stars, the sun, and moon all travel in exact circles, as should the planets. Everything else functions as expected."

The astronomer-docent patted Owen on the shoulder. "But you can rest assured, young man, the Watchmaker has his best engineers working on calculations. He saved Albion with his Stability, and now he has turned his sights on the universe itself. Sooner or later, our loving Watchmaker will find a way to make the planets travel in circular orbits."

"I have no doubt of it," Owen said. And he meant it. Even the Watchmaker couldn't stop thinking big.

CHAPTER 8

The joy and pain that we receive
Must be what we deserve

By the time night fell at the end of such a long day, Owen's body was exhausted from helping on the docks, and his mind was exhausted from seeing the great Orrery, not to mention the deluge of other amazing sights in the city. Thanks to the astronomer-docent, however, Owen was out of money, so he could not afford a room at any inn, nor did he have any friends here who might let him sleep in a spare bed.

He heard a town crier striding down the streets, calling out in a loud voice, "Ten o'clock, and all is for the best!" even though the clocks chimed on the hour throughout the city. As the crier walked away, Owen kept his eyes open for a place where he might find shelter. He would make do. "All is for the best," he muttered to himself.

The streets had fallen quiet for the night; people returned to their homes to set their clocks, go to bed, and wake with their alarms the next morning. The city seemed large and crowded around him, and he felt small and alone. He walked along the boulevards, as if he had every reason to be there. He knew that a determined stride implied that he had a real destination. Maybe he would just keep walking until dawn. Under the glowing streetlight spheres of coldfire, the night was bright.

As he passed a shadowy alley that connected two main streets, he came upon a furtive figure, heard a rattle and a concentrated hiss. Though a tingle of fear went down his spine, Owen stepped closer. The man kept busy moving in the dimness, waving his hand in wild gestures as if performing some kind of incantation. Along with the thin hissing sound, Owen smelled paint.

"Hello? What are you doing there?" He tried to sound brave and important. He stood at the opening of the alley, where his dark silhouette must have made him look ominous.

Startled, the shadowy figure dropped something that made a metallic clatter on the alley pavement, then he bolted away with feral speed, dashing out the opposite end of the alley and into the street beyond.

Owen ventured into the alley, where he found a copper cylinder with a thumbwheel on the top; this must be what the man had dropped, the source of the metallic clang. He touched the thumbwheel, found a levered nozzle; when he depressed it, a spurt of bright paint emerged: scarlet. The stain spread like a splatter of blood across the bricks. Curious, Owen looked at the canister. A spray-dispensing device? He turned the thumbwheel to another setting, toyed with the lever again, and this time a blob of citrus green spattered the wall.

Then he recalled the graffiti symbol the two workers had been scrubbing so vigorously on his first day in Crown City, and the offending, provocative words the Anarchist had scrawled on the building across from the inn.

With eyes now adjusted to the alley's gloom, he looked up to see the encircled "A" symbol prominent on the wall, along with another bold pronouncement: *The Stability makes time stand still!* and again, *Who made the Watchmaker?*

Now that he knew the "A" symbol was a signature of the

Anarchist, he shuddered with the cold realization that he'd been within a few paces of the murderous man who was causing mayhem across Albion! The man who set bombs, blew up steamliner tracks, created havoc in daily life.

He heard marching footsteps out on the boulevard from which he had entered the alley, and he could tell by their perfect rhythm, a syncopated echo of boot heels, that this was the Blue Watch marching on their rounds, guarding the city against criminals . . . like the Anarchist.

Owen could sound the alarm, send the Regulators chasing after the criminal. The Anarchist had been here only moments ago! And if they apprehended the most-wanted man, Owen would be a hero, maybe even receive a medal from the Watchmaker himself.

But he suddenly realized that *he* was here in the alley, holding a copper paint sprayer, in front of freshly written treasonous statements.

He dropped the copper cylinder and bolted out through the alley. Behind him he heard the marching boot steps stop, then a succession of angry shouts, but he kept running so that the Watch would not see him. . . .

Panting and flushed, he returned to the tree-studded park where the carnival had performed. There were walking paths and flower gardens, as well as the expansive performing area where the Magnusson Carnival Extravaganza had set up. With droopy eyelids, shaking and exhausted, Owen sat beneath a large tree. This would be an adequate bed. He could lie back on the grass, look up through the branches at the night sky where the constellations were washed out by the glow of city lights.

He knew his adventure was almost over, and he would have to go home soon, but he was determined not to return to Barrel Arbor before he had a chance to see the Clockwork Angels. After many inquiries, he had learned that everyone in Crown City received tickets and dispensations according to their addresses, their professions, their stations in the city, as well as the day of the week. It was a complex formula, comprehensible only to the Regulators and the Watchmaker.

But Owen had come here on impulse, so he did not fit anywhere in the standard equation. He was a gear that had jumped loose from its train; he wasn't supposed to be in Crown City. It was unsettling and certainly argued for following the Watchmaker's perfect plan.

However, if he had remained content, hadn't dared to break the rules, he would never have seen the most wonderful things in his life. Now, he lay back on the moist grass and decided that he had to stick it out. The universe had a plan.

After full dark, the empty park was quiet and peaceful—but the Blue Watch continued on their rounds with their lockstep gait, walking down the paths, following their precise route, regardless of the hour. Owen had dozed off but woke when a gruff-sounding Watch patrolman barked out, "Citizen, where is your place?"

Owen scrambled to his feet, brushing grass from his rumpled homespun clothes. "Why, right here under the tree, sir."

"Your card, your papers, your ticket!"

"I don't have any, sir. I'm from a country village, here to pay my respects to the Watchmaker."

"Pay your respects? Did the Watchmaker send you a bill?" The Regulators seemed flustered. "You're not allowed to sleep here— it's a public park."

"I'm part of the public," Owen said, "and I was tired."

The Blue Watch grabbed him by the arms and marched him out under the bright light of coldfire streetlamps. They frisked him, searched his pockets for money, weapons, or papers, but found only the wilted rose from Francesca, nothing else, which they considered even more suspicious.

Owen realized they must be wary because of the dangerous mayhem caused by the Anarchist, the violent explosions and sabotage, even the troubling graffiti. "I didn't mean any harm, sir."

"Nevertheless, you don't belong here. Your very presence disrupts the Stability. We are required to escort you from the city."

Owen had always considered "escorting" to be a more pleasant process. As they marched him roughly along the path, he feared he had gotten in over his head yet again. He pleaded with the Watch captain to let him go. The uniformed man said, "That is precisely our intention."

For some reason, the prospect did not gladden Owen.

His unauthorized presence in the park had disrupted the timing of their rounds, which made the Watch members surly. "Now we will have to include this in our report," complained the captain. "We've had no incidents in more than a month."

Owen did his best to be rushed along. "No incidents? But didn't the Anarchist blow up a steamliner rail just inside the city? And what about all that writing on the wall?"

The Watch captain sniffed. "Anarchist incidents fall into an entirely different category. None of our concern."

They placed him in the back compartment of a chugging vehicle, which rolled down the empty streets. His retreat from Crown City was not at all like his arrival. In daylight, these streets were filled with vendors, performers, and pedestrians. But now Owen was no tourist, and the shadows seemed dark and frightening.

The Regulators were very efficient. Before 11:00 p.m., according to the clock faces he could see on the buildings as the vehicle rumbled along, they had evicted him from the city. They stopped the vehicle on the outskirts and unlocked the back compartment to let him out. Disoriented, he had no idea where he was or how he could make his way to his village. Without answering further questions, the Blue Watch climbed aboard their chugging vehicle again, reversed the wheels, and rushed back into the city, eager to catch up with their rounds. They had a schedule to keep.

Owen stood blinking, hungry and lost. His father would have

said that he had gotten exactly what he deserved. He never should have left Barrel Arbor, never should have broken with his past and ventured to the city where he didn't belong. The barren outskirts felt primitive, barbaric. This was the way people had lived before the Stability, and he remembered the horrific images and stories from the pedlar's book. How could a simple person survive alone out here? Where would he go?

Sooner or later, he would have to find a steamliner to take him back home; he had learned his lesson and would put away thoughts of such "foolishness," as his father insisted, although he would secretly revel in his memories of adventure for a long time to come. At the moment, however, the experience did not feel particularly enjoyable.

Many steamlines radiated in all directions from the city, and the Blue Watch had dumped him far from where he'd first arrived. In order to identify the correct rail line to take him back to Barrel Arbor, he would have to go back to the central station in Crown City. What if the Regulators drove him out again?

He had always been taught that the universe had a plan, but Owen didn't like the plan much right now.

He struck out away from the city in search of a friendly, well-lit home, even though everyone should be asleep by now. His muscles ached, and his stomach growled, and he wandered along. It was nearly midnight when he saw a glow up ahead; he didn't wonder whether it might be solace or threat. He climbed the grassy hill and gazed down at a sprawling camp where the carnival had set up, brightly lit and full of activity even at this improbable hour of the night.

Owen blinked, then smiled. After all the surprises he had experienced, he did not question what he saw. He hurried down the hillside and out of the night shadows until he was bathed in the glow of carnival lights.

The Magnusson Carnival Extravaganza was not set up for a performance, but merely camped on the open field in between destinations. Even so, the carnies seemed as exuberant as they had been before an audience. They had set up bright pavilions, game tents, the fortune teller's booth, even a practice wire for the trapeze and tightrope, as well as homey trailers and sleeping tents. Coldfire lanterns dangled from posts, but much of the light and warmth came from actual campfires, flames that burned real wood. The cheery orange glow and scent of smoke warmed Owen's heart.

He ventured into the camp, waiting to be noticed, but no one challenged him. The carnies played their own games, throwing balls to knock down the stacked but reinforced beakers, which had caused such consternation to the customers. At the spinning clock wheel with colored prize sections, a gamer threw sharpened daggers instead of darts; each knife whistled through the air and thunked into the spinning wheel with a meaty sound, a prize every time.

The three carnival clowns hunched on the ground, dressed in vests and bright pantaloons; they passed a cup around in which they rattled lumpy, odd-shaped dice, each face marked with a tiny alchemical symbol. "Roll the bones," one of the clowns said and spilled the dice onto the flattened dirt. Two of the men whistled, one grumbled in defeat; Owen couldn't tell how the game was played.

Looking up, he caught his breath as he saw Francesca flipping on the trapeze, performing for an audience of stars. She swung back and forth, doing part of her routine and then simply playing, enjoying her own movements, the grace of acrobatics. She wore not the angelic white outfit, but a patched practice leotard. Her hair flew behind her like the tail of a black comet. Two other young carnies caught the trapeze as Francesca passed it to them. A little girl attempted to walk on the low practice tightrope, but fell; she caught herself on the rope, and then dropped the five feet to the ground. Unhurt, she scrambled up the pole to try again.

These people were not going through the show according to the Watchmaker's approved routine; they were simply performing for the fun of it, the joy of doing what they wanted to do—an improvisation.

His face filled with silent laughter. He turned and suddenly found himself facing the tip of a pointed sword like the stinger of a mythical beast. The narrow blade twirled in the air, deftly missing him in a playful threat. "Who goes there?"

He recognized the handsome man who had ingested alchemical powders and then breathed out fire. The man was lean, with a tight tunic and black hose. His patchy beard gave him a rakish look.

Owen backed away, raised his hands. "I saw the lights—I just came to see."

The man danced with his sword, stepped back, bounded forward in a comical caricature of practiced swordsmanship; he intimidated Owen, but left not so much as a scratch on his skin. The swordsman swirled the tip of the blade and circled Owen, who turned in an attempt to keep his eyes on him. "Our next show is not scheduled yet, stranger. The price for the performance is . . ." His voice lilted upward. "Your name."

"I'm Owen—Owen Hardy." His nervousness made him blurt out the name as quickly as he could.

The swordsman cut and thrust, then danced back, grinning all the while. "So, Owenhardy, I am Tomio—fire-eater, sword-swallower, and soon to be expert fencer." He twirled his blade again.

A rude snort came from the left. "He only calls himself an expert because he has no one to practice with. That way, he can claim to be the best among us."

Owen spun again, feeling hunted and trapped. The speaker was the dapper César Magnusson, still dressed in black tails and top hat, but the handlebar mustache looked cockeyed, as if hastily applied.

"I am expanding my skills," Tomio said. "Finding new things to incorporate into our act." He bent backward like a willow bowing in a wind, tilted his head up to the sky, and opened his mouth wide as he stretched out his arms. The tip of the thin blade wavered a little as he lowered it into his mouth. He plunged the sword down until Owen couldn't bear to watch. Impaling oneself through the stomach—even via this unusual direction—was a skill that not many audiences would appreciate.

Tomio's performance, however, did quiet the other carnies, who watched in respectful silence. In deep concentration, he slowly withdrew the sword, bent over, swallowed hard, and took a bow. He said in a roughened voice, "I am also a night watchman, apparently, for I discovered this stranger wandering in our camp."

"I'm not a stranger—I'm Owen Hardy. At least I'm not a stranger to myself."

"But why are you here, Owenhardy?" asked César Magnusson.

"Because I'm . . ." The full explanation—his long story, his tribulations and adventures, and all the sights he had seen—built up within him and paralyzed his wit. Unable to provide a detailed explanation, he said only, "Because I'm here."

"You'll have to do better than that," said another voice. Francesca.

"I saw you perform!" He fumbled in his shirt, where he found the now wilted and rumpled rose. "You gave me this."

Francesca chuckled. "You kept it. That's sweet."

Tomio raised his eyebrows. "You've been flirting again, dear Francesca."

Owen finally got up his nerve and rattled off an abbreviated description of how he had left his village to see Crown City, but once he'd exhausted his money, the Regulators had driven him out of town.

"And then I saw you," he said. "Can I stay with you?"

César Magnusson crossed his arms over his chest and regarded Owen. "Don't you have anywhere else to go?"

Owen shook his head. "No."

With a toss of her dark hair, Francesca said, "Then this is exactly where you belong."

CHAPTER 9

Each moment a memory in flight

It was a strange and refreshing sort of freedom. When they finally settled down for the night, the carnies didn't mind that Owen stretched out wherever he liked, exhausted from his journeys and travails. No Regulators chased him from the mound of grass where he curled up near a warm campfire. The wonders, excitement, and uncertainty of the past few days caught up with him; he pulled the porkpie hat over his face and quickly drifted off.

Though Owen got very little sleep—as measured by hours—he awoke energized. Maybe the carnies had discovered how to turn the valve on some underground reservoir to let alchemical energy bubble up from the ground. . . .

When he rolled over to blink up at the brightening sky, he half-expected the carnival camp to have been a dream. But he rubbed his eyes and saw the people preparing for the new day, talking and laughing as they went about their chores.

Over by the wagons he saw Francesca, who seemed like sunrise incarnate. She had a smile that filled her entire body, and even when she walked she seemed to be dancing. Every step was an acrobatic performance.

She paused to talk with the dashingly handsome Tomio, who swept his arm around her waist and swirled her in a half circle. Laughing, she kissed him on the cheek, then went over to talk to Mr. Magnusson. Owen felt a twinge of jealousy and disappointment to watch the close connection she had with the fire-eater and swordsman.

"Join us for breakfast, young Owenhardy."

He turned, recognizing the woman who spoke instantly. Louisa was handsome, and not only because of her beard. Owen had stared at her at the carnival gateway back in Crown City, but now she had brushed out her brown hair and beard, not bothering with the lavender ribbons. Her blue eyes twinkled.

"I'd like that very much." His stomach rumbled in agreement as soon as he said it. The bearded lady took his arm like a matronly escort—not at all the way the Blue Watch had escorted him out of the city—and led him to a group of plank tables set up on sawhorses.

The gathered carnies slid over to give him and Louisa a place to sit on the benches. He ate a wonderful repast of eggs, bacon, and toasted bread, all heated on a thermal plate powered by reacting packets of chemicals. He listened to their conversations about the upcoming day, the next scheduled performance, and the verified permits, as if the frenetic activity were as much of a routine for them as his own daily chores in the orchard.

Feeling homesick, he told Louisa about Barrel Arbor, and she listened politely, stroking her beard as she munched on a rasher of bacon. "I know exactly what Barrel Arbor is like," Louisa said.

Owen brightened. "You've been there?" He couldn't remember the last time a carnival had come to town.

"We've been to the same village hundreds of times. Maybe it wasn't called Barrel Arbor, but all country villages are designed on the same master plan. So, yes, we've been there."

Owen had not considered this. Since he had never left Barrel Arbor before, how would he know that the next village up the river or in the hills looked exactly the same? Owen wondered if he had an identical counterpart there—another young assistant manager of the town orchard with a beautiful girl in his heart, the daughter of the local newsgraph operators.

He finished his breakfast, wiped his mouth with a napkin, and didn't have the slightest idea what to do next or where he should go. Without asking, he helped scrub pots in a basin of dishwater, and no one complained that he wasn't scheduled to do so. It was unsettling but liberating. Then he looked around for some other way to earn his keep and repay their hospitality.

Afterward, hoping to find a way to fit in here, he asked Louisa, "Is there any way I could help you with your show?" He did not want to leave, not yet.

She smiled beneath her lavish beard. "Oh, I'm not a performer, young man, I'm just a showpiece. People stare at me and move on."

Ahead, Owen and Louisa heard a clang of metal plates as Golson, the burly strongman, flexed his muscles, bent over to slide two more iron disks onto his barbell, and strained to lift it. Golson did not acknowledge them, though he seemed to draw strength from having even this small audience. He had loaded his bar with every weight on the stack except for the last two, which rested off to the side, bound with a chain and padlock.

Finding this very curious, Owen whispered to Louisa, "Does he have a story?"

"Everyone has a story, but not all are worth telling or listening to." She smiled and continued, "Golson is just a performer's name, a patchwork of Goliath and Samson, because he says he draws the best qualities of both. His mentor was the greatest weightlifter of all time—our previous strongman." Louisa lowered her eyes and dropped her voice. "Golson could be even stronger, I think, but he won't push himself—he refuses to."

"Why not?" Owen asked.

"It's fear, plain and simple, although we all sympathize. His mentor was killed when he pushed himself too hard and tried to beat his personal best. He added more weight than he could tolerate, managed to lift it . . . but he couldn't hold all that weight. He was crushed right there in front of a large audience."

"That's horrible!"

Louisa nodded. "And that's why Golson keeps those last plates padlocked, so he's never tempted to go too far."

Owen swallowed hard. When he had first attended the carnival, he had seen these performers as bright distractions, but now he realized they were people with their own lives, their own tragedies. Maybe some of them had their own picture books given to them by mothers who'd gone away early in their . . .

Tomio emerged from his private wagon, which had several small shuttered windows. Tiny smokestacks and air vents protruded from the roof. The wagon had its own motivating engine and large tires balanced on an intricate network of springs, so as to minimize shocks from a rough road.

The graceful swordsman concealed something in the palm of his hand; when he hurled it down at the ground, a bright flash of light was accompanied by a puff of purple smoke. "Presto!" He strutted along, brandishing his thin sword like a magic wand and tossing tiny packets with the other hand; he timed his cuts and thrusts to punctuate them with colored smoke. "Presto!" When he had expended his packets of powder, Tomio ducked back inside his trailer to continue more experiments.

Life was so much more exciting outside of Barrel Arbor, Owen realized.

"Francesca!" The bearded lady waved, and the dark-haired acrobat came over from her practice area. Owen's heart started beating more rapidly. "Young Owenhardy wants to participate in an act."

"I . . . didn't exactly say that," he said, but before he could make further excuses, Louisa left him. His tongue suddenly became stupid, connected to a brain that could not remember how to form conversation.

"You'll have to earn your keep if you're going to stay with us," Francesca said. "Plenty of work to do."

Owen was caught off guard by the implicit invitation. He hadn't planned on staying long, just needed a place until he could figure out how to get back home. "I'm . . . I'm always happy to help," he finally managed to say.

Francesca placed her hands on her hips. "Well, what can you do?" She was a saucy, energetic, and independent woman—in every way the opposite of Lavinia. Her very presence seemed to sparkle.

Owen wished more than ever that he knew poetry. "I was the assistant manager of an orchard."

"Excellent," Francesca said. "Unfortunately, the carnival has no orchard to tend, so we'll have to find something else for you to do."

A loud but muffled thump came from Tomio's trailer. With a clatter, the window shutters blasted open, and curls of smoke wafted into the air. Owen's mouth dropped open. "Should we go see if he's all right?"

Francesca wasn't concerned. "That's only the first of the daily explosions. We don't come running unless there's a much bigger boom. Otherwise, we'd spend all day, every day, rushing to rescue Tomio." They watched the smoke change colors as it curled from the rooftop vent stacks.

The trailer door opened, and Tomio staggered out, coughing, rubbing his eyes, but he waved to show he was unharmed. He waited for the fumes to clear from his trailer before he ducked back inside and closed the door.

Francesca cocked her head. "He insists that if I worry about his experiments, then he'll worry about me practicing on the high wire, and I can't allow that. So we've made an accommodation. We have to accept who we are, or it's not worth being ourselves."

Near the cook tent, she spied a basket of apples that had been set out for the breakfast hour. She snatched one from the top of the pile. "So, you picked apples?"

"Yes—Sunrise, Red Flush, Ruby Delicious, Tartfire. We had different varieties on the trees." He was about to relate to her which type of apples made the best fresh eating, which made the best cider, which were most appropriate for pies, and which created potent vinegar. She tossed him an apple, and he instinctively caught it.

"And you cared for the apples?"

"I was a very diligent assistant orchard manager." She tossed him a second apple, and he caught it.

"Then you should never let the fruit fall on the ground. Don't let it get bruised."

"I wouldn't let any apples get bruised!" He scrambled to catch the third apple she tossed.

"You'd better not." Francesca grabbed another apple from the basket. "So you'll have to learn how to catch them all."

She tossed the fourth one, and Owen had to release one of the apples into the air so he could catch the new one, but then he caught the apple falling down, scrambled to catch another one. But he could not keep the rhythm going, and they all came tumbling down in a disappointing mess.

Francesca chuckled, but it was not mocking laughter. "Needs some work, but it's a good start." She picked up the apples and stepped back. "We could use a juggler." She tossed the apples at him again.

CHAPTER 10

Clockwork angels, spread their arms and sing
Synchronized and graceful, they move like living things

When the carnival packed up to move on, the flurry looked like a random whirlwind but had a choreographed efficiency. César Magnusson had filled out the proper paperwork, paid the appropriate fees, and received permission to perform in a different sector of Crown City.

Without being asked, Owen helped the carnies wherever he saw work that needed to be done. They loaded the tents, the game booths, the disassembled whirling rides on flatcars. Tomio packed up his wagon, powered up its engine to join the line of vehicles, and the caravan puttered back toward the city like a long, slow exhale.

In spare moments, Owen practiced tossing apples into the air and was dismayed each time he dropped one. His fruit was bruised and battered by now, so he suggested to Francesca that he should try juggling with rubber balls. She dismissed the suggestion. "Absolutely not."

"But then I wouldn't bruise any apples."

"Correct—and then you wouldn't *care*. That's more important than a few apples."

As the carnival followed the curving arc of an outer road in toward Crown City, Owen walked beside the vehicles. Cautious, he juggled with only two apples, but he was growing more proficient. He understood the parabolic arc, the gentle path of gravity. He strode along while maintaining his intense concentration: he watched each apple as it rose and fell, considered the symphony of his muscles, his fingers, his wrists, the palms of his hands. It was like one of the Watchmaker's equations that governed the universe.

When Francesca was nearby, though, he had a hard time thinking of anything but her. She rode aboard a rolling wagon that slowly passed him, and she laughed when he dropped the apples again. He scurried to pick them up from the dusty side of the road as he followed the moving carts. After he had retrieved the apples, she patted the bench beside her. "Up here."

"You want me to ride with you?" he said.

"I want you to *talk* with me." She patted the seat again, and Owen grabbed a rung on the side of the wagon, stepped on the running board, and swung himself up; somehow, he managed to keep hold of his two apples. As he settled himself beside her, Francesca took one of the apples, polished it on her sleeve, and took a bite.

"I could get you a better apple, one that's not bruised." Owen turned around, looking back to the food wagon.

Francesca shrugged. "Nothing in life survives without a few scuffs and dents. It adds character, and it tastes just as good, maybe a little better."

Owen ate the other apple, and it did taste better, but primarily because he was sitting beside her.

He told her about his disappointment at not being able to see the fabled Clockwork Angels. "Ah, I do enjoy the Angels,"

Francesca said. "And when I see how wonderstruck you are by simple everyday things, I'm afraid you'll become euphoric and useless when you see them."

He sighed. "Yes, it sounds wonderful."

She took pity on him. "Owenhardy, I love your optimism and your innocence. We don't see much of that." His ears buzzed after she said the word love, and he had to concentrate to understand the rest of her words. He didn't even catch that she had used the teasing contraction of his name. "I do remember you from the audience a few days ago, when I flew down on angel wings and landed in front of you."

"I'm keeping the rose," Owen said, patting his homespun shirt.

"That sort of wonder and appreciation is usually reserved for children, but sometimes adults can experience it."

"I'm not an adult," Owen admitted. "Not quite yet. My birthday is in a little more than a week. I should probably go home before then. . . ." He looked ahead as the tall buildings of Crown City grew larger. "But I haven't seen the Clockwork Angels yet."

Francesca reached into the folds of her peasant dress, found a pocket that he had never suspected was there, and withdrew two tickets etched on metallic paper, embossed with the honeybee symbol of the Watchmaker. The tickets shimmered like a prismatic illusion. "Hmm, I just happen to have these tickets, and I'll take you to see the Clockwork Angels tonight."

Overhead, the stars were aglow like scattered sparks. As Francesca led him into the city, toward Chronos Square, Owen didn't even need a tightrope to walk on air. He was in the most fabulous city in the world, going to see the Clockwork Angels at last, in the company of the most beautiful and fascinating woman he had ever met.

During his travels so far, he might have become bruised and scuffed like a dropped apple, but none of that mattered. Surely, this was part of the Watchmaker's perfect plan. All had indeed turned out for the best.

As he and Francesca flowed along with the people approaching the center of the city, Owen held his ticket as if it were a talisman. It felt slick and electric in his fingertips. He told her, "It's lucky you have a ticket for this performance! I tried so hard to get one, but didn't have the proper address or the correct day."

Francesca chuckled. "Oh, we always carry tickets—they're counterfeit, but the Red Watch will never notice the difference."

Owen gripped the ticket as if the bee symbol might sting him. "A . . . counterfeit?"

Francesca did not seem at all concerned. "No one's ever questioned it. Why would the Regulators imagine there could be a fake?"

His excitement was now tainted with trepidation, but Francesca slipped her arm through his. He was so close to her, touching her, that he felt an alchemical reaction building between them. She seemed as much at ease with him as when she'd given Tomio a kiss on the cheek. He didn't want to ask her about the handsome fire-eater, didn't want to think about anything except her—and the Angels.

Feeling a flicker of guilt, he was sure that Lavinia must be worried about him back at the village. Had she decided that the betrothal wasn't going to happen? What about the printed card from the Watchmaker, promising them happiness? Neither she nor Owen had ever had any doubt. According to the plan, he was supposed to get married to his true love . . . but now he was far from Barrel Arbor and with someone else entirely.

With a burst of realization, Owen wondered if he had been thinking of the wrong betrothal all along. If these unexpected events were part of a grand plan, what if . . . ? He turned to look at Francesca with a new kind of wonder, but she tugged on his arm before he could speak. They reached the line of stern Red Watchmen, who took their counterfeit tickets without objection. They each received a program card printed from a newsgraph—that evening's scheduled pronouncements from the Angels, which Owen pocketed, waiting for the proper time. Finally, they passed through the last archway.

Chronos Square was enclosed by ornate government buildings, the Watchmaker's ministries, the Cathedral of the Timekeepers. The main clocktower loomed like a wise parent over the crowd that had come to see the spiritual machinery. Each building bore honeybee markings in various places of prominence. Globes of pulsing coldfire hovered in the air like private suns crackling with elemental lightning.

Francesca helped him worm his way through the crowd to get the best possible view. Power shimmered in the air—an excitement, a personal energy from the eager onlookers. Through cracks between the flagstones, faint blue light seeped upward as if the Angels had summoned so much energy from the gathered people that the city itself might catch fire. The nexus of coldfire lay right beneath them! Owen felt a tingling in his feet.

Sweet-smelling smoke wafted out of vents, making the air thick and heady. When Owen inhaled, he felt giddy—more than could be explained by the sheer joy of being here. His vision fuzzed, and he became calmer, both more content and more ecstatic at the same time.

The floating globes sparked, and dazzling arcs of light leaped from one to the next to the next in a spectacular show, imposing a hush on the crowd. Chain lightning bound the globes together, pulsing.

"It's about to start," Francesca whispered. Even she sounded fascinated, though she had seen the spectacle many times before.

Owen stared up at the Watchmaker's tower, concentrating on the immense doors beneath the clock face. With a rattling, mechanical rhythm, internal gears turned, and the doors began to open. The crowd inhaled in eerie unison.

Bathed in light, the four Clockwork Angels emerged from their alcoves within the tower: four beautiful women the size of Titans, with flowing stone robes, majestic wings. Their bodies sparkled such a dazzling white that even alabaster was put to shame. From the foundations of the alchemy by which the Watchmaker had saved the world from barbarism, these four figures represented the four basic elements of the universe, light, sea, sky, and land. These four elements encompassed the whole world, regardless of what additional nuances the Alchemy College teased out and dissected from the chemistry of the Creation.

People gazed up with mouths slack and eyes wide open, full of love. Owen couldn't breathe; the others were so close, so enraptured, that they propped him up when he swayed. When he gazed upon the Angels, he realized that even his fondest dreams of his mother's face were not so beautiful.

The Angels glided on their clockwork mechanism, spread their wings, raised their arms—and Owen could do nothing but stare. Though these were just immense clockwork automatons, they moved like living things.

As the silent Angels stood in position, everyone in the crowd held their breath. Owen felt moved to worship, overwhelmed by the grandeur, dizzy and disoriented. He closed his eyes and bowed. All around him people fell to their knees.

Gliding forward on smooth hydraulics, the first Angel took prominence. She did not speak, and her face remained chiseled, impassive, achingly beautiful . . . yet somehow he heard hollow, vibrating voices in his head. He felt strange, and the smoke in the air made his eyes water, his ears ring.

He looked down at the printed card, the program given to him in exchange for his precious ticket, and the Angels made the words there come alive: *Lean not upon your own understanding.*

The second Angel rotated into position, and Owen felt compelled to look at the printed words again. *Ignorance is well and truly blessed.*

But the words were just letters, lines of ink. What he read, heard, experienced, and *understood* held so much more, as if the Angels had hooked up a hydraulic conduit to his mind and poured revelations into him. "Ignorance" was not just an empty lack of knowledge, but an acceptance of the world's vast incomprehensibility, a broad cosmic safety net that caught and cradled common people like himself. He was not being kept in the dark; the Angels were shielding him from all the things he didn't understand, the things he didn't need to understand. The Watchmaker was loving and omniscient, and *that* was all he needed to know. Owen's responsibility was just to be content. . . .

Accompanied by words thrumming through his head, the third Angel's pronouncement read, *Trust in perfect love and perfect planning.* He wondered if the Watchmaker used some trick, acoustical vibrations that made the words *mean* more. The effect was all enveloping: moving, sensual, pervasive, emotional, intense . . . intoxicating.

Owen squinted up, trying to see more. Though the faces didn't change, a collective voice emanated from the figures, an unearthly soprano, sometimes solo, then in unison, then breaking into heart-rending harmonies. Together, it created an effect that assaulted his entire being—sensory, physical, emotional. As he listened, he could imagine that the Angels, so delicate and so grand, were indeed divinely inspired.

The smoke grew thicker in the air, and finally the fourth Angel came into position to give a reassuring benediction: *Everything will turn out for the best.*

The crowd mumbled aloud in response, "Everything will turn out for the best."

The Angels ratcheted forward to loom down from the clock-tower platform, and they spread their wings as if to fly. The starry-eyed crowd surged to their feet, and everyone held out their arms as well, spreading their fingers and reaching toward the universe, as if they too could fly.

The hovering blue globes dimmed, and the arcing sparks faded from sphere to sphere, disconnecting the lightning. The Clockwork Angels folded their wings again, bowed as if to acknowledge the audience's adulation, then retreated into the clocktower. The doors closed, like hands folding in prayer.

Owen realized he had been holding his breath, and he inhaled deeply. Only then did he remember Francesca beside him—and that, in itself, demonstrated how wonderful the Clockwork Angels were, the perfect manifestation of the fundamental elements, light, sea, sky, land.

But Francesca had been watching *him* instead of the Angels. "I've never seen a look of such pure amazement in my life, Owenhardy." She laughed and bent to kiss him on the cheek. "Thank you," she said.

The Anarchist

The lenses inside of me that paint the world black

The Anarchist walked through the streets of Crown City, wearing a standard timekeeper's uniform, a dark green jumpsuit with three synchronized pocketwatches clipped to his belt. He carried a kit with appropriate tools to adjust the springs and pendulums of the large public clocks. In his pocket were forged work orders. No one would question his presence.

Businesses welcomed the regular inspections of a timekeeper. Clocks did not set themselves. Although time was perfect and unchanging, like the Watchmaker himself, human mechanisms were fallible and needed to be double-checked, every timepiece tuned and adjusted accordingly. If the Watchmaker had his way, every person's pulse would tick to the same heartbeat.

Nobody noticed the Anarchist on the streets, because he looked just like everyone else, but he was very different inside.

His intellect and his imagination were a special set of inner lenses through which he could spot imperfections in the Watchmaker's Stability. Alas, those lenses did not increase the colors or sharpen the focus; instead, they painted the world black and allowed him to see only the rotten heart of too much order, too much oppression. He saw the sad details of mass-produced lives.

In a city like this, he could have walked along the streets with his eyes closed, because everyone moved with mechanical precision, following exact schedules. It was as if the Watchmaker had inserted a key into their backs, wound them up, and set them loose to go about their daily lives. A small part of him—a very small part—envied such people for their blissful acceptance. *Ignorance is well and truly blessed*, as the Angels said.

Inner rage drowned out his other emotions, but he held it inside, gave no outward indication that anything was wrong. He was like a steam boiler reinforced to contain extreme passions.

Even in this work uniform, he wore a seemingly unremarkable pin on his lapel, a misshapen uncut diamond with a reddish tinge. No jeweler would have looked twice at it, but *he* had created the gem. A diamond, a simple, efficient crystal lattice of carbon atoms, tempered with blood, *his* blood, in an experiment that had gone violently wrong. The surgeons had dug the small diamond out of the bone, plucking it from the mangled flesh of his wrist. How could he not wear it as a badge of honor? He touched the pin to remind himself of his purpose as he went to work.

He slipped his burned, scarred hand into a dark glove, but not out of embarrassment. He just didn't want others to see the evidence of the accident. The *transformation*.

The other hand, clutching the toolkit, had a tattoo, an alchemical symbol that he had chosen from obscure texts he had studied when he was a student at the Alchemy College—something he'd never forgotten. The symbol was an open-ended rectangle that enclosed six dots stacked in a pyramid. Among alchemy students, such a sign indicated a precipitate. *A solid separated from a solution*, as the alchemist-priests taught. *A product resulting from a process, event, or course of action.*

He slid his tattooed hand into a glove as well.

All the ingredients of his life had filled an empty part within him, had precipitated a new personality from the neutral, homogeneous Stability—a creature unlike these other sheep. A man who appreciated freedom to its extremes. *I am what my life has made me.*

He would never forget that lesson, the *process* or *event* that had marked his left hand: the searing white-hot fire, the acid flames that ate down to his bones. But a part of him had been annealed, which made him strong enough to do what had to be done. The others wouldn't do it. No one else wanted to make the terrible choice on the price of being free.

The Anarchist had no family to applaud his acts, not even to decry him. He had flung away his name long ago like a man emptying a chamber pot. That had been his first step toward freedom.

But it was such a burden to be the only one in the world who wasn't a fool. The Anarchist longed for an ally who had the same perceptive dark lenses, the same drive, even if he had to create such an ally himself. He had already set events in motion, begun preparing a candidate, a blank slate, an everyman . . . hoping to precipitate out another one like himself.

It couldn't be too difficult. After all, the Watchmaker had created *him.*

He heard a clanging handbell and a hissing, chugging sound. Amidst the metronomic bustle of the city, an old pedlar with a stovepipe hat, twisted gray hair, and an eye patch accompanied an automated cart down the street. The cart was mounded high with unusual trinkets, kegs, packages, contraptions. The old man called out, "What do you lack?" From the tone of his voice, it sounded as if he actually wanted to know.

What do I lack? What an annoying, ridiculous question! He bit back his answer, keeping the words to himself. He muttered in a low voice for his ears alone, since no one would understand anyway. "I lack freedom. All these people lack freedom. If a man has a perfect life but cannot make his own choices, then what good is that life?" Oh, they had their clothes and their comforts, their families, their pocketwatches and cheap gold, their smiles and their diamonds. But above all that, *he* would choose free will. They didn't even know what it was.

But the pedlar found no customers in the crowded streets. No one even answered the old man's question—the Anarchist wasn't surprised, since the people didn't have the imagination to wonder what might be missing in their lives.

The pedlar turned to him with a piercing gaze as if he saw something there, recognized him, regardless of the work uniform and disguise. The Anarchist flinched, retreated behind a mask of *normality*, betraying no atypical expression; self-consciously, he tugged the gloves that covered both hands. He sensed something odd about the old pedlar, too, but could not identify it.

"What do you lack?" the old man repeated, seemingly speaking to anyone in earshot, but his words were directed only to the Anarchist.

Far too many things for you to comprehend, he thought, but at the moment what he lacked was the freedom to speak. Their eyes met, and after a strange moment the pedlar moved on without receiving an answer.

Unsettled, the Anarchist fumed and strode off in the other direction. The people lacked a great deal, whether or not they could see it. Like sheep, they assumed the Watchmaker wanted them only for their wool, when in truth he was hungry for mutton.

In his previous unsuccessful attempts to awaken the populace, the Anarchist had broken steamliner rails, disrupted vital deliveries, thrown ritualized meetings into mayhem. He would strive for greater things. He would wake them up even if it killed them. He had been about his work all day.

He smiled as he entered another clocktower with his toolkit and his timekeeping instruments. It required great effort and attention to keep a city running in perfect synchrony. Tick. Tock. Tick. Tock.

Far easier to disrupt it all.

He presented his work order to the building superintendent, who let him up the winding metal stairs to the attic chamber behind the public clock. Whistling without a tune, he set to work with his tools. . . .

Back at the Alchemy College, he'd been a student with such aspirations! Expecting to excel, he had set a goal of drawing the Watchmaker's attention, maybe becoming his successor one day. He had indeed attracted that attention, too much of it. He had done extra work, *superior* work . . . and he had been punished for it. In the Watchmaker's Stability, any irregularity—even an obvious improvement—was not rewarded. In a field of poppies, if one flower grew taller than the rest, it would be hacked down to size.

With secret messages of encouragement, notes sent for his eyes alone, the Watchmaker had celebrated the student's glorious rise. And when that student grew too tall, the Watchmaker hacked him down. Thinking himself special, nudged along by confidential communications, the student had performed his own experiments, tested new elemental combinations, liberated more energy . . . with disastrous results.

The Anarchist flexed his burned hand.

They had drummed him out of the Alchemy College, muttering in a superior tone that he had gotten what he deserved. After his exile, he wandered across Albion and fell in with a traveling carnival. He saw those people as kindred spirits, lovers of true freedom—at first. He stayed with them for a season, performing in their shows and contributing his ideas. They were receptive, until they claimed that he had gone too far.

Now, the Anarchist realized that even the painful accident and its consequences were for the best, because those experiences had made him what he was, had precipitated out his true personality. . . .

Inside the attic clock room, the Anarchist adjusted the swinging and clicking pendulum, inspected the gears, compared the hands of time with the three accurate pocketwatches at his belt.

A simple wrench thrown into the gears would have changed all that, but that was far too crude a disruption, little more than a prank. Unworthy of his cause. Instead, the Anarchist attached wires, connected a complex device of his own making into the intricate machinery of the public clock. His schemes had to rival the Watchmaker's.

Finished with his work in the clocktower, he packed up his tools and left without speaking to the building superintendent. He had enough time to adjust one more building clock before the appointed hour. Disorder would strike at precisely five o'clock.

After he was finished, satisfied but eager, he bought an apple from a fruit vendor, sat down on a bench from which he could see many of the public clock faces in Crown City. It was the best view to encompass the scope of what he had achieved.

At five o'clock, the towers began to chime in perfect harmony, but the notes suddenly turned into a dissonant jangle. The hands of many clocks crept forward, while others spun backward, marching to an utterly imprecise drummer.

Each one of the clocks he had "inspected" now lurched to different times, some hours off, a few only minutes behind. The death knell was that they were *inaccurate*.

As soon as the people in the city realized what was happening, cries of dismay lofted into the air like dissonant music from a suicidal choir. Members of the Blue Watch moved through the streets trying to maintain order, but they didn't know what to do. No one could be certain of the correct time. Even the accurate clocks were viewed with uneasiness and suspicion.

Perfect. Tick. Tock. Tick. Tock.

The Anarchist finished his apple and watched calmly for a long time.

CHAPTER 11

Find a measure of love and laughter
And another measure to give

Owen traveled with the carnival as they put on performance after performance for appreciative crowds. He watched, he learned, and he fit in. Even though they became part of his everyday life, he never grew indifferent to the wonders. His optimism was infectious; the carnies laughed with him, teased him, and he laughed right back.

He got to know the three carny clowns—Deke, Leke, and Peke—and was surprised to learn that despite their humorous pratfalls during performances, all three were serious and intelligent men. Before each appearance among the crowds, they would apply their makeup to perfection and stitch fine wires and trip-springs into their costumes for surprise effects. Although the audiences never realized it, the clowns were as adept in their acrobatics as the trapeze performers, but they preferred the reward of laughter to awed applause.

He came to realize how much planning and interaction each performance required, especially the ones that seemed easiest and most casual. For every star performer who evoked whistles of appreciation from the crowd—like Golson the strongman, or Tomio with his fire-eating act, or Francesca's trapeze feats—ten others helped set up the tents, rig the ropes, build the game booths, take the money, and prepare food for the crew.

The carnies accepted Owen without questions, without permits or dispensations from the Watchmaker. They knew he had run away from his mundane life, and they never inquired how long he might stay. He did not ask to be paid, although Magnusson put him on the payroll along with everyone else.

In one town, trying to show a glimmer of responsibility, he did stop at a newsgraph office and pay to send a message home. By now, his father and Lavinia must be frantic. Since he did not have the money to transmit a full book of his exploits, he merely reassured everyone that he was safe and happy, told them not to worry. Mr. Paquette would take the printed sheet to the Tick Tock Tavern, brush down his lavish sideburns, and read the message to a room full of eager listeners.

Someday, whenever he did get back to Barrel Arbor, Owen would tell his adventures in full detail. Sitting in the Tavern drinking hard cider—a man, now—he would talk about the Clockwork Angels, the Orrery, the ships in port, the carnival and all its charms, and Francesca.

For a week, he practiced his juggling and bruised more than a few apples, but he soon became good enough to impress and amuse spectators (provided they did not have high expectations). Most of the time, though, if he tried juggling while walking among the crowds, he became nervous and blundered badly; few people actually believed he was part of the act.

Francesca spent many hours in Tomio's private wagon, sometimes not departing until late at night, but she also talked with Owen, ate with him, laughed at some of his fumbling, innocent jokes (he didn't tell her that he wasn't always trying to be funny).

One day while she practiced her tightrope act, Owen climbed up to bring her a cup of water. She stood facing him halfway across the rope, balanced on her two feet, and beckoned. "Bring it out here to me, Owenhardy."

He looked down at the rope, his feet, and the water in his hands; though he longed more than anything to go meet her, he couldn't summon the nerve, even though the practice rope was only six feet off the ground. Finally, she relented and flitted back to the platform where she took the water.

"Maybe someday," she said.

After breakfast one day, Louisa strolled over to Tomio's wagon, and Owen trotted beside her. The bearded lady indulged him. "Why would you be interested in a woman's efforts to maintain her beautiful appearance?"

"I'm interested in all aspects of a woman's beauty." Owen's response came automatically, since he was thinking of Francesca. He was also curious to see what Tomio did in his wagon with those alchemical experiments.

Louisa rapped on the trailer door, and Tomio opened up to grin at the bearded lady. "I knew you'd come this morning. I fixed a brand-new batch." He handed Louisa a small pot of lotion that smelled like vanilla, rhubarb, and a hint of brimstone.

"Thank you. My beard has been feeling thin." She dipped her fingers into the pot and smeared lotion on her face. She winked at Owen. "This tonic keeps my beard full and lush—it's my livelihood, you know."

That wasn't the answer Owen had expected. Noting his interest, Tomio laughed. "Maybe you should let young Owenhardy try the tonic to see if he can grow a beard!"

Owen self-consciously stroked the corn silk on his cheeks. "Would it make me look older and more handsome?"

"It would make you look *hairier*, that's for certain."

Louisa walked away with her lotion, massaging the cream into her skin, but Owen hovered by the wagon door. Tomio looked down at him with an amused expression. "Clearly that wasn't the reason you came here."

Owen tried to catch a glimpse of the trailer's interior. "I . . . I was just curious about your wagon. It's very mysterious."

"I'm a showman," Tomio said. "I'm supposed to be mysterious."

"The smoke from last night smelled particularly foul," Owen said.

Tomio gave a grave nod. "Yes, yak fur covered with pitch—a revolting combination. Nothing I intend to use again, I promise you. Come inside if you'd like to see my library." Owen entered, as hesitant as if he were stepping into some monster's den.

Tomio had an impressive collection of volumes filled with alchemical symbols, lists of elements, charts of metals and salts and powders, as well as guidelines for remarkable chemical reactions. In addition, the fire-eater had a "library" of organized and catalogued chemical samples, cross-referenced by color, reaction types, and level of hazard.

"Did you go to the Alchemy College?" Owen asked. "I saw the buildings when I first entered Crown City."

"I wasn't chosen for Alchemy College, but I made my own choice."

"I didn't choose to become the assistant manager of an orchard either," Owen admitted.

"And look where you are now!" Tomio paged through his books, looking up a recipe, then began pulling samples from the chemical library. "Look where we all are now. The universe has a plan, but it seems a disordered one. I think someone is making it up as he goes along."

Owen was startled to hear such sacrilege against the Watchmaker. Tomio mixed a pinch of powder in a crucible, added four drops of blue liquid from an eyedropper, then used tongs to hold the crucible over a burner flame powered by a coldfire battery. He continued to talk as he worked: "The carnival is a place for misfits, not Stability. You've joined us, and we'll remember you, but sooner or later you'll go do something else."

An image came unbidden to Owen's eyes: Francesca on the tightrope extending her hand to him. "I haven't decided yet," he said, "although I do turn seventeen tomorrow. That's when my life changes, and I become an adult."

"That's when the *calendar* says your life should change. For the rest of us, it will likely be just another day." He removed the crucible from the flames. "We've seen other people join us and then move on. It always happens. One season, I had a particularly driven assistant, someone who said he'd been trained at the Alchemy College but wouldn't talk about it. I could read in his eyes—and in his scarred hand—that something terrible happened there, but the scars in him went far deeper than a patch of burned skin."

Owen recalled the stranger who had helped him aboard the steamliner when he left Barrel Arbor.

"There was something *missing* inside of him." Tomio shook his head. "He loved the spectacular, took a stage name—*D'Angelo Misterioso.*"

Owen frowned. "The Mysterious Angel?"

As it cooled, the substance in the crucible burst into a sparkling, orange flame, a pinwheel that bounced in the tiny bowl like a living sprite. It capered, sparked, and finally ricocheted toward the ceiling, but dissipated before it could catch anything on fire. Tomio laughed, then grew serious again.

"At first, he and I were kindred spirits, but he wasn't so much interested in performing and entertaining as he was in his explosions for their own sake. D'Angelo Misterioso proposed an astonishing show of pyrotechnics, a dangerous one. The slightest miscalculation, the tiniest inconsistency in the mixture, could have resulted in a fireball that would incinerate an audience. When I refused to add that to our act, he lectured, and he ranted, and he finally went on his way. I can't say I was sorry to see him go."

"I hope I'm not like that," Owen said.

Tomio chuckled. "No, you aren't, young Owenhardy—not at all." He gave him a considering look, then opened a drawer to withdraw six delicate balls, one at a time. He placed them into a sack. They seemed as fragile as soap bubbles. "These are to help you with your juggling. They'll provide you with incentive."

"I juggle with them?"

"Just like with apples. Only better."

Owen couldn't imagine what Tomio meant, but he accepted the gift of soap-bubble juggling balls, thanking him. Outside, he gingerly removed three from the sack and tossed one, then another, and a third into the air. They began to glow as he juggled them, shining bright like miniature suns, but when he dropped one through a momentary lapse of concentration, the bubble burst with a puff of green smoke that smelled like pickles and stung like nettles. Chastened, he practiced with the remaining balls, and when he eventually dropped another one, it exploded with a similar embarrassing mess.

From that point, he learned his lesson and did not drop any of the remaining four.

Intrigued by the clockwork gypsy fortune teller enclosed in her booth, Owen was even more amazed to learn that the old woman was Francesca's great-great-grandmother, her head kept alive by rare and secret alchemy attached to a mechanical simulacrum of her body. None of the carnies would explain further; they seemed embarrassed or frightened by the extreme measures that had been taken to preserve her.

"One of the Watchmaker's early experiments," said César Magnusson. "He was desperate."

Owen didn't understand. "Desperate? How could the Watchmaker be desperate?"

But Magnusson merely stroked his extravagant mustache, pulling down the strands as if to cover a troubled frown. "Part of carnival life, young Owenhardy, is that we live in the present. Our timepieces always say *now*. Your past is not our concern, and you should not be concerned with ours. . . ."

So Owen remained curious, yet cautious. The old woman continued to live her sedentary life, to think her thoughts, and to dispense wisdom. Now that she had been disembodied, her brain was more attuned to cosmic vibrations and the thrumming threads of fate. She saw things that others didn't.

On some quiet evenings Owen would wind the key on the side of the booth and keep the old gypsy woman company. While the anchors held her neck in place, the old woman conversed with him in a hollow, papery voice.

"You're so old, madam," Owen said. "Do you remember the world before the Stability?"

"Yes, I remember it." Her wrinkled lips formed a smile, and her mechanical arms twitched and fidgeted. She turned her face as much as she could, given the constraints of her clockwork body.

"Was it ever so horrible?" Owen asked. "Savage and frightening? I read a book about it." He shivered to think of the murder, starvation, and lawlessness.

Oddly, the gypsy woman smiled at his question. "I was young then, and the world seemed bright. So many things to see, places to explore, and friends . . . I had so many friends."

Owen hunkered down. "But wasn't it a nightmare, disorganized and dangerous? Barbaric."

The clockwork woman made an odd, disrespectful sound. "It was a little of both—tedious at times, unpredictable at times.

Normal life. The Watchmaker drew a tight box around society, but people are people." A rattling sound came from her throat as the slowly turning key on the side of the booth wound down. "I wish that I could live it all again."

The carnies gave Owen a seventeenth birthday celebration that was stranger, and more wonderful, than he could possibly have had in Barrel Arbor. If he'd been back home, he would have given his betrothal to Lavinia, with pre-scripted words, according to plan. He felt a pang to think of his true love, but then he paused, surprised to realize that he could barely remember what Lavinia looked like.

The carny cooks had baked a cake for him and presented it on the long plank table. In his booming voice, César Magnusson declared that "*young* Owenhardy" was henceforth to be referred to, with great respect, as simply "Owenhardy."

To celebrate, Tomio created dozens of his small flaming sprites, which he set loose to dance and twirl in the air. The clowns Leke, Deke, and Peke performed pratfalls that made him laugh.

Deke snatched Tomio's sword, puffed up his chest, and swaggered, slashing with the blade, pretending to trip and finishing with a brilliant somersault that landed him on his tiptoes. Then Deke demonstrated his own alchemical prowess. Miming a retching convulsion, he burped up a cloud of colored smoke.

Leke stuffed rags in his shirt sleeves and padded his shoulders to the point of absurdity, then strutted around like Golson, making a great show of lifting pieces of cake as if they were tremendous weights.

Peke appeared with a long dark wig, flouncing and swaying his hips and walking an imaginary line on the ground, obviously pretending to be Francesca. And then Deke snatched Owen's porkpie hat and stared at the faux Francesca, eyes round, mouth gaping like a mooncalf. Deke pretended to swoon, falling on his back, and "Francesca" simply walked over the top of him. All the carnies laughed along with Owen (though he was the only one who blushed).

Everyone sang to him, out of tune but with great heart. Louisa even shared a small jug of hard cider she had procured in one of the recent towns. She poured him a mug to celebrate, and Owen's voice caught in his throat. "This is the next best thing to the Tick Tock Tavern!" he said, and then realized it was untrue. This was even better.

Best of all, after he had eaten a second piece of cake and felt the warm satisfaction of a full belly and a warm heart, Francesca wiped a stray bit of frosting from his mouth and licked it off her finger. Then she leaned forward and kissed him full on the lips to whistles and catcalls from the other carnies.

Though he might have been homesick on his birthday, Owen gazed at Francesca and decided to stay with the carnival for a while longer.

CHAPTER 12

I learned to fight, I learned to love and learned to feel

Over the course of the touring season, the Magnusson Carnival Extravaganza traveled a route that was like a pendulum—swinging outward to villages that radiated away from Crown City, then back into the capital, then outward along a different line of identical villages for the next set of performances.

Crowds of families with smiling children came out to enjoy the games and performances. By now Owen was even earning a few coins by juggling (when he managed not to drop his apples), passing around his porkpie hat for donations. He included Tomio's special soap-bubble spheres in his little show and, thankfully, did not drop another one.

Each day offered another adventure, never quite the same. Twice, Francesca even lured him out onto the practice tightrope. She stood just out of his reach, beckoning him, smiling. "Look at me." She pointed her fingers at her dark, hypnotic eyes. "Focus on *me*, not on the fall."

"That I'll gladly do." He stepped forward, one foot in front of the other. But he wavered, overcompensated, wavered even more, and then fell, every time. The drop was only five feet, however, so other than a few bruises, he injured only his pride. It was no worse than Tomio's stinkbomb bubbles.

Francesca laughed as he picked himself up off the ground, but not *at* him. "A few scuffs will only bring out your character. One of the first skills to learn in tightrope walking is how to fall with grace."

"I'll keep practicing," he said.

From the platform, Francesca called down. "I watched your expression—what were you thinking when you tried to walk the tightrope?"

He brushed himself off, ignored the soreness of what would surely become a bruise. "I was thinking, *Don't fall.*"

She tossed her hair. "Instead of fearing what might happen, what should you be thinking about?"

He climbed the pole again and guessed, "Getting to the other side."

"Wrong again—you should not have any goals. Just clear your mind, enjoy the sensation of your feet on the wire, the wind blowing through your hair. Think of *nothing* and let your feet do what they already know how to do."

He fell again the next few times but made it farther, more than halfway across. And when he finally did succeed, Francesca didn't drown him in celebration. "That's once. Now do it again. And do it every time." She took a bite of an apple she had carried up with her. "When you've practiced enough, we can start you juggling at the same time."

--------- ◆◆◆ ---------

Several more times, Owen sent brief messages home to Barrel Arbor, but there was so much to tell that he felt he couldn't get across much of anything at all. He came to consider the carnies his extended family, making friends with the game runners, the performers, the roustabouts.

At each show, Tomio teased carnival attendees with his sword, dancing about in playful challenges and then startling them with bursts of colored smoke. He developed an amusing routine with the three clowns, chasing them, slashing at the backs of their trousers until they dropped flaps to reveal polka-dotted underwear.

Owen continued to watch the relationship between Tomio and Francesca, and his heart ached every time she laughed with the handsome swordsman. She would brush against Tomio, elbow him, and walk close by his side with a carefree grace. Tomio didn't even seem to notice. But when Francesca did such things to Owen— and he remembered every single instance—he was unable to think straight. Her kiss on his birthday was a moment as profound to him as when he'd first seen the Clockwork Angels. . . .

Burly Golson took it upon himself to strengthen Owen, encouraging the young man to swing the huge mallets and drive tent stakes into the ground each time the carnival set up in a new place. Though Owen's arms and shoulders ached, Golson pronounced his work satisfactory, promising that it would get better through practice. Only later did Owen realize that the strongman had tricked him into doing some of his chores, but he didn't mind. Golson repaid him in many ways, and Owen was eager to learn.

The strongman had him practice light sparring to improve his reflexes and strength. Owen pummeled a suspended leather bag filled with sawdust, defeating the imaginary enemy; after the young man was exhausted and his knuckles sore, Golson nudged him aside. "It's acceptable to win by wearing down your opponent, but I find it much less tiring to do it in one blow."

He cocked back his fist and delivered a punch as hard as a steam-driven pile driver—so hard, in fact, that the stitching split and sawdust spilled out of the stuffed leather bag. "It's not so much your muscles or your actual strength. Your *confidence* can be all you need." He pushed the punching bag close so that Owen could take another swing. "Now, I'm large enough that I don't have to prove myself." He pinched the young man's biceps, which were still rather scrawny. "*You*, on the other hand, might have to rely more on confidence."

———◆◆◆———

Late one night after a busy show in another village, César Magnusson rounded up the carnies and said in his booming voice, "A Regulator courier delivered a special newsgraph printout!" Beneath the extravagant handlebar mustache, Magnusson showed perfect white teeth. "In one week's time, in honor of the summer solstice, the Magnusson Carnival Extravaganza has been requested to perform in Chronos Square!" A perfect showman, the ringmaster paused for the flood of gasps, chuckles, and applause. "We will be seen by the Clockwork Angels and even our loving Watchmaker from his high tower!"

Owen's heart pounded; this was more than he had ever dreamed. The summer solstice was one of the most important days of the year, when the sun stopped in its path and switched direction to sweep toward winter. Not only would Owen see the Angels again, but he would be part of the show!

With a flourish, Magnusson reached into his tuxedo jacket and withdrew a stack of prismatic tickets, which he handed around to the carnies. "A special pass for each of you."

Owen took his ticket as if he had won a prize and placed it with the now-dried rose that Francesca had given him.

———◆◆◆———

The caravan of chugging flatbeds and rolling wagons crossed the countryside to the next destination. Owen hadn't even asked the town's name. Before jumping aboard the nighttime steamliner that one surprising night, he had never traveled beyond Barrel

Arbor, but now he had visited so many identical villages that they blended together.

This town specialized in pig farming, and when they arrived, the sign *Welcome to Ashkelon* seemed somehow insincere. A weathered stone angel figure stood at the entrance to the town, but she seemed to be facing in the wrong direction. Although the village had its standard clocktower, tavern, and small newsgraph office, the smell of the place was anything but standard.

And Owen found that those who herded, wrestled, and slaughtered pigs had a different character from assistant managers of apple orchards. He found them to be ruder, edgier. Very few of them gave him appreciative tips, but they laughed at every small mistake he made—laughter that sounded like derision rather than enjoyment.

The Cage of Imaginary Creatures was a sturdy rectangular vault with reinforced metal walls. It groaned and rocked as if it contained something large, powerful, and restless, and various lenses of distorted colored glass provided peepholes into the box. Once a visitor paid the price, he or she could look through the shifting lenses to see the mythical creatures imprisoned within. The prominent warning was meant to tantalize rather than frighten. *Do You Dare Look Inside Your Imagination?*

During the Ashkelon show, one shrill woman paced around the attraction, her face flush with anger. "I want my money back. There's nothing inside!"

As she excoriated the ticket-taker, more audience members gathered around, angry on their neighbor's behalf, immediately turning against the carnies. Striding along with top hat in place, César Magnusson stopped to calm the disturbance. "We are a carnival extravaganza, madam. You are to expect the unexpected!"

"There's nothing inside that box! I can look into an empty box at home without having to pay for it." She planted her hands on wide hips and looked like a bull about to charge.

Magnusson bowed. "For you, madam, I have no doubt there is nothing within the Cage of Imaginary Creatures. Please accept this refund." He reached into his pocket, withdrew a coin, and placed it in the woman's hand. She wrapped her fingers around it like a Venus flytrap closing, then stalked off.

Owen had watched the exchange with growing uneasiness, and the people from Ashkelon moved away from the attraction. The ringmaster regarded them with disappointment.

Having never gotten a chance to look inside before, Owen gathered his nerve and stepped up to the cage. "What is inside it, sir? Is it a trick?"

"No trick at all, Owenhardy. It is a standard imaginarium." He twirled his mustache. "Have a look and see what you see."

Owen flinched when the solid metal walls of the cage groaned, but the ringmaster encouraged him again. He peered through one of the distorted glass lenses and saw the murky, rippled form of a muscular centaur, a human body joined with a fine stallion's body. He drew back in amazement.

Magnusson smiled. "Try another one."

Owen walked around the box to a different window, a green-tinted lens. This time he saw a reptilian form with great bat wings, a long scaly tail tipped with an arrowhead barb, and a narrow head that was majestic and terrifying at the same time. "A dragon! But dragons aren't real!"

"Your imagination is real," the ringmaster said.

Other windows showed him a basilisk, a griffin, a unicorn. "How can they all be inside this one vault?"

Magnusson brushed his black jacket. "They don't exist in the vault, but in your mind. The Cage of Imaginary Creatures is an imagination amplifier. You see expansions of the wonder that is inside yourself." He looked up, sniffed. "Some people, like that woman, have no imagination to amplify. Alas."

Owen understood, and was sad that he did.

Francesca had ascended to the platform to begin her act for the people of Ashkelon. When two unbathed pig farmer lads dared each other to climb the trapeze pole, Owen ceased his juggling routine and hurried over to stop them. "You're not allowed to do that!"

The two young men sneered at him, "Look, he thinks he's the Watchmaker and can lay down the rules."

"The carnival has its own rules." His heart pounded; he had never been in a full confrontation before. He remembered what Golson had told him, and he stood straight, not backing down, as he repeated, "You're not allowed to climb that."

The two pig farmers leered up at Francesca, who was stretching against the trapeze bar. Hearing Owen's tone of voice and sensing the argument, she looked down.

One of the young men grabbed the ladder knobs and began to ascend, but Owen ran forward. "*Don't* do that!"

"You're not going to stop him," said the second pig farmer.

"Yes, I am." But with his arms full of apples and one of Tomio's soap-bubble spheres, it was hard to muster much of an intimidating presence.

The second pig farmer rounded on him. "Not gonna take that from a carny." Since a brawl with Owen was less daunting than climbing the trapeze pole, the first young man dropped to the ground, also closing in.

Then, like an angel gliding down from heaven, Francesca snagged a dangling rope and slid down to drop in front of them. Her voice was haughty. "I'm offended. Isn't my performance enough to hold your interest? Or would you boys rather play with each other?"

The two pig farmers looked at Francesca in a way that Owen definitely did not like. One of them answered, "We'd rather wrestle with you." He laughed with a sound that reminded Owen of the seagulls at the river docks.

Francesca gave a breezy laugh, not bothered by the comment, but Owen was furious. Why didn't Tomio arrive like a dashing hero and chase away these unsavory men with his sword? Then again, Owen didn't really want Tomio there—he wanted to defend Francesca himself.

He stepped forward. "That is uncalled for in the presence of a lady!" He hurled the soap-bubble sphere, which burst at the feet of the two pig farmers and doused them with foul smoke that smelled of pickles. The aroma was a considerable improvement over pig shit, but the green dye and stinging fumes set them howling in anger. As they backed away and fled into the crowd, Owen pelted them with his apples, even though Francesca yelled for him to stop. When his hands were empty, he balled his fists.

He looked up to see two blue-uniformed Regulators marching up to him. "There is a specified fine for harassing people."

Owen pointed and blurted, "But they're the ones harassing— they started it." The Blue Watch captain turned, but the two pig farmers had disappeared.

"Ashkelon is their town. They are citizens of the area. You are guests."

Francesca grabbed Owen's arm and spoke to the Watch captain. "Just give us the citation. We'll pay it."

Owen caught his breath. His pulse was racing and his face felt hot. He did not regret his actions because they proved his love for Francesca; he had shown he would come to her defense, as her hero.

But to his surprise, she looked disappointed instead of starry-eyed.

———— ◆•◆ ————

Magnusson paid the fine without complaint. Tomio hurried over to make sure that Francesca was all right, and when she confirmed the story but laughed it off, Tomio seemed to worry no more about it. Golson was proud of Owen and clapped him on the shoulder hard enough to spin him around.

But why did Francesca seem to be avoiding him? Finally, after dark that night, he went to her tent, anxious to talk with her. She met him and placed her hands on her skirts and tossed her head, her raven hair long and loose. "Well, what have you got to say for yourself?"

Owen remained tongue-tied and befuddled. "I'm sorry for whatever I did, but I don't understand. Those young men were being cruel to you. They said terrible things. I defended your honor!"

She raised her eyebrows at him. "You don't think I could have protected myself?"

Owen considered this. Lavinia would never have been able to fend for herself. "I . . . I just felt so angry. Tomio wasn't there— if he loves you, he should have come to your rescue." He took a breath, reminded himself that Golson had told him to exude confidence. "I love you more than he does." His heart fluttered as he said the words.

Francesca laughed. "Of course Tomio loves me."

"So do I! I plan to prove myself. I will win your heart, and you'll choose me over him."

Francesca's dark eyes widened, and her smile was warm now. She reached out to wrap her arms around him, and Owen didn't know what was happening. "Oh, you silly fool! Tomio is my brother."

Owen thought his knees might buckle, but Francesca was holding him, and he embraced her back. She kissed him on the mouth, and it was even more wonderful than the time on his birthday. And the next kiss was better still.

She led him into her tent.

CHAPTER 13

All my illusions
Projected on her
The ideal, that I wanted to see

The next day of traveling brought them to the outskirts of Crown City, and their excitement built with the upcoming summer solstice performance for the Watchmaker. Before they arrived in the zoned city area, where they would require permits, the carnies camped in an open field near one of the steamliner rails. They would put on one last show before their grand performance in Chronos Square.

His companions were hard at work, oiling and polishing the components of the Ferris wheel and the whirling rides, topping off the hydraulics in all the machinery, wiping down the game apparatus, repainting the gypsy fortune teller's red booth. The equipment had to be spotless, every act flawless for the solstice show. The Watchmaker would expect nothing less. From the way César Magnusson spoke of the Watchmaker, it was as if he had some sort of personal affinity for the carnival.

While the carnies were focused on the grand show, Owen found it hard to concentrate. He wandered around carrying a stack of freshly printed broadsheets to celebrate the Chronos Square performance, but found no place to post them. He didn't realize that his giddy mood was so obvious to the others until Tomio and Louisa stopped him.

The bearded lady sounded sincere and caring. "Be careful you don't get in over your head, Owenhardy." He didn't know what she was talking about.

"It's not his *head* he's thinking with." Tomio let out a good-natured snort. "Francesca is my sister, and I know her well. Take care for your own sake. She's one of us—independent, full of life, passionate. Don't expect her to think like a girl from a quiet, small town."

Owen grinned, unable to help himself. He couldn't disagree with Tomio's characterization of her as *passionate*. "Francesca . . ."

Letting out a concerned sigh, Louisa shook her head. "I doubt there's anything we could say that'll reach him." Tomio shrugged, and they left him to wander about with his broadsheets. He paid little attention to what they had said to him, and in less than an hour he forgot the conversation had even occurred.

Owen came upon César Magnusson sitting outside the carnival's main office tent, poring over lists of towns, marking destinations on a map of Albion. He joined the ringmaster, curious to look at all the names of places he had never thought he would see.

"It's been a busy season," Magnusson said conversationally. "We have to fit in as many villages as possible before we go up the coast for winter."

Owen studied the marked route, the list of towns Magnusson had compiled—and his heart leapt when he saw that Barrel Arbor was one of their upcoming destinations. After such a long time away and everything he had experienced, he was going to go home. He laughed out loud at the thought of seeing everyone again, and he realized that he could have everything a man could ever want.

When the ringmaster didn't understand why he was chuckling, Owen said merely, "Yes, the Watchmaker does have a perfect plan."

Even though the carnival was set up on the outskirts of the city, a surprisingly large crowd came out to see them. By now, every newsgraph office had carried the announcement that the Magnusson Carnival Extravaganza would perform for the summer solstice, but since most people could not get tickets for the show in Chronos Square, they came to watch this local performance instead.

Owen felt happier than he had ever been, still enchanted from his night with Francesca. Now he knew that she was, indeed, his true love. They were connected, as if magnetic field lines bound them together. Lavinia could never hold a spark to Francesca! How he had fooled himself back in Barrel Arbor.

During the afternoon performance, he walked through the carnival crowd as if floating. Even though he fumbled his apples more than usual, he laughed at himself, and his lovestruck grin was so bright and charming that no one seemed to mind.

Out of the corner of his eye, he glimpsed someone who looked familiar—the nameless stranger who had pulled him aboard the steamliner. Before Owen could turn, the man melted into the crowd so quickly that Owen thought he must have imagined him.

Half an hour later, though, he found Tomio, obviously unsettled. "D'Angelo Misterioso was here—the one I told you about."

"Oh, I know who you mean! Maybe he came to see the show."

"Maybe, or maybe he was up to no good." Tomio's expression was grave. "Keep alert. If you see him, come and find me."

The rest of the show passed without incident, however, and Owen noticed very little—beyond occasional glimpses of Francesca. When she performed her act on the trapeze, he felt he was witnessing a miracle. No wonder the Watchmaker embraced perfection in all things—but had even the wise old man seen perfection to match Francesca's?

Owen thought beyond the big show in Chronos Square. Since

the carnival's route would take him back to Barrel Arbor, like the weighty pendulum of destiny, he had so much to plan. He had the printed congratulatory card the Watchmaker had sent him in preparation for his birthday, promising him happiness. A life perfectly planned. Now, the unexpected prospect of returning home was a sign that told him all was indeed for the best.

An adult, like Owen, was supposed to become betrothed to his true love; he had never questioned that, but he had been too calm and accepting, waiting for life to happen to him. He had almost made a terrible mistake with Lavinia, because she had been there in Barrel Arbor, and the obvious choice. Fortunately, life's roundabout journey had conspired to bring him to Francesca instead—and that was exactly what he needed.

She was engaging, independent, *alive* in a way that made Owen feel alive. She would crook her finger, beckon him across the tightrope of his own future, and he would meet her there halfway . . . not over a precipice, but high in the air. Like the Angels. He couldn't stop smiling as he thought of the comparison.

He would walk across that tightrope for her.

Late that night, after the show had wound down and the crowds wandered home, Owen screwed up his courage, drew a deep breath. He knew what he had to do. He took out the now-dried rose that he had kept for months, and it still had a faint beautiful smell that, for him, was inextricably connected with Francesca. He found his resolve, reminding himself of what Golson had told him about confidence being his greatest weapon.

He made his way to Francesca's tent, each step careful, precarious, as if there were a terrible fall on either side. But he focused ahead, cleared his mind . . . called out her name.

She opened the flap of the tent and met him with a smile full of hints and meanings, enough to make Owen imagine his own love poetry. She teased, "Hmm, and what could you be here for, young man? I don't believe I extended a permanent invitation."

Owen's throat went dry, but he lifted his chin, just as Tomio would have done. "You're the one who taught me to bring my own ticket even if I wasn't given one."

She chuckled. "Aren't you cocky!" She held open the tent flap.

Instead of entering, Owen dropped to his knee and extended the dried rose. "You gave me this when I first saw you. I kept it." Her eyes sparkled with amusement, and for a moment she seemed embarrassed, surprised.

He continued in a flood of words he had practiced too many times. "I've been in love with you every second I've known you, and I hope you've come to love me as well." He swallowed hard and continued. "After I left Barrel Arbor, saw Crown City, and joined the carnival, it was all a bright, dizzy dream. And now the show route is going to take us back to Barrel Arbor. Back *home*. You and I are like two gears fitting together, perfectly matched. I . . . I joined your life, now will you join mine?"

He held out the rose. "When we get back to Barrel Arbor, will you stay with me? I have a cottage there. We can be married, have children, tend the apple orchard." He heaved a pleasant sigh. "As it should be."

He expected her warm laughter, then an embrace; she was supposed to hold him close, give him a long kiss. Maybe tears would even come to her eyes as she nodded yes. He had so much to offer her, and he knew that the two of them were meant to be together.

Instead, she drew back in disbelief. "Oh, Owen, you're sweet, but I'd never let myself be trapped like that!" Her laugh was quick and loud, and she tried to brush his question aside. She held the tent flap open wider. "Now, let's have no more of this foolishness."

Her words were dismissive, and he heard them as hurtful, a betrayal. She thought he was joking! He had the card from the Watchmaker—everything was supposed to go according to plan. "But, that's not the way—"

She chuckled again. "Now, Owenhardy, you should know me better than that!" Her words thrust like Tomio's sword, straight through his heart. She faltered, as if she didn't know what to say. "How can you even imagine—"

He dropped the dried rose on the ground and turned, blinded by the tears that sprang to his eyes. He stumbled into the night, running away as far and as fast as possible.

He didn't think he could bear to hear Francesca's voice again, but it hurt him even more when she didn't call after him.

CHAPTER 14

What did I see
Fool that I was?

Heavy-hearted and disillusioned, Owen left the lights of the carnival camp behind. He was unable to see where he was going, nor did he care. *I'd never let myself be trapped like that!*

Marriage to one's true love? He had never thought of it as a trap! Or as foolishness. But that was what Francesca saw. She was not the person he had believed her to be. How could he have been so deluded?

Now he regretted his impulse. He shouldn't have proposed to Francesca—it had ruined everything. He should have guarded his feelings and waited. Now it was too late to withdraw the question.

He hurried past the last line of tents, practically running. Did the other carnies consider him a naïve child as well? He had felt so comfortable with Tomio, Louisa, Golson, César Magnusson, the clowns—everyone in the carnival. They were like family to him, sharing, loving, supporting.

He remembered Francesca's kisses, the smell of her hair, the grace of her every move, her laugh, the light in her eyes. But now he knew what Francesca thought of him and his "foolish" ideas. Such a bitter discovery.

His throat went dry as he recalled the carnival's imaginarium, the Cage of Mythical Creatures. Had he been looking at Francesca through the distorted lenses of unrealistic love, seeing only what he wanted to see? Had she been the woman he imagined all along, or had he merely projected his fanciful illusions onto her?

When he stumbled upon a set of steamliner tracks, he followed them toward the distant glow of Crown City. Now that his own life had been so disrupted, he took comfort in any straight and perfect path. He walked along on the rough gravel of the siding, letting the cool glow of the coldfire-infused rails draw him onward. With the carnival camp well behind him, he glanced over his shoulder, paused for a long moment, then walked on again.

When Lavinia had failed to meet him on the orchard hill, he felt disappointment, but not a bottomless loss like this. Lavinia had been pleasant and pretty (or so he remembered; her features were faded like a ghost in his memory). Lavinia had not engaged his imagination, his conversation, but he saw signs of Francesca everywhere, in a whiff of night-damp grass, a whisper of wind that sounded like her voice close to his ear.

He was a naïve young man unschooled in the ways of the world, ill equipped for what he had encountered after leaving the safety net of his small village. This was supposed to have been a great adventure, but at the moment it didn't seem that way.

The carnies lived differently, laughed differently, played by their own rules, and Owen had danced blindly on the eggshells of misconceptions. He had thought he belonged here, and that he belonged with her.

He kept walking into the night. Moonlight washed out the stars, but he no longer looked overhead at the constellations, no longer imagined his own patterns in the stars. He saw only the ground in front of his feet.

Why had no one warned him? Surely his love for Francesca had been obvious to everyone in the carnival. He remembered the clowns and their pantomime of him at his birthday party, when the faux Francesca had blithely walked over him. Stepping on his heart.

Alas, if anyone *had* pointed out his foolishness and unrealistic dreams, he wouldn't have listened anyway. Yes, Tomio and Louisa had cautioned him, he now remembered—too late—but their words had rolled off him like rain. Maybe naïve optimism was his defining force of character, and he had continued on his euphoric, hopeful path right over a cliff. . . .

We get what we deserve: the Watchmaker had said that, both as a promise and as a threat. Owen broke the rules, followed his sense of adventure, and wandered far from the plan. And now he'd been ruined for it.

Owen had not gone far along the steamliner tracks before he encountered a shadowy man. The stranger stood on the siding, as if waiting for him. Though startled, Owen was too wrapped in his own worries to be terrified. "Who are you? Why are you out here at night?"

"I could ask the same question," said the man.

Owen recognized the lean face, the significant eyebrows, the pointed beard and mustache, and dapper businesslike clothes so unsuited to camping on the ground. "You're the man from the steamliner car!" he blurted out.

"And you're the boy from the steamliner car—though older now, aren't you? A fair distance from your tiny apple-orchard village?"

"A fair distance from all of that," Owen agreed. "I never should have left."

"Now, that's a foolish statement, my good friend." The stranger's voice dripped with acid. Owen flinched at the word *foolish*, but the stranger did not pause. "Since you left your humdrum home, you have seen wondrous sights, have you not? You've done exciting things, experienced *life* instead of just bland existence."

"How would you know that?" Owen asked, then hung his head. "My heart is broken. I was spurned by my true love. And before that, I abandoned my father and my home. I lost everything through a series of bad decisions."

The man's laughter sounded mocking. "You've been brainwashed by the Stability, boy. Think what you have now that you didn't have before. The Watchmaker gives us a steady routine, tells us all is for the best. He puts out the beautiful Clockwork Angels, but their beauty masks a cold machine inside."

"I won't believe that!" Owen stumbled on a rock at the side of the tracks as they trudged along. The stranger did not reach out, did not even try to steady him; instead, he let Owen catch his own balance or fall.

"People don't understand freedom," the man continued as Owen caught up with him. "They use the Stability as a crutch instead of walking on their own—or running." He lowered his voice. "*Or flying!* You've been blindfolded so long you forgot how to see. I've watched the carnival, watched you."

Owen noticed a striking tattoo on the back of the man's pale, unscarred hand, a symbol like an open box containing a triangular pattern of dots. "What does that mark mean?"

The stranger looked at his hand, folded his fingers into a fist to make the tattoo dance. "Alchemists call it a precipitate. The solid from a solution. It always reminded me of blood from a stone. Or more properly, a stone made from blood—*my* blood." The man toyed with his collar, adjusting an artless stickpin set with a murky diamond.

"Tomio warned me about you," Owen said with an uncertain glance back at the lights from the carnival camp. "D'Angelo Misterioso, that was your stage name, wasn't it? He said there's something missing inside of you."

The suspicious-looking stranger flashed him a dangerous grin. "There's something missing in the Watchmaker's society. Extreme order will kill us all."

"Extreme freedom sounds just as dangerous." Owen recalled the words the baker had said in the Tick Tock Tavern. "You're a . . . a freedom extremist! I like to know that the sun is coming up the next morning."

"You think the Watchmaker controls the sun? He's not that powerful," the man scoffed. "The sun comes up, and the sun goes down—then there's all the time in between. Think about the summer solstice performance in Chronos Square, so many people—even the Watchmaker himself from his tower." He jabbed his finger at Owen. "And do you know what's beneath Chronos Square? The nexus of coldfire, the heart of the Watchmaker's schemes, the power that drives the city, the machinery, the steam-liners, industry! If such a thing could be disrupted . . ."

Owen was horrified. "That would shut down Crown City, send civilization back to chaos. It would be like . . . *Before the Stability.*"

"Well, yes, young man. Yes, it would—like resetting a clock. And we'd start with a clean slate."

In the distance, Owen heard a whooshing sound, and the metal tracks began to shimmer with a lambent blue glow. Far away, he could see the line of sparks and the inflated zeppelin bags, could hear the distant rumble of pistons as the steamliners drifted down from the sky and alighted on the tracks. The whole train rolled toward Crown City.

"If we're free to do whatever we want, we are responsible to no one but ourselves," the stranger said. "Only that way can we under-stand the joys and obligations of true liberty. Each person should succeed because of who *she is*, or fail because of what *he lacks*, and not have some cruel Watchmaker coddle us through life."

Owen had already experienced an awful night of collapsing dreams, and he remembered how Golson had told him to stand up for himself. "Some people want order and predictability, a life they can rely on." The steamliner caravan was rumbling closer, and he had to continue in a shout, "Otherwise they might become lovesick fools and get hurt!"

"Strange," the man said. "The last time we spoke, you wanted to leave all that predictability."

Owen backed away from the tracks as the steamliner approached. He could hear the passage bell clanging. "Maybe I changed my mind. Maybe I'd like a normal life after all. I have faith in the Watchmaker!"

The man said, "I have no faith in faith. I have faith in *myself* and what I can accomplish."

The front car of the steamliner shot past them, wheels thundering, the swollen airship bags rocking. Sparks flew from the steel wheels as the line of passenger gondolas and cargo cars slowed on its approach to the city.

"Without the plan, there would be anarchy!" Owen called.

"Yes . . . anarchy! And all is for the best."

Owen suddenly realized who he was talking to. He should have seen it from the beginning.

The Anarchist stepped close to the rails and the shuddering steamliner. Barely looking behind him, as if he knew exactly what was coming and where to reach, he snagged the side of a cargo car and swung himself up.

Owen stared at the pale flash of the stranger's face as he smiled and ducked onto the train that headed into Crown City.

The Watchmaker

The Watchmaker has time up his sleeve

In the well-lit workroom chamber in his clocktower, the Watchmaker surveyed the tiny components spread out on the table. He alone understood the intricacies and precision required to keep the perfect machinery in motion.

Sloppy work was the work of chaos, and he assembled the components of his devices—of his world—as if life itself depended on his attention and care. Indeed, sometimes it did. The Stability depended on him. All of Albion depended on him.

He was proud of his accomplishments, and he rewarded his alchemist-priests. His Regulators maintained order in every aspect of daily life. Everything worked exactly as it should, according to plan. He saw that it was good, but a truly loving Watchmaker could not grow complacent.

A wide band of leather circled his thin white hair, mounting a complex arrangement of lenses on his brow. The lenses were rimmed discs of polished crystal, some colorless, some ruby, sapphire, or amber. They sparkled in the glare of coldfire globes floating above the bench. Pairs of short copper cylinders held compound lenses for higher magnification.

With his right hand, the Watchmaker lowered a pair of eye-pieces. Simultaneously, with the same precise and steady motion, his left hand selected a miniature tool from the bench.

His fingers moved unerringly, his concentration complete, as he guided the tool into the heart of the complicated mechanism. The device was a fist-sized, egg-shaped armature of machined gold that surrounded a complexity of tiny gears and jewel bearings. Precision diamonds, faceted redfire opals from the distant mines in Atlantis. A bubble of coldfire glowed at the mechanism's heart.

"Wheels within wheels," he muttered, exactly the way he perceived his clockwork universe, and the personal world he had created within it.

Tick. Tock. Tick. Tock.

Facing away from him in the tower chamber, the four Clockwork Angels stood in their alcoves, full of beauty and majesty. He adored them—they were the closest things to perfection he had ever created. Light. Sea. Sky. Land. One Angel to represent each of the four elements.

And only he controlled the fifth element. *Life.*

More than two hundred years after he had learned how to create gold, the gold itself had lost its interest for him. He had controlled its supply, and thus its value, but a now-commonplace yellow metal was no longer "precious" to the Watchmaker. Even coldfire—a simple mixture of acids, bases, and catalysts that could evoke energy out of silica, the basest substance—had lost its luminescence.

The Watchmaker's dreams were grander than that. With even rarer elements—moonstone, sunstone, bloodstone, dreamstone—he continued his quest for the essential presence of existence, the bio-alchemical force that was the heart of everything and everyone. The animating force, the fifth element—the *quintessence.*

The Watchmaker raised his right hand with a smooth motion

to select a different pair of lenses, red ones, to see deeper into the spectrum. In the same moment, his left hand reached out to select a tiny file from the array of miniature tools. He leaned closer to the device and lovingly filed smooth the edges of tiny gear teeth in the escapement. Setting it in motion, he judged its perfect rhythm and released a long slow breath that was like a prayer.

The Watchmaker viewed his devices as mirrors of life—life the way it ought to be—action and reaction in a balance that was precise, controlled, reliable. Not like the unruly humans he tried to guide and keep content, although their simple needs were not difficult to understand and provide for. He remembered an ancient piece of wisdom for rulers: "Give them bread and circuses, and they will never revolt." Coldfire provided for all their energy needs. His alchemically controlled weather patterns kept the farms productive, and the people well fed. Traveling roadshows like the Magnusson Carnival Extravaganza kept them entertained. All was for the best.

Even so, a few rogues and renegades insisted on disrupting his Stability, but he would deal with them soon. For now, he had to tend his beautiful Angels.

Viewed through the powerful magnifiers, the intricate mechanism filled the Watchmaker's eyes and delighted his mind. Spiritual machinery, possessed of a life force he himself had instilled, and of which he was both master and servant.

It could not exist without him—but he could not exist without it.

In youth, one might search for riches. In middle age, a man might want power. But now, after more than two centuries, the Watchmaker considered life itself most precious. Time was most precious.

Long ago, the Watchmaker had discovered a primitive form of the quintessence and used it to keep his own daughter alive when a cruel disease tried to take her from the world; he force-fed her the energy, kept her head alive even when the rest of her body failed. Back then, the quintessence was only a raw distillate, powerful but unrefined, and she did indeed still live—after a fashion—but it was only an early experiment. It had not turned out well, and he had lost her anyway. It had been so many years. How much of her still remained? His daughter would never forgive him . . . but he was not in the business of giving or receiving forgiveness.

Even so, he wished he could do it all again.

The Watchmaker had caught glimpses of her over the years while walking in one of his disguises, and he had invited the carnival to perform at the summer solstice mainly because he wanted to see her again. She had never forgiven him, would not talk with him—of that he was sure—but at least she would be here in Chronos Square. At least she was still alive. Did she not appreciate that? The success of the experimental procedure was a tribute to his own abilities.

But he had gotten better over the years.

At the workbench, he turned his attention to the most delicate of the movement's complications, the *tourbillon*, the "whirlwind." Its rotating cage would counteract the effects of gravity on the escapement and balance wheel, keeping the interlocking gears, springs, and wheels accurate at any angle, any temperature, any altitude. Wheels within wheels. Just as the tourbillon controlled the machinery, he himself could control the most chaotic of nature's powers. He could reap the whirlwind.

He held up a larger implement, and his thumb pressed a lever to spark flint and steel. He touched it to the gold, egg-shaped armature, and blue lightning flickered in tiny arcs deep in the mechanism. Finally, he snapped the backplate on the energized clockwork device, and he set to work on the tiny hydraulic pump it would control.

The Watchmaker had kept himself alive by making all the necessary calculations and bargains. Mere humans might have to live and die in their limited spans, but not the Watchmaker. Albion simply couldn't function without him, and the Stability would fall apart under the guidance of imperfect people. Therefore, he had an obligation to stay alive.

Taking the throbbing device, he walked over to the nearest Clockwork Angel, the figure made of pure white, her clothes lustrous, her skin turned to simulated stone. Between the beautiful wings on her back, he opened the access hatch where her activating machinery sat motionless. She was a Titan, a giant among humans, filled with the energy and grace his experiments had given her.

All four of these clockwork beauties had been volunteers a long time ago, starry-eyed followers who believed in every detail of his plan. At one time they'd been partly human, but they were now much more than that. As he connected the clockwork heart to the cavity in her chest, released the quintessence, and set the wheels in motion, he whispered, "Animate!" The power source sparked life into the Angel.

With the smoothest vibration, her wings extended, then folded again, as if stretching. The Angel swiveled her head and blinked her beautiful, glassy eyes. Looking at him with love in a gaze so powerful and ethereal, the Clockwork Angel nearly hypnotized *him*. He felt a thrill run through his own body, his own systems.

For an instant so brief that it might have been an illusion—*had* to be an illusion—her normally serene expression changed to a shocking flicker of utter hatred and despair.

The Watchmaker's arms stuttered and jittered in unexpected reaction. An unevenness occurred in his own delicately aligned gears. With his other hand, he forcibly straightened his arm, bent his wrist, and felt the gears move smoothly again. He tugged down his sleeve to cover his enhancements and fastidiously brushed away specks of imagined dust. Soon, he would have to replace his own quintessence animator.

Smiling with perfect love and adoration again, the Clockwork Angel faced forward and returned to rest.

His bees buzzed around the hives, a white noise that he found soothing. In the large enclosed courtyard gardens of the Cathedral of the Timekeepers, the Watchmaker kept his own beehives, an array of conical structures with hinged backs for the removal of the combs. The structures were made of delicate and pure wax, filled to dripping with the gold manufactured by his perfect insect pets. And while he admired their uniform behavior and natural precision, the bees operated on their own Stability, unrelated to his personal wishes. When viewed through the bees' multifaceted eyes, even the Watchmaker's world must seem an uncooperative, disordered place.

But he was doing his best.

As he approached the thrumming hives, the Watchmaker needed no protection, just his confidence and his gentle nature. Little enough of him was still human anyway; why would the bees bother to sting him? After opening the hinged door, he bent to watch all the busy little creatures chasing out their destinies. Marvelous.

Even so, he had never been able to determine why his hives produced significantly less honey than most others. He had studied the best volumes on the science, devoted much time to becoming the best possible apiarist, but his bees seemed to lack proper incentive. Given the smaller volume of honey, however, the Watchmaker declared it rare and consumed it on only the most special of occasions.

He leaned closer, and the throbbing buzz increased as the bees became agitated, but not yet aggressive. He viewed the hexagonal chambers interlocked like gears and admired what they represented to him. Out of the seeming chaos they created not just order, but *beauty*. Bees understood the perfection of geometry. They created something useful, which also happened to be beautiful. If only people could learn the lesson of lowly insects. Yes, the honeybee was the perfect symbol for him.

He recalled the intricate chronometers he had built more than a century ago, early in his career, early in his existence: timepieces of such accuracy and craft that they went far beyond their original intent, not just to tell time but to instill awe through their

perfection. He had always considered that a laudable goal for its own sake, whether or not others could understand all the intricate connections and symbology.

He looked up from his study of the hives as his loyal commander of the Black Watch entered the courtyard garden. Seeing the bees whirling through the air like static, the commander stopped at a safe distance, raised his voice. "Watchmaker, sir, a fresh report from our scouts on the Western Sea. Our long-range military ships have completed another section of the ordered grid mapping."

"And have they found the Wreckers?" The droning sound of the bees blurred his words.

"No, sir, but they continue the search." The man flapped a hand in front of his face, though he should have known that too much motion might intimidate the bees.

The Watchmaker nodded. "Even an empty data set provides important information. We know where they are *not*, so that limits the areas of the sea where they can *be*."

The Watchmaker was eager to find the pirates who kept attacking his cargo steamers, costing him fortunes in essential resources from Atlantis: the jewels he needed for his most precise watches; the moonstones, bloodstones, and dreamstones necessary for his quintessence research. The Wreckers must have a lair somewhere out on all that open water, but the Watchmaker's airships were hindered by their range from the coldfire pivot points. The new ones under construction, though . . .

Impatient, he was tempted to have the scout fleet broaden their sweeps and loosen the net, but he was not a haphazard man. "The search has to be done properly, according to the pattern. And when the Wreckers are found—no matter how long it takes—we must descend upon them with an irresistible force."

As his anger increased, he felt his metronome pulse picking up speed; energy gathered in his veins. Whenever the attack happened, he would join them for that assault. The Wreckers and the monstrous Anarchist were a personal affront to him.

Bees swirled around him, unnoticed.

The provocative graffiti had been removed, the sabotage of steamliner rails repaired. The recent mayhem caused by the Anarchist's stunt of resetting so many clocks had been more dramatic, because it shook the citizens' faith in time. But the Watchmaker reassured everyone. He would be victorious in the end. He was an intelligent man, not a wild animal. Civilization must triumph over barbarism. Order had to succeed above chaos.

"Thank you, Commander," he said as the insects swirled around him. "Continue your search with due diligence."

The black-uniformed Regulator turned on his heel and departed from the garden, glad to be away from the bees.

The Watchmaker entered the well-lit analysis halls with more than curiosity; he suspected that the fate of the world might be at stake, thanks to the interactions of seemingly trivial people.

For many days now he had set his destiny calculators to work— sealed, energized engines that scanned and calculated timelines, like cosmic clocks that could be set forward in time to capture glimpses of the future. If properly aligned, with the compass needle set, the destiny calculators were alchemical crystal balls that could predict—with fair accuracy—what a target person would do.

The Watchmaker followed the blueprint of a person's life, a complex decision-tree diagram that extended the length of the hall and around the corner. He followed the branch points, each intersection marking a choice that led to other choices in a widening cascade. The stagger-path mapped out possibilities, decisions made and not made, like the chemical reactions of fate.

The Watchmaker had been keeping his eye on one young man. At the beginning, his pattern had been perfectly regular, just like everyone else's, until several months ago, when suddenly the branch points shattered in surprising directions, like the crystalline angles of a snowflake.

From his destiny calculators, the Watchmaker knew that was the point at which the Anarchist had decided to recruit the young man. Owen Hardy from Barrel Arbor. A nobody, a common villager, a human grain of sand on a vast beach; he had merited no special attention whatsoever, but was made significant because the Anarchist had noticed him.

And so the Watchmaker had to notice the young man as well, so he could tug him in the opposite direction with subtle grandiosity. Not only would he steal back Owen Hardy's loyalty and contentment, as it should be, he would also impose a devastating symbolic defeat on his rival. With his destiny calculators, the Watchmaker could plan every tiny event in detail, forward and backward, decision and consequence, first order, second order, third order.

The Anarchist had no such powerful tool; he had only *unpredictability*. And the Watchmaker vowed that would not be enough.

That impulsively chosen young man, Owen Hardy, could be a key to continued Stability, or a horrific reign of chaos and disorder. The young man's decisions could make him important in different ways, depending on his choices.

Owen Hardy was such a tiny speck of dust that none of the Watchmaker's Regulators, analysts, or calculating experts understood how he could possibly be important.

Even a pebble could disrupt the most delicate gears.

He walked down the hall, paying careful attention to the geometrical river of branchpoints. He followed Owen Hardy's journey, tracing the path with his eyes, until he reached the current end, the decision point the young man faced now: either to go home to his calm and stable life in Barrel Arbor, or to sneak back into Crown City and see the carnival again.

He touched his finger to the vertex on the wall, the possible paths Owen could take, but he knew exactly which direction the young man would choose. With his fingertip, he erased the alternate decision point and stood back to assess the young man's future.

Of course, Owen would choose to see the carnival again.

CHAPTER 15

Deadly confrontation
Such a dangerous device

Owen trudged all night long, following the steamliner tracks and looking more at his feet than at the glow of Crown City ahead. His encounter with the Anarchist had disturbed him like a stick hammering the beehive of his thoughts, and now he couldn't calm himself. Owen did not like this, didn't like it at all.

He was lost in the countryside, lost inside his ideas and experiences . . . Francesca, his imagined happy future, Barrel Arbor, the carnies, the Anarchist and his plans, the Watchmaker. Only yesterday, he had been in the center of the most marvelous universe of happiness, and now . . .

How could all be for the best? And who decided that?

He thought of the great mechanical Orrery. His entire life—like all those planets, stars, sun, and moon—had been affixed to a regular course, but now because of his impulsive decision to jump on the steamliner and leave his home, all those celestial bodies had flown loose from their connecting arms and tumbled everywhere, causing the end of his personal universe.

At dawn, another steamliner thundered past, but he had already reached the outskirts of Crown City. He no longer belonged with the carnies. The image of Francesca hovered before him, burned in his memory. He saw her in his mind's eye, and in his heart's eye, but he didn't know what others saw when they looked at her. She had smiled at him, standing on her tightrope, beckoning him to step out on a precarious path, *luring* him. But it had turned out to be much higher up than a mere practice rope, without any safety net, and he fell. . . .

By now, the Magnusson Carnival Extravaganza would have packed up their camp and loaded their wagons and steam trucks. Within hours, they would roll into Chronos Square. He knew the routine so well. He should have been helping them, and he wondered if the carnies even noticed his absence.

After first learning of the summer solstice performance, Owen had imagined it was going to be—yet again—one of the most wonderful days of his life. But he wasn't part of the show. Not today . . . maybe not ever again.

He did have his ticket, however, so he could get in, be part of the crowd. And he did want to see.

For years as he grew up, Owen had looked at his mother's books, studied the chronotypes of the city, dreamed about the Angels. They had drawn him along with their benevolent mercy, blessed him with wonder. The Clockwork Angels, more than anything else, had tempted him to jump aboard a steamliner and ride off into the night to the city of his dreams.

He'd seen the Angels once with Francesca, but those memories were now tainted because of how she had scorned him. Tonight, with the carnival performing, he could go to the Square, lose himself among the people, and watch the beautiful Angels again, one more experience to catalog in his memory and in his heart.

Francesca had changed everything for him, first for the better, then for the worse. He had never met anyone like her, had never felt such a surge of real feelings. She was his *lover* . . . yet she had laughed at his suggestion that they be married, had shown him what a fool he was. *I'd never let myself be trapped like that!*

He wondered what she had told the carnies about why he was gone, if she had made up some story about how he abandoned the show. Or maybe she had told them all just how foolish he was. They would have had a deep belly laugh at his naiveté.

Or maybe that wasn't what had happened at all.

They were his friends, and he wanted to see them again, even if just to say goodbye. He missed them already. The carnival was more than Francesca; there was also Louisa, Golson, Tomio, César Magnusson, the clowns, the barkers—more than just coworkers, they were friends. They were part of his family.

If he was brave enough, maybe he could be part of that family again. He had concluded that *not knowing* was worse than *hurting*. Maybe Francesca could explain herself . . . or maybe he was the one who needed to do the explaining. Perhaps he had misunderstood, overreacted, or just expected too much. Maybe he could have another chance, or maybe he should just take his bruises. He still felt he belonged among the carnies. And he could never forget about Francesca, no matter what. . . .

At the appointed hour the following night, Owen kept his head down, his porkpie hat pulled low. As he made his way to Chronos Square, he did not stare like a fool at every shiny object. In the surging crowds, he felt like a fallen leaf drifting down the river.

When he held up his ticket, the Red Watch guards showed no particular interest in him, and he slipped into the Square. The carnival had just opened for business, and Owen moved among the smiling, wide-eyed attendees, but he walked on eggshells, afraid to see how the carnies would react to him, but afraid to stay away.

Around the great square, under the glow of the dazzling cold-fire globes, solstice banners had been strung across the faces of government buildings, with a particularly colorful one across the Cathedral of the Timekeepers. Ropes dangled from each banner, an odd and messy loose end that should have been tied up out of the way. He looked up at the clocktower from which the Angels would emerge. Somewhere up there, hidden from view, the Watchmaker himself would be observing the spectacle. . . .

As he wandered, letting the crowd keep him invisible, Owen walked past the bright red booth of the clockwork gypsy fortune teller. Though no customer had activated the mechanism of her body, her organic head was turned up toward the high tower. The ancient woman stared longingly, her eyes focused—as if she knew the Watchmaker was there somehow. He sensed some unspoken connection.

He wondered how old she was, if the Watchmaker's specialized alchemy had anything to do with the arcane science that kept her alive. The fortune teller's gaze did not waver from the closed tower windows, but the hint of a blue-tinged tear sparkled in her eyes. Owen slipped away before the fortune teller could notice him.

As part of his performance, the knife thrower made a great show of sharpening his blades on an alchemically driven grinding wheel that made blue-tinged sparks fly from the razor edges. Finished, he stood up and asked for a volunteer who might be willing to be cuffed onto the Wheel of Fate. "I promise, my daggers will strike only the wheel, no body parts whatsoever!" He looked around and teasingly reassured them by saying, "I usually don't miss." It was all an act, though. When no one stepped forward, he threw his knives in rapid succession, and they thunked into the center of the wheel, exactly on target.

Tomio walked about, tossing his colored powders, cutting and thrusting with his sword as he yelled, "Presto!" in time with each small explosion. Owen nearly bumped into the bearded lady, but turned the other way. He longed to run to Louisa, laughing, to tell her he was back. But he didn't want to answer her questions or, worse, hear her sympathy, should she have any for him.

How he missed these people, even after only a day. Owen strengthened his resolve to see them again, talk with them, but he couldn't interrupt the show. He would wait until the performance was over, after the solstice festival wrapped up, and the Watchmaker had been pleased with the show. He would join them for the tear-down, pitch in, and hope that they welcomed him back—if they had even noticed he was gone!

As the crowds grew, the carnival continued building in color and intensity. Levitating blue spheres shone down to illuminate the games, the clockwork Ferris wheel, and the other spinning, whirling rides. Golson flexed his muscles and awed the bystanders by lifting an unbelievable amount of weight on his barbell. In the audience, Owen was probably the only one who knew about the two plates Golson always kept padlocked together so he would never be tempted to use them.

People won prizes at the game booths, or lost to peals of laughter. Keeping his porkpie hat tugged low, Owen drifted along with a heart that felt warm but also heavy.

Even if Francesca didn't love him, maybe he could find enough of a home here to make him stay. The alternative, he supposed, was Barrel Arbor, being an assistant orchard manager, marrying Lavinia, and spending the rest of his life remembering *these* days. . . .

He smiled to see the three clowns flitting, dancing, bouncing, and tripping through the crowd. Leke carried a swagger stick and was accompanied by Deke in common homespun clothes, walking stiff armed and stiff legged as if he were an automaton; Peke, meanwhile, wearing a colorful piebald costume adorned with feathers, frolicked and somersaulted along with them. Owen suddenly realized that they were meant to represent the efficient Watchmaker, a citizen like an automaton, and the wild

Anarchist—although the symbolism went unnoticed by the common folk.

In his Anarchist act, Peke pulled feathers and colored kerchiefs from hidden pockets in his costume, tossing them every which way like explosions. Then he tickled a little girl's face with a feather. She giggled, and the three clowns scampered off.

Members of the Blue Watch roved through the crowd. The uniformed men stopped at specific intervals and announced to the noisy crowd, "Citizens, remain vigilant! There has been a sighting of the Anarchist. He is wearing a brown hooded cloak to hide his features. We believe he intends to disrupt our loving Watchmaker's great celebration."

The news sent a ripple of anxiety through the people. No one knew what the Anarchist looked like, but Owen did. He felt a chill. Based on the man's conversation the night before, he might indeed intend to do mischief at the performance. Owen looked around the sea of faces, searching for D'Angelo Misterioso.

If he reported to the Regulators, however, then he would have to identify himself, and the Watch would know he didn't belong here, that he had no business being away from Barrel Arbor. The last time the Blue Watch had found him, they had escorted him promptly out of the city. His stomach twisted, as if the knife thrower had stabbed him with one of his blades and turned it. Owen kept his eyes open but saw nothing suspicious.

Owen made his way over to where the carnival trailers and equipment were set up. Since the carnies were performing, he knew that the place would be safe and out of the way. The trailers looked so familiar—the folded tarpaulins, the flatbeds, the temporary pavilions—that he felt a pang in his heart.

In the center of Chronos Square, César Magnusson called the crowd to attention, and their excited murmur quieted as all eyes turned to the trapeze and high wire. Floating coldfire globes drifted closer to the high wire, brightening into spotlights.

Owen caught his breath as Francesca climbed the wooden pole up to the first platform, as he had seen her do many times before. Now he looked through stinging tears, and she seemed to shimmer.

Her voice was so clear in his memory. *I'd never let myself be trapped like that!*

He almost turned away but found his strength. He wanted to be here. Francesca was stunning in her white leotard and short skirt—he would never think otherwise. Inky black hair fell down over the hidden pack of angel wings on her shoulders; she was confident, completely professional.

After he had stupidly opened his soul to her, Owen had run headlong into the night, all his dreams dashed. Francesca, though, didn't seem bothered in the least. There she was, ready to perform difficult acrobatic maneuvers, not preoccupied at all. Did she even think about it? Did she feel even a fraction of the ache he carried with him?

Perhaps she had forgotten him already. Perhaps she had never thought of him much at all. . . .

Although breathing hard, he forced himself to watch as she stepped onto the thin rope. She was so beautiful, a goddess with wings on her heels. Francesca raised her hands, as if to fly.

Then the Clockwork Angels upstaged her. The glow brightened from beneath the flagstones of Chronos Square, and faint, sweet-smelling smoke wafted up. A kind of synergistic power rose from the crowd, all those hearts and minds giving their complete focus to the same thing.

Francesca paused where she was, suspended in midair.

Under the dark sky, the clocktower doors glided open with the ratcheting sound of an escapement clicking along gear teeth. Huge wheels turned in the tower—and the four beautiful female figures emerged to stare down at the imminent performance, as if they were Francesca's most appreciative audience. The people caught their breath in awe, transfixed.

Keeping his gaze turned up toward the Angels, Owen drifted to the edge of the crowd. The four figures came forward and spread their wings, as if to diminish the small costume wings Francesca would reveal at the end of her performance.

While balanced on the rope, Francesca gave the Angels a deep, respectful bow and took gliding, even steps forward to cross the rope to the opposite platform, where she retrieved her trapeze, ready to begin her act.

While everyone's gaze was turned upward, Owen spotted something out of the corner of his eye—furtive movement near Tomio's wagon. Already sensitive to being where he should not be, Owen instantly became suspicious. He noticed small wooden barrels stacked against and beneath Tomio's trailer. Out of place. Owen knew how protective Tomio was of his alchemical library in his wagon. Spare supplies were never stacked outside it. Ever. More troubling, the barrels were connected with wires to a mechanical striking gadget. On the opposite side, a shadowy figure was bent over, intent on attaching some strange device.

The man spun and looked up at him. A brown hooded cloak lay discarded on the ground near the wired barrels. He had covered the lower part of his face with some sort of filter mechanism, plugs in his nose, copper tubes extending to the breathing mask. Owen wondered if it was to keep himself from inhaling the giddy, suggestive smoke in the air. Owen could see only the man's eyes—black coals, obsidian fire—a face of naked evil that turned his blood to ice.

"I know who you are!" Owen said.

In his tattooed hand, the Anarchist held a complex contraption, a set of braided pocketwatches, interconnected like Siamese twins, the hands of clocks set with winding screws and spinning gears.

Seeing the kegs, the wires, the detonator, Owen rushed forward. "Stop!"

He knew that what the Anarchist was doing now was far more

dangerous than spraying treasonous graffiti or disrupting Crown City's clocks. Those barrels were surely packed with explosives to create a bomb that would kill countless people crowded in the square for the solstice festival—including Francesca, Tomio, and all the others! It could also cause a chain reaction in the nexus of coldfire that simmered beneath Chronos Square.

The Anarchist had described such a scenario just before leaping aboard the rushing steamliner last night, but Owen couldn't believe even a madman would cause such a disaster. Taking a step backward, the Anarchist adjusted the detonator.

Owen knew he had to save everyone—the whole crowd. No matter what happened, he could not let them come to harm!

The Anarchist actuated the device in his hand with a *scritch*, a smell of flint and steel. A liberated spark sustained across the poles set the clockface hands whirling, aligning.

High above and far away, the Clockwork Angels looked down at the crowd, captivating all of the spectators as Francesca started her act. They weren't paying any attention to his struggle here. Owen yelled out an alarm. "Help! The Anarchist! He's here!"

Even then, the Anarchist didn't seem to panic; instead, he smiled. He tossed the dangerous device toward Owen—who, with the reflexes he'd developed as a juggler, instinctively caught it.

A companion device was mounted to the wired barrels, a sympathetic contraption with its own building arcs of lightning. While Owen stood by the wired barrels, struggling to disarm the detonator and save everyone, the Anarchist fled.

"Somebody, help!"

Fumbling with the device, Owen saw the clockwheels spinning, the second hand whirling about, all the times converging. Not much time! He turned the winding screw, tried to pry off the crystal face, anything to stop the hands. The sustained lightning that arced across the poles burned his finger when he attempted to smother it.

With only seconds remaining, he smashed the crystal face

against Tomio's iron-shod wagon wheel. The watchface cracked, the back of the detonator popped off; gears and springs spilled out. The sparks died.

In response to his shouts, the crowd turned toward the disturbance, and Regulators marched forward in double time. Breathing
hard, hoping he had stopped the explosion, Owen stood near the
brown hooded cloak that lay on the ground. Relieved, he held out
the smashed detonator. "Nothing to worry about," he wheezed.

"The Anarchist!" someone in the crowd shouted. The
Regulators surged toward Owen like a battering ram, and someone
else took up the cry.

Owen looked at the detonator in his hand.

"Get the Anarchist!" someone yelled.

He realized they were talking about *him*.

CHAPTER 16

How I prayed just to get away
To carry me anywhere

He froze in shock for an instant, just enough time for a watch gear to click ahead by one tooth, to release and catch an escapement, and drive a second hand one mark forward around the circle. Owen held up the detonator he had just smashed. "No, it was someone else! I saved everyone!"

But the real Anarchist was long gone.

The Regulators took out long, black nightsticks and stalked toward him; Owen had never noticed them carrying sticks before. The crowd closed in on him, their eyes shining, energized by their worship of the Clockwork Angels and the colorful frenzy of the carnival, as well as the intoxicating fumes in the air.

Everything happened in a flash, although Owen felt enough fear to last him a lifetime. For a fleeting instant, he expected Tomio to arrive with his dashing sword and save him. Or would Tomio—Francesca's brother—be among the foremost who wanted to tear him limb from limb?

As the mob came at him like predators, he decided against

further explanations and dropped the detonator. He ran.

The Regulators shouted after him. Shrill whistles punctuated the square.

Above the growing, angry roar, Owen thought he could hear the Anarchist laughing.

In the confusion, Owen took advantage of the splashes of shadows in the night. Around the square, uniformed Regulators went on the alert, guarding all exits, standing shoulder to shoulder to prevent the fugitive's escape. Groups of determined Blue Watch elbowed through the crowd as the mob pursued Owen on their own, wanting him punished.

And the Clockwork Angels looked down upon it all, no longer seeming benevolent; they were goddesses of vengeance now.

As people closed in, Owen knew he couldn't get out to the open streets. He was cornered, trapped against the tall ministry buildings. Above him, strung across the stone façade of the Cathedral of the Timekeepers, was the bright fabric banner commemorating the solstice—and the dangling rope.

Thankful for his practice in the carnival, he seized the rope and scrambled up. Within moments, he had climbed halfway up the side of the building. He looked down at the angry faces of the shouting crowd; they raised their fists, cursed him, and began hurling stones, fruit, anything they could find. Owen ducked as rocks clacked against the stone blocks next to his head, and he continued to pull himself up the rope until he reached the banner, which gave him little protection. From there, he stepped onto a stone windowsill. He dug his fingers into cracks in the blocks, pulled himself along.

He had never entirely mastered his fear of heights, but now his fear of the crowd was much greater. He inched along, his toes wedged into cracks in the stone blocks, holding the fabric banner for balance, until he reached another windowsill. The thick cornerstones on the side of the building let him climb even higher, swinging up like an acrobat until he reached the rooftop. His heart beat furiously, pounding in his temples, and he felt a surge of adrenalin.

From the top of the Cathedral of the Timekeepers, he gazed down on Chronos Square and the crowd that hated him so much, so suddenly. From there, he could see the bright lights of the carnival, the tents, the game booths, the whirling rides, the high wire and trapeze—and the tiny figure of Francesca looking up at him.

He stared at her across the open distance, sure that he could see her face, imagining that her eyes met his. He saw her mouth but could not hear her words, if she said anything at all.

Turning his back, he fled across the rooftop like a footpad in the night, slid down sloping tin shingles to a gutter, and inched his way along until he reached the far corner of the building—and a dead end. This cathedral was connected to another rooftop by a set of newsgraph cables: thick, insulated black cords that appeared even more dangerous than the high wire Francesca walked. The shadowy street below looked like a deep, endless canyon.

Bells rang out like dissonant gongs from the Watchmaker's clocktower, calling the city to arms. He could imagine the Angels themselves pointing accusatory hands in his direction. Owen had never heard such a clamor before. Uniformed Regulators flowed in from the streets and boulevards, the Red Watch, Blue Watch, even the elite Black Watch. All hunting him.

Owen stared at the newsgraph cable and knew that he had to walk it. If he could reach the other building, he could cross the rooftop, find his way inside and down the stairs, then vanish into the streets. It was the only way to escape from Chronos Square. The newsgraph cable looked no wider than a knife edge.

He had seen Francesca do it so many times without even losing her breath. He had done it himself, but had been unsuccessful more often than not, and this time he had no safety net, no one to coach him, only hard paving stones to meet him if he fell. Francesca had gestured to him, beckoning him to walk out to her across the rope, encouraging him, taunting him, until he did exactly as she wanted.

Now he placed his right foot on the flexible tension of the cable, hoping his weight would not uproot it from its anchors.

Behind him, he heard shouts accompanied by the thundering of booted feet. A group of guards must have gotten inside the ministry building and were storming up to the roof. If he didn't get away now, they would corner him.

Owen placed his left foot in front of his right, stretched out his arms for balance—like angel wings spread out to fly. He refused to look down, refused to think. This was just *walking*, one step after another. He imagined Francesca smiling at him, urging him along. *I would never let myself be trapped like that!* He wavered but drove away the distracting thoughts, blinked his burning eyes and focused ahead, focused on *nothing*.

Countless times he had seen Francesca stroll along the wire as easily as he walked a street. He told himself he could do it. He swayed, gingerly lifted his right foot, and swung it in front of his left. Another step, and he was halfway across, although the gap still looked like an infinite gulf. His vision was fuzzed with black, his concentration as channeled as the view through a natural scientist's magnifying tube. Each step brought him nearer to the other side. Another step and another.

He was walking on air. He was absolutely terrified.

He collapsed onto the other rooftop, surprised that he had crossed the entire distance. He huddled on the solid tin shingles, breathing heavily.

A door burst open on the dark cathedral rooftop behind him, and Regulators marched out, searching for him. They shouted when they caught sight of him on the opposite building.

Owen heaved himself to his feet and continued his headlong flight, although he still felt dizzy, and his knees were weak.

The clocktower bells continued to clang an alarm. All across the city, newsgraphs rattled out a notice for his capture and arrest.

Someone would already be sketching his likeness based on eyewitness descriptions.

The Regulators would probably round up the carnies to interview them about him. Would any of his friends—former friends?—believe he was secretly the Anarchist? Tomio had known the real D'Angelo Misterioso, but even if the carnies insisted Owen was innocent, would anyone believe mere *carnies*? Owen swallowed hard, wondering what Francesca would say about him. "A foolish boy, but I never believed he was *dangerous!*"

With two sharp kicks, he broke open a rooftop door, pelted down the stairs, and burst out onto the street. He ran in a random direction, down one street, turning a corner and heading away from the square. He ducked through an alley and emerged onto a wide road. He wanted to go home but knew he couldn't—Owen didn't even remember what home was. He couldn't rejoin the carnival or go back to Barrel Arbor. There would no longer be any routine life of picking apples in a peaceful orchard. There'd be no simple cottage, no evenings in the Tick Tock Tavern, no bland and unchallenging Lavinia at his side.

He had longed for adventure. *Sometimes the Angels punish us by answering our prayers.*

He had to get away, to go anywhere. His running feet carried him down to the river and the docks. Alarms rang from other clocktowers in the city, but this late at night, people so comfortable with their unwavering schedules would take a while to understand the reason for the disruption.

He made his way to the docks at the wide mouth of the Winding Pinion River. Several cargo barges were tied up at the piers, and the bustle of dockworkers loading cargo under bright coldfire lights reminded Owen of the happy day he had spent among them.

More important, though, he saw a cargo steamer ready to push off into the night. White vapors coughed out of the cylindrical smokestacks, backlit by glowing docklights. The ship's boilers had been pumped up to high pressure, and the cargo steamer's air horn blatted even louder than the gongs on the Watchmaker's clocktower.

Dockworkers were removing cables as thick as Owen's leg from dock stanchions, ready to cast off. He stared for a moment at the great ship's beautiful lines, the hull designed to glide like a spear-point through the Western Sea, taking everyone aboard to exotic lands. He began to run.

All but the last gangplank had been removed, and he charged toward it, using his final reserves of energy. His lungs burned and his heart pounded. "Wait! I need to get aboard." No one could see him in the long dock shadows made by the garish coldfire lights. "Wait!"

He had dreamed of riding cargo steamers to Atlantis, of setting foot on the distant lands mentioned in his mother's book. Poseidon, Atlantis, the Seven Cities of Gold, and places not even named. He didn't know where this vessel was bound, but he knew he could not stay in Crown City. Alarm bells continued ringing from clocktowers.

Where would he rather be? He made up his mind—*anywhere but here.*

The dockworkers looked at him in surprise as he ran up the gangplank, flushed, holding his porkpie cap to his head. One burly man paused while working at an enormous knot next to the gangplank, and Owen recognized him as the one who had introduced him to pineapples. The burly man's brow furrowed, then smoothed open with realization. "Ah, I know you!" He called up to the steamer in a thunderous voice. "Hold up, you got one more to come aboard!"

The steamer crew came out and gathered at the rail to see the cause of the commotion. Owen ran up the gangplank before he had time to think—*confidence,* Golson would have reminded him. The crew didn't know who he was, and he didn't have a story— not yet.

After all that had happened, he could not believe this was what he deserved. He thought of the Watchmaker's supposed plan and decided he no longer believed that all this was for the best.

But he knew that *they* believed it. And that was his story. . . .

As he burst onto the deck and the steamer's engines heated up to full power, the workers detached the gangplank and threw off the final docking ropes. The vessel drifted into the channel and steamed away into the night.

Heaving enormous breaths, Owen presented himself to the curious captain. Unable to bring himself to tell an outright lie, he chose his words carefully, "I've come from Chronos Square and the Clockwork Angels." He sucked in a deep breath, swallowed hard. "I'm supposed to be here."

The captain gave a brusque, accepting nod. That was all Owen needed to say.

INTERLUDE

The Anarchist

The things I've always been denied
An early promise that somehow died

Wearing a well-tailored suit and carrying his leather valise, the Anarchist made his way toward the Alchemy College. He had more than his share of vendettas, for he was an ambitious man. So many people had wronged him that it was a challenge just to keep track of the list.

Most of all, he wanted to punish the great, yet flawed, Watchmaker—that much went without saying. Also, he had never forgiven the carnival, especially Tomio. He could have made the carnival show so spectacular, if only their imaginations had been greater than their fears—breathtaking alchemical reactions igniting in a blaze like a thousand bonfires, converting base powders, rare earths, and a chain reaction of catalysts! Through the transformative ignition of powders, he would have showered the audience with sparkling, new-formed diamonds, precipitate gems that even the Watchmaker could not create! Transmuting cheap metals into gold was a mere parlor trick by comparison. Yes, the reaction was as dangerous as it was spectacular, but what was life without risk? Tomio had driven him out just like those small-minded philosopher-professors, had insisted that he was being too brash and reckless, that he was showing off.

No one understood him. He did not need to show off for the crowds, since his greatness was inherent. Even the Watchmaker had spotted his talent back at the Alchemy College. And when the student had become too talented, the Watchmaker set out to destroy him.

But after being expelled, he had survived, and thrived, and changed. The Anarchist glanced down at the alchemical symbol on his hand. He was a precipitate, a new being, created by a set of reactions. He flexed his other hand, the scarred one, felt a twinge of blind pain that went as deep as the bone. Such fire could change a person and change a civilization.

The Anarchist sought to create a new world order, an Instability that ran counter to the Watchmaker's repressive Stability. He did it for the good of the human race, not just for revenge . . . although revenge had to be satisfied as well.

He had already left his mark by scrambling clocks in the city, turning the sedate march of time into a drunkard's walk. That had shaken the everyday people from their deep slumber, though it did not entirely awaken them. He could count the stunt as one little victory, but it was not sufficient to end the war. In the grandest spectacle of all, he had attempted to destroy the coldfire nexus beneath Chronos Square, along with the Watchmaker's tower and the Clockwork Angels—a setback that would have brought down civilization in Albion.

As he strode down the street, eyes fixed forward, he drew in a deep breath. The resulting chaos would have been its own reward, a dash of cold water or a bracing shot of whiskey! The turmoil would strengthen human hearts and minds, cure them of the deadly effects of apathy and atrophy, stability and stagnation. His neat and efficient vengeance would have hurt all those who had harmed him—the Watchmaker, the carnival, and the populace of sheep.

Every piece in its place, every action leading to a reaction. Like clockwork. Only he understood the irony.

Even such a neat plan was not without its risks, however. When naïve and innocent Owen Hardy (his unwitting protégé) had discovered the plot—not entirely by accident—the Anarchist had been content to turn to his secondary plan. A man like him had to embrace random acts.

He was alone—always alone. Yes, with so much work to do, he longed for an apprentice. He needed someone, anyone, to help his fight. He could not be the only person in all of Albion with the acuity to recognize the flaws of Stability. And if he could make even a small, insignificant, *normal* man see what the whole world lacked, then the battle was half won.

By tossing the detonator to the young scapegoat, he had set the wheels in motion, giving Owen another sharp shove toward his destiny, an alchemical reaction that might precipitate another Anarchist, someone against whom the world had unjustly turned. The mob and the Regulators had pursued him, howling for blood.

Owen Hardy had the potential to be an important catalyst, but he needed to be awakened. Optimism was such an insidious venom that it left a person too cheerful to know he had been poisoned. The young man was now awake, although not ready. Not yet . . . but the Anarchist had faith in entropy.

Eventually, experience would shape the young man into an ally.

That had been three days ago. Owen Hardy was gone, fled across the sea and out of the Anarchist's reach—for now—but he would be back. Or the Anarchist would find another candidate. And there were always the Wreckers.

Today's demonstration might wake someone else among the sheep. . . .

Now, as the Anarchist reached the huddled buildings of the

Alchemy College, he found a quiet alley, opened his valise, removed his disguise. Before he could pass through the school gates, he had to become someone else entirely.

He shucked out of his business clothes and donned a traditional white robe adorned with alchemical symbols. He tugged a conical hat onto his head, tied the robe with a green sash that denoted his rank as a mid-level official alchemist from the Watchmaker's headquarters, a person with sufficient authority to go where he liked, but not impressive enough to attract too much attention.

The Anarchist pulled the other part of himself inside, stuffed his real thoughts and feelings out of sight, and arranged his expression to match the rest of his disguise. He arched his significant eyebrows, twisted his lips in a haughty, critical air, and walked with a mean stride to the school's cut-stone gates.

From years ago, he knew the schedule of classes and study times, and he knew they would never change. Timekeeping was the hobgoblin of little minds, and every person here was completely predictable. Like honeybees. He walked up to the school at the precise time when his work could have the most impact.

While studying at the Alchemy College, he had done such great work that the philosopher-professors were at first impressed, then intimidated. When he remained persistent, proposing ideas for unorthodox experiments that were not part of the curriculum, they had reprimanded him.

But he had drawn the secret attention of someone far superior to their closed minds and small dreams. He discovered mysterious, unsigned notes smuggled into his books and under his pillow in the dormitory—quiet encouragement, suggestions of possible chemical mixtures for him to try, questions that even the philosopher-professors or the alchemist-priests could not answer. And he *knew* the secret communications came from the Watchmaker himself.

More than two centuries ago, that man had rewritten the

economy of Albion when he'd discovered how to create gold. The alchemist-priests who created and maintained the coldfire nexus beneath Crown City had long since stopped making new discoveries. No one else had the imagination even to try. The Watchmaker surely must be frustrated, needing fresh blood and new ideas.

He had continued to send surreptitious suggestions to that ambitious and talented student. In all his years of continuing research, the Watchmaker was never able to create diamonds or precision jewels; instead, he had to purchase them at a dear price from the mines in far-off Atlantis. So, he had coaxed the talented student to concoct an unauthorized experiment. If successful, it should have created a wealth of gems; instead, it had resulted in a massive explosion, one that burned and disfigured his hand, earned him severe reprimands and expulsion from the school.

None of the philosopher-professors believed him when he claimed that the Watchmaker was a catalyst for his experiments. They laughed at the very idea. They called him insane. They insisted that the Watchmaker did not communicate directly with everyday people, that he had no contact whatsoever with mere students.

Only later did he realize that the Watchmaker was so intimidated by his protégé's talent and potential that the experiment itself had been sabotaged. . . .

Now, wrapped in his own physical and mental disguise, the Anarchist tightened the green sash holding his robe together and presented himself at the college gates. The red-uniformed Regulator glanced at his outfit and rank and allowed him through without question.

"All is for the best," the Anarchist muttered, and the guard acknowledged him.

At half past the hour, classes ended, doors opened, and alchemy students marched out of their lecture halls to the assigned study chambers where they would memorize alchemical symbols, copy down approved reactions, and complete the designated tasks they needed to finish before they could be certified for the next level of study.

As he looked at them now, the students reminded him of himself. Years ago, when he was one of them, he had worn the same uniform every day. He had read the same texts, heard the same lectures, mouthed the same rote responses. The philosopher-professors wanted him to think like a scientist, and yet accept every discovery without question. The Alchemy College was designed to unlock the secrets of the universe; instead, without allowing the students to think for themselves, the classes did nothing more than reinforce ignorance.

Well and truly blessed, indeed.

The students gave the Anarchist respectful bows as they passed, making way for him to continue down the halls. Seeing his stolen robe, they were impressed by him, wanted to *be* him after they graduated. If only . . .

He walked without hesitation to the guarded chemical storage vault. A gold disk emblazoned with the familiar stylized honeybee had been affixed to its exterior. Hydraulic tubes ran to pistons that pressed long locking pins into the floor and ceiling, with crossbars thrust into sockets in the jamb. Large-diameter gears connected to one another in a special combination, metal teeth biting into the locking pins. A pad glowed with blue coldfire, waiting for someone to input the proper code.

Even with all the intertwined security systems, a Red Watchman also stood straight-backed at the door, arms at his side, gaze forward. The Anarchist walked up to him, impatient to see someone standing in his way. He ran his gaze across the red uniform, deliberately looking for the rank insignia.

"Lieutenant, I require access to the vault. The Watchmaker suspects irregularities in the accounting of certain rare earths and precision jewels imported from the Atlantis mines. I am here to complete a full inventory on his behalf."

Noting the alchemist-priest's robe and the green rank sash, the Regulator fished out a key from a ring on his belt. He inserted the key into the control pad, which made the coldfire glow brighter. He twisted a valve to release steam, making the gears turn; teeth retracted the locking pins from floor and ceiling; another system withdrew the side bars. Finally, with a hiss of equalizing pressure, the heavy vault door unsealed and swung inside with the force of heavy pistons.

The Red Watchman stepped aside to let him enter. "Do you require my assistance?"

The Anarchist gave a sharp shake of his head. "That is expressly forbidden. The Watchmaker assigned me alone to perform this task—undisturbed." He glanced down the hall, where clocks were mounted every twenty paces. "Leave me for an hour. I will secure the door when I have finished."

Reluctant to abandon his post, but more reluctant to question the Watchmaker's instructions, the red-jacketed guard marched off like a windup soldier.

Inside the large vault, the Anarchist drew a breath filled with secrets. The chamber was lit by the eerie glow of floating coldfire globes, and he paused a moment just to drink it all in. He had been in the alchemy vault only once during his first year as an acolyte, when he'd assisted his philosopher-professor in organizing the treasures and dangerous supplies that crowded the shelves.

He had seen so much more since then. After being expelled from the Alchemy College, severely burned in body and soul, he had fled across the sea, worked like a slave, and nearly starved. But he went where he wanted, learned what he wished, and discovered that there were ways of life other than the Watchmaker's Stability, other lands and other cultures beyond Albion. More than that, according to an eccentric bookseller who owned a shop in a back alley of Poseidon City, there were other possible worlds as well, not just this one.

The bookseller was a very tall, lean woman with short gray-brown hair in a mass of chaotic curls. She wore a pair of spectacles that left angry red pinch marks on her nose. On the dusty shelves in her dim shop, she carried arcane volumes in many languages, including treatises from scientists both great and obscure.

Back during his days of exile from Albion, the Anarchist had spent afternoons in the shop perusing the volumes until the bookseller scolded him to buy the tomes if he wanted to study them. "I respect a seeker of knowledge," she had said, "but I am not a library." So, he stole enough money to buy the books that most intrigued him.

The bookseller told him that they came from other earths, worlds where the laws of physics and chemistry might be different than here, that their conclusions might not be valid everywhere, but he didn't listen to her warning. With such a wealth of knowledge, he was sure he could recreate powerful but forgotten discoveries. Preparing for a triumphant return, he stowed away aboard a ship bound for Albion; he smuggled not only the books but also rare and necessary alchemical resources from Atlantis. He returned to the land of the Watchmaker not as a prodigal son, but as a vengeful one.

The stern bookseller had been right, though. When he arrived at Crown City and practiced his demonstrations, the resulting chemical reactions were different from what the book told him to expect. Many of the Anarchist's "triumphant demonstrations" were sad failures; one disaster resulted in two deaths, which forced him to change his identity and hide among the people. He had intended to create diamonds with his experiments, but the accidental discovery of such amazingly explosive chemical reactions served him in a different stead.

If the Watchmaker used his destiny calculators to see

everything, did he know that the Anarchist had returned, the nemesis that he himself had created? Or were his own actions too random to be predicted?

Now, inside the alchemical vault, he found the powders he needed, the boxes of elemental salts, sealed beakers of acids, humors of green sulfur, and rare ingredients shipped at great expense from the continent across the sea: powdered dreamstones, distillate of red coal, oil of moonstone. Working like a chef preparing for a state banquet, he recreated his forbidden experiment, but on a much larger scale.

This would be no mere exothermic reaction, but one that would ricochet like chain lightning among the volatile chemicals inside the vault—natrium, saltpeter, magnesium, wolfram, kalium. He stepped back as the mixture began to rumble, releasing a scarlet mist. Distillates leaked onto the floor in bubbling pools of poison, like chemical symbols of his rage.

And that was just the beginning.

On top of the mounded chemicals he placed a beaker of dissolved redfire opals, the final reactive component. Now he required absolute precision—which was all part of the grand joke on the Watchmaker.

From a pocket inside his white robe, the Anarchist removed a device of his own invention, a pocketwatch with a secondary timepiece attached, connected to thin activator rings and powered jointly by a wound-tight watchspring and a chemical battery. A detonator ... a small thing, but sufficient to create a shock at the desired time to spill the beaker of dissolved redfire opals into the remaining chemical mixture. Flint and steel to *liberate*—beautiful word!—a spark. The energy slumbering within the elements would awaken with a roar.

As the detonator ticked, he turned to depart, not just taking his time but stealing it. Just inside the vault door, though, he spotted a complex, intriguing device on an equipment shelf, placed safely away from the chemicals. A newly tuned but inactive machine.

He had seen a destiny calculator only once before, but there it was! He caught his breath. This was a small device with a limited temporal range . . . but if he could set the needle to focus on a particular person, he would be able to monitor Owen Hardy's future before the young man made it for himself. Then the Anarchist could make the proper adjustments, or at least put himself in the right places.

He carefully removed the destiny calculator from its storage shelf, held it in one hand, hid it by pulling down his padded sleeve, and hurried out of the vault. Behind him, the detonator continued its countdown.

As he left the chemical supply chamber, he reset the coldfire control pad so that the crossbars and locking pins snicked back into place; the hydraulics pressed the door into its seal; steam vented with a sigh of relief for a job well done. A last careful detail: he smashed the coldfire control pad, which sparked, sputtered, and died.

He had set the device for eight minutes, and the Red Watchman was due back in ten, but in such a random and exuberant experiment, one could not be precise.

Carrying the stolen destiny calculator, the Anarchist moved with a quick step down the college halls, past the closed doors where students were studying for their examinations. He kept his eye on the clocks, watching each second tick away, trying not to look hurried. Once outside the school buildings, he passed the Regulator guards at the entrance gate; they did not impede or even acknowledge his departure.

A long time ago, he had been driven from the Alchemy College, chased off the grounds. Now, he felt like a conquering hero.

He found his valise exactly where he'd left it in the alley—no one in Crown City would even think to steal. He shucked off his alchemist-priest's robe and cap and donned the formal suit again, his well-dressed disguise. He stored the destiny calculator, straightened his hair, and reentered the streets, melting into the crowd just like everyone else, invisible and unnoticed. He had just enough time.

Behind him the Alchemy College exploded.

There were shouts and shrieks. People came running toward the smoke and flames, but he just smiled and walked on. He heard a pattering on the ground and looked down to see a sparkle . . . tiny diamonds, an unexpected residue of the spectacular chemical reaction. He snorted; and the Watchmaker could create only *gold*.

Oh, they would never forget him.

CHAPTER 17

Sometimes the Angels punish us
By answering our prayers

Since childhood, Owen had dreamed about exciting sea voyages, but he never imagined just how miserable such journeys could be.

The cargo vessel steamed away from the nightmarish memories of Crown City, exiting the mouth of the Winding Pinion River, and headed out to the open sea. The ship's hold was full of machines and equipment manufactured by Albion industries, as well as crates of gold created by the Watchmaker's alchemist-priests, which would be used to buy valuable items from Atlantis.

The captain, a stoop-shouldered and lonely seeming man named Lochs, had accepted Owen's story without question; if the young man said he was supposed to ride aboard the vessel to Poseidon City, who was he to question the Watchmaker's plan?

Feeling guilty that he had tricked his way aboard, Owen offered his help in the galley or on deck. Captain Lochs was surprised—apparently, previous representatives from the government had expected fine staterooms and pampering. He already had a full crew, but he did ask the young man to write down a long-overdue inventory of the ship's stores. Owen took his pad and clipboard, feeling important and relieved that he could do something in exchange for his passage. He finished the detailed list in a few hours, marking down their food stores, spare parts, coldfire batteries in the engine room, water-storage tanks, barrels of grease, coils of rope, clean hydraulic tubing to be used for repairs, piston jackets, turbines, and drums of paint. He frequently had to ask one of the crew to explain what a particular item was, and he learned a great deal.

Each hour carried the ship farther from the coast of Albion, from the Anarchist and the Regulators—each of whom wanted Owen in their own ways—and farther from Barrel Arbor, from the carnival, and from Francesca. In a storybook, she would have come to the docks to wave goodbye to him, but Owen now understood how foolish storybooks were.

Still, thinking of the chronotypes in his mother's volumes, he was off in search of a different dream. True love had turned out to be an illusion. Now, feeling stung, he hoped to gain wisdom from his youthful mistakes. He vowed never to let himself be so deceived again . . . but he knew himself better than that. Sooner or later, he would fall in love, with all its illusions, all over again.

For now, he would follow the course of winds and sea, see the shores of Atlantis and fabled Poseidon City. Maybe, if he showed Captain Lochs he was a hard worker, trustworthy, companionable, Owen could find a place aboard the cargo steamer, spend his life traveling from Albion to exotic ports. He smiled at the possibility; *that* truly seemed the best of all possible worlds.

But on the second day, as the winds picked up outside, Owen became so ferociously seasick that he was incapable of performing any task more challenging than emptying his own vomit bucket.

None of the other sailors seemed affected in the least, but Owen curled up and felt more miserable than he had ever been.

The cargo vessel bounced across choppy seas like a steamliner with a broken wheel, rising up to the crest of a wave and plunging down into the trough again and again.

Captain Lochs and his crew strolled about in the bridge house or out on the open deck, nonchalant about the turmoil of the water. Two men had set up a chessboard on a crate and moved their pieces from square to square, catching them each time they threatened to tip over.

Meanwhile, Owen stayed in his own small cabin. Though it was no larger than a closet, Owen had felt guilty when Captain Lochs assigned him the cramped quarters. As an uninvited passenger, he had expected to bunk with the crew. But Captain Lochs had insisted that Owen was a guest sent by the Watchmaker and must therefore accept at least the minimal hospitality of the tiny cabin. Especially now that he was experiencing the full effects of seasickness, Owen was thankful for the privacy.

He clutched his stomach and his pounding head, rolled from his bunk to the deck, threw up in the bucket, and crawled back into the bunk. He felt so sick, he couldn't even think of Francesca. He was not quite the dashing heroic figure he had imagined himself to be.

By now, his preconceptions had been shattered many times. He couldn't believe that he was a fugitive, wanted by the Watchmaker himself, that the Regulators considered *him* to be the murderous Anarchist—when, in fact, he had prevented the explosion in Chronos Square! He had saved the Clockwork Angels, the Watchmaker, the carnival, and everyone there.

When the seas finally calmed, at least for a few hours, he went out on deck at night to look for the stars. Taking deep breaths of the chill, salty air, he distracted himself by picking out constellations; he was surprised to see that the star patterns looked different here, far from Crown City. But clouds scudded across the sky, obscuring the constellations. He glimpsed a bright light off in the distance at the waterline . . . some other ship, perhaps, or a mysterious fire out at sea. The cargo steamer voyaged on.

Though weak and pallid, he climbed up to the bridge deck and asked Captain Lochs for a few sheets of paper and a lead pencil. Clutching his writing materials like a lifeline, he crept back to his cabin and in between bouts of nausea and misery, he wrote a letter to his father, detailing his adventures, explaining where he had been, what he had seen. He hoped Anton Hardy had received his other newsgraph letters, which he'd written among the carnies. Owen didn't know what his father would think of him, what Lavinia was doing, or how the rest of Barrel Arbor would react to his fall from grace. Maybe Barrel Arbor had already forgotten him, quietly sweeping the embarrassment under a rug.

Finished with the letter, and exhausted from the effort, he gathered his strength and struck out to the bridge deck again. Captain Lochs promised to forward the letter to Barrel Arbor as soon as the cargo steamer returned to Albion.

On the fifth day of the voyage, knowing they would soon be in sight of land, Owen worked his way out onto the deck, hoping that the sunshine and fresh air would revive him.

The steam curling up from the great stacks looked like celebration streamers. The two men continued to play their game of chess, moving wobbly pawns and bishops.

As waves crashed against the bow and sent up a diamond sparkle of spindrift, the beautiful sight captivated him . . . until he rushed to clutch the deck rail like a strangler with a reluctant victim and tried to re-empty his already empty stomach over the side.

Captain Lochs looked at him with sympathy. "Maybe for this secret mission, the Watchmaker should have chosen someone less inclined to seasickness, eh?"

"All is for the best." Owen choked out the words and wiped his mouth.

"We'll reach Poseidon by late afternoon, don't you worry,"

Captain Lochs said. "You'll have your feet on solid ground soon."

Owen felt relieved and then nauseated again. He looked at his pocketwatch ticking down the hours. He couldn't wait until they reached the marvelous city of Poseidon, so that he could be off this hellish ship.

But when Owen arrived, Poseidon City was even worse.

———◆———

He walked down the gangplank in port—he had intended to *bound* down and set foot on a new continent, but with his weak legs, he managed little more than swaying and staggering—and entered a city he had imagined since he was a boy.

Worried about him, Captain Lochs called down from the deck, "Will you be all right, lad?"

Although Owen was nervous about the dramatic changes in his life, he straightened his shoulders, shored up his confidence, and maintained the fiction that he had genuine business here. This was a new land and a new hope for him—what he deserved. And the Angels had granted him his wish.

He was not under any illusions about how difficult it was going to be to establish a new life, though. "I could, however, use a small loan to tide me over until I get settled. I will pay you back next time I see you."

Without objection, nor expectation of repayment, the captain gave him enough money for a few days' worth of expenses, provided he was frugal. Owen knew how to be frugal. He was struck by an unpleasant thought: the Anarchist had given him a few coins to help him out for the first few days in Crown City, saying, "Maybe I just like the idea that you'll owe me." Owen had not felt comfortable with that.

Now, as he waved goodbye to Captain Lochs, he vowed that he would not forget to repay his debt. He pushed all thoughts of the Anarchist from his mind.

In the port of Crown City, every docking slip had been organized and numbered, the cargo ships laid out like merchandise on a warehouse shelf. Poseidon was exactly the opposite: disordered, loud, and smelly, beset with rough-looking people who had no interest in keeping a schedule or feeling the joy of a job well done.

After Crown City's neat street grid and the ordered assembly of buildings, Poseidon looked as if some giant had picked up armloads of buildings from a stockpile and simply dumped them, letting them rest where they fell. Ramshackle structures leaned together on the steep hills, and narrow streets wound up from the harbor.

Owen walked into the city, eyes open, ready for anything. He saw no emblems of bright, perfect honeybees; no hexagonal windows; no efficient bustle of busy workers in newsgraph offices. This was a different sort of city altogether.

As he walked along a seemingly endless promenade of taverns, two unshaven men jostled him, then apologized by patting him as if they were old friends. Their breath smelled of pickled cabbage and fish, two aromas that did not blend well together. Owen was friendly to the men, since he had no acquaintances here, but he didn't see the two as likely comrades. They were gone down the street before he could ask their names.

Not long afterward, Owen found an inn. After so many days vomiting up anything he tried to eat, he was hungry and weak. Only when he tried to buy food did he discover that the two overly friendly men had robbed him of the coins Captain Lochs had loaned him.

When he told his pitiable story to the innkeeper, hoping for just a few scraps of bread or maybe a soupbone, the man chased him away with a broomstick.

Owen huddled on a crate outside of a smoking house where rumpled-looking businessmen paid the doorman to let them in; later, they staggered out, reeking of acrid smoke. He put his head in his hands, wondering what was to become of him now. The doorman let him loiter for half an hour before telling him to be on his way.

It seemed like a lifetime ago that Owen had jumped aboard a night steamliner to leave his village and start his adventure. "On my way at last!" Now he had arrived at a new part of his journey, but he didn't see the point of all his tribulations. Where was he supposed to go?

He faced up to his situation and went from door to door, offering to work if the proprietor would give him food and shelter. At the docks in Crown City, the porters and laborers had been happy to accept a willingly offered hand, but these suspicious business owners chased him away. One threw a sloshing chamberpot at him, but he dodged the mess.

A café owner told him he could help himself to the fine banquet out back, but when he went behind the building, he found only a garbage heap with vegetable peelings, rotten fruit, and a great many flies.

As full night closed in, the inns and drinking establishments grew louder. Lanterns were lit with hot-burning red coal from veins in the foothills; fights broke out, and Owen huddled in the street shadows, afraid. He found an alley and curled up there to sleep, drawing his knees to his chest, leaning against a brick wall. Though he now had the freedom to sleep wherever he wanted, with no Regulators to harass him, he took no comfort in his supposed peace. He closed his eyes and tried to imagine that he was under an apple tree on top of orchard hill. The memory didn't help much, but he dozed off nevertheless.

By the following morning, he was so hungry that he did venture back to the garbage heap behind the café. He sorted through the scraps to find a few bites that would fill his rumbling stomach; he barely managed to keep the food down, but it was food.

He went back to the docks, thinking maybe he could get help

from Captain Lochs again, but the cargo steamer had already set sail, loaded with a hold full of alchemical supplies, obsidian, agate, jasper, redfire opals, and even rarer minerals from outposts in the mountains. The dockworkers jealously guarded their own wages against interlopers, and they chased him away when he volunteered to lend a hand.

The next day, he encountered a group of feral young boys, the oldest of whom couldn't have been more than twelve. They surrounded him, jeered at him, and tried to rob him. When he emptied his pockets to show that he had nothing of value other than his pocketwatch, they stole his watch out of spite and beat him up. But they had little heart for the wasted effort and left him bruised and aching on the ground.

He no longer knew what time it was, and the city seemed indifferent to clocktowers.

This was a far cry from the picture of Poseidon City painted by the legends. He wanted to weep for the loss of the wondrous place from his mother's books. He was glad she had never been able to see the real Poseidon for herself; better that she had died of a fever with her dreams intact.

CHAPTER 18

In this one of many possible worlds, all for the best,
or some bizarre test?

Though the days in Poseidon City were without order and without a routine, they had a bleak sameness. Owen had no goal beyond finding food, scrabbling for money, and keeping himself safe.

Never before had he lived in the shadows. He searched for a warm place to sleep, like a rabbit desperate for a cozy warren. More often than he could count, he escaped into the memory of that one night in Francesca's warm and welcoming tent, and the memory was sweeter and more golden than the Watchmaker's finest honey.

Each time he found even a marginally comfortable spot, though, someone else found it soon after, usually someone stronger than he was. Three of those times, Owen fought to protect his meager scrap of normalcy, but each time he failed and found himself bruised and bloody, thrown out to search for something else. The others living on the streets of Poseidon did not fight according to the rules that Golson had taught him. Confidence alone did not serve Owen well, and his confidence soon waned.

One day in the back of a crooked alley where he hoped to find a sheltered stoop, perhaps some piled old crates and shadows for a blanket, he discovered a storefront with a grime-streaked window and a hanging wooden placard. *Underworld Books.* The entrance was set down two steps into the ground as if the shop itself were sinking into a new subterranean location.

A book propped inside the window caught his eye, its colors faded from long exposure to sunlight, although Owen couldn't imagine how sunlight could ever penetrate the alley's shadows. He recognized the cover: it was his mother's book, the illustrated volume containing chronotypes of Crown City.

He froze, astonished. After all he'd been through since fleeing Albion, the experiences that had to be categorized as *ordeals* rather than adventures, this bookstore, this *book*, shone like a bright beacon on a dark, stormy night. He touched fingers against the window, unable to reach the volume on display. The grime and dust were on the inside of the glass.

Gathering his nerve, Owen brushed off his rumpled and unlaundered clothes, adjusted the porkpie cap to cover his dirty and mussed hair, and pulled open the door of Underworld Books.

Inside at a front desk he saw a tall woman with a tangle of short, gray-brown curls and ill-fitting glasses that pinched her nose. She glanced at him with the automatic welcoming expression of a shopkeeper who saw too few customers. At the moment, she was dealing with a broad-shouldered, bearlike man with a huge beard, bald pate, and rich, dark skin.

Owen did his best to put confidence into his voice. "Excuse me, could I look at the book in the window?"

"Help yourself," said the bookseller, who turned back to finish wrapping up a package of small volumes for the bald man and deftly tied twine in perpendicular loops. "Just be sure your fingers are clean."

Owen wiped his hands on his trousers and gave an earnest nod. "I'll be careful. I . . . I know this book."

He removed the volume from its display stand in the window, and with trembling fingers, hungry for a reminder of familiarity, he turned the pages. In quieter days, he had spent endless hours pouring his imagination into the intense chronotypes: the Watchmaker's clocktower, the ornate Hall of Regulators, the Cathedral of Timekeepers, the façades of the ministry buildings, and the lovely Clockwork Angels.

But the images in this book did not show the Crown City he remembered. The plates sewn into the binding were not the deep alchemically treated photographs from his mother's book, and certainly did not show the sights he had seen with his own eyes.

The bald, bearded man tucked the package of books under his arm and turned to go. "Thank you, Mrs. Courier. These will keep me busy on a dozen more runs."

"It's just Courier, Commodore, you know that. And I know I shall see you again."

He smiled at the bookseller. "Too many books to read in this one universe, but I have plenty of time on my hands—and, thanks to you, I've got the choice of libraries from many possible worlds."

On his way to the door, the bearded man gave Owen a polite nod, as if to encourage a fellow literary traveler. "That's an excellent book, young man," he said. "I have one of the variations myself."

Focused on the book in his hands, Owen stared at the images, bewildered, even distraught. "This is different." Owen looked up at the bookseller—Mrs. Courier, or just Courier. "It's not the Crown City I know."

She pushed her spectacles up on her nose then rubbed at the angry red mark. "Maybe it's from a different Crown City."

"How many Crown Cities are there?" he asked. "I've only heard of the one."

"There are as many Crown Cities as there are worlds."

He turned the page, found another unsettling image. "And how many worlds are there?"

The bearded man—the Commodore—laughed. "More than you can imagine."

Owen frowned. "I can imagine a lot."

Holding his package, the Commodore smiled and tipped an imaginary hat. "That explains it then." He pushed open the door and left the bookstore.

Owen didn't understand the explanation at all.

The bookseller jotted down a notation in her thick ledger. "It's an import," she said without looking up, and then quoted him a price he could not possibly have afforded, even back when he had money from the carnival. "You're welcome to look at it . . . for now. Just be aware that it'll be nearly impossible to replace." She pushed her glasses up on her nose. "In fact, I don't even know if I could find that particular world again."

She glanced with incomprehensible meaning at a large looking-glass that stood next to the bookseller's front desk. It was unlike any mirror Owen had ever seen—taller than Courier, the size of a door, and it reflected no image. Instead, it was a single flawless piece of polished moonstone. She stroked the edge of the moonstone looking-glass. "Few people ever visit those other worlds from here."

Nervously, Owen closed the book and placed it back on the shelf. "The Watchmaker says that this is the best of all possible worlds."

"And how would he know that? Has he visited them all?" She clucked her tongue. "Absurd." She marked another notation in her ledger, then closed the book. "Did you have a specific request, young man? I can find you any book from anywhere, although it might take me a while to search the alternative locations."

"I couldn't pay you anyway," he said with a sigh.

"I didn't think so." Courier, neither surprised nor disappointed by his lack of funds, seemed content just to be compensated by seeing his love for books. "And if you did have the money, young man, I would recommend that you spend it on fresh clothes and a hot meal rather than a book . . . although some days I would rather go hungry than give up books."

His stomach growled as if to disagree with her assessment. From what he had experienced so far, pity seemed to be a rare commodity in Poseidon City, but Courier took pity on him. She handed him a stack of flat crackers and a small bunch of grapes from a plate by her desk. "I can't give you the book, but I can give you my lunch."

Upon consideration, Owen appreciated that more. "I don't know how to thank you, ma'am."

She regarded him, seemed to see—or imagine—something there. "Maybe you'll write a book of your own one day."

Less than a week later, feeling a homesick need to look at the illustrated book again, even though it showed the wrong version of Crown City, Owen tried to find Underworld Books again.

Though he searched from street to street, wandering down alleys that had become all too familiar, he simply could not locate the bookshop. Either he did not remember where it was, or the shop had closed, or the entire alley had disappeared.

CHAPTER 19

In a world where all must fail
Heaven's justice will prevail

He spent weeks and then months learning a new kind of life. He grew tough and wary, first questioning what he had known from the innocent village of Barrel Arbor, then forgetting it entirely. He was never lost because it made no difference where he was. One street was the same as another.

Chasing a new idea, just trying to survive, he found four suitably round stones. He stood on a corner and practiced his juggling, one rock after another in a smooth clockwork arc. With a pang, he thought of Francesca there watching him, teaching him, but then he drove all thought of her from his head and concentrated on nothing.

People stopped to watch him, curious. (Poseidon City must not host many carnivals, he decided.) With an audience, he juggled at the best of his ability, saw some of the faces nodding, and he smiled back at them. When he finished and caught the juggling stones with grace, he bowed. He set the stones at his feet, whisked off his porkpie hat, and passed it around, hoping for a few coins. Most of the people just looked at him; several walked away, as if called to pressing business. Finally, he received two copper coins—grudgingly given—from a pair of old men, who walked away without a word to him.

He started juggling again, maintaining his smile, remembering how the carnies performed. Sweat trickled down his forehead, but he put on the best possible show. Another small crowd gathered to watch him, but they kept to the opposite side of the street, well beyond the reach of his extended hat.

Pressing the coppers in his fist, so no one could pick his pocket, Owen walked down the street, looking at the shops until he came upon a bakery. The smell of bread and pastries intoxicated him, sharpening the knot of hunger. The baker was a jowly man whose ruddy complexion showed through an unintentional dusting of flour. While Owen looked at the loaves of bread, the rolls, the tarts, the baker watched him with suspicion. He was very different from Mr. Oliveira, the baker in Barrel Arbor.

Extending the two copper coins, Owen asked, "I'd like to buy some bread, please. What can you sell me?"

The baker frowned at the copper coins as if they were unclean, but he took them anyway. "That'll buy you a stale roll, and you're lucky for it." The man fished around behind the counter and produced a hard lump of bread, probably several days old; at least it wasn't moldy.

"Thank you." Owen took the bread without arguing and stood in the street outside the bakery, and he started wolfing it down. He forced himself to slow down, to savor every bite.

In an alley across the street, he glimpsed a rangy tow-headed young man about his age. He had strikingly blue eyes and a hungry look that was calculating rather than desperate. Owen ate the rest of his bread, afraid that if he didn't it would be stolen from him.

The baker started sweeping inside his shop, stirring up a cloud of flour and powdered sugar rather than dirt and dust. The man grumbled to himself.

Owen licked his fingers, getting the last crumbs from the dry bread. He glanced across the street, but the blond-haired boy had vanished into the alley. So Owen screwed up his courage and stepped back into the bakery. The man frowned at him again—it seemed to be his natural expression—in response to Owen's smile. "I can sweep for you, if you like."

Though the baker hesitated, Owen stepped forward and relieved him of his broom. He applied himself with great energy to sweeping the floor, while the baker stared at him and reluctantly nodded. "Mind you do a good job."

"Yes, sir."

Owen swept, and the smells of the bakery made him dizzy. Though he had eaten the stale bread, it had done little—nothing, actually—to dampen his hunger; it merely made him realize how very little he'd eaten in a long time. And there was so much bounty here.

"And do the walk in front, too," the baker said as soon as Owen had finished sweeping the shop floor. So Owen did. He worked up a sweat, but he was satisfied with the job he had done. He came back inside, and the baker extended his hand. "Give me back my broom." Owen returned it and waited, but the baker shooed him away. "Now out of my shop before you scare any customers."

Owen's heart fell. "But I was hoping . . . could you spare another roll? Or maybe one of those pastries?"

The baker looked offended. "No. Those are for sale."

"But I just did the sweeping! I helped you—"

"I never promised you payment. If you're fool enough to do work for free, I'd be a fool not to take advantage of it."

Owen was as confused as he was indignant. No one in Barrel Arbor would ever be so ungrateful, and none of the carnies would have treated him so badly. When he'd pitched in with the dockworkers in Crown City, they had happily let him eat whatever fruit he liked. "But that's not fair!"

The baker let out a sharp-edged chuckle. "If you think I'll pay you just because you make me laugh, you're sorely mistaken."

Owen could not believe his ears. He had already endured a great deal, had been cheated repeatedly and robbed more than once. The baker had to have known that Owen expected payment. Why else would he have told Owen to sweep the front walk? If the man had taken his work with no intention of paying, then he had "robbed" Owen as surely as any other thief had. Anger simmered deep in Owen's empty stomach. He didn't like the way people lived here in Poseidon, or the rules by which they played. This was a barbaric society, just like the one he'd read about in the book the strange pedlar had given him before the rainshower.

As if wiping excrement from his shoe, the baker dismissed Owen and went back behind the counter. He chortled again, louder this time.

In a flash of poor judgment, Owen grabbed one of the pies on the bakery counter and pelted from the shop. His vision had focused down to a pinprick, and he ran down the street, clutching his stolen pie.

The baker burst out of the door of his shop, yelling, "Thief!" The word sounded *wrong*. The man was talking about *him*, and Owen had never been a thief, never even considered stealing. Nevertheless, he kept running, dodged into an alley, crossed to another street, and finally found a dark, quiet overhang, where he caught his breath, let his heart stop thudding. Then—even though he felt sick for having stolen—he ate his pie, a mixture of tart berries, all of which had large crunchy seeds, and very little sweetening. Nevertheless, to Owen, it was delicious, and when he finished devouring it, he looked up to see the tow-headed young man watching him.

Owen sprang to his feet. His hands and face were sticky. The other young man laughed. "I hoped to get here before you finished it all. Next time you'll have to share."

"Next time?" There wasn't going to be a next time. "I earned this!"

"Oh, I'm sure the baker would agree," he said facetiously and rolled his eyes. "It was a good act, though. I liked it." The young man hunkered down next to Owen, who flicked his glance from side to side. "I'm Guerrero. What's your name?"

"Owen. Owen Hardy from Barrel Arbor—in Albion. I was the assistant apple-orchard—"

"I asked your name, not your life story."

Owen clamped his lips together.

The two young men spent the rest of the afternoon together, but Guerrero told nothing of his own story. "Where do you live?" Owen finally asked.

"Depends."

"Depends on what?"

"The day of the week . . . who's home and who isn't. Who has something they're not using." Guerrero did not ask Owen to stay with him, nor did Owen ask permission, but he had no friends and it felt as if he'd been a long time without companionship.

As night closed like a stranglehold on the city, Guerrero took him to a set of dark homes on the outskirts of the city. "This is where you live?" Owen asked.

"Tonight. These people have a lake cottage. I've been watching them for weeks, and they often leave for days at a time." He jimmied open a window in the back. "See? Not even locked."

"But we can't just—"

Guerrero looked at him with his piercing blue eyes. "I can. And you're welcome to join me . . . or not, as you prefer. Look around you—the owners have so much they won't even miss it, so long as we cover our tracks. Don't you want somewhere to sleep that's warm and safe, a place to clean yourself up? A decent meal big enough for you to feel full?"

Owen's eyes stung, and he realized tears had sprung to them.

"Yes, more than I can say." He had been brought up to believe that each person would get what he deserved, and the devil could take the rest. For his own survival, whether or not he deserved it, Owen had to take what he could, for himself.

Guerrero knew exactly where to look. The two feasted on stored food in the larder, careful to take apples, carrots, and potatoes only from the back barrels, and to rearrange the pantry shelves afterward so nothing was obviously missing. "See how much they have?" Guerrero said. "It's not really stealing if they can do without it."

"But it's not *ours*," Owen said.

The other young man shrugged. "Who's to say they deserved it? And why do they deserve it more than we do?"

Owen hung his head. "It's still stealing. They earned it or bought it." Before the incident in the bakery, he had never stolen in his life, and the thought of what he'd done nauseated him . . . but it made sense that this was a crime that hurt no one.

Guerrero watched him closely. "You got a better way to survive?"

"No . . . not yet."

Despite having a roof over his head and a bed to sleep in, Owen spent a restless night, and even after eating his fill of good food, his stomach knotted and roiled. They crept away at sunrise, just in case the owners came home early. "I try not to leave any trace," Guerrero said. "Good places like this, I can stop by three, maybe four times before they get wise."

Back on the streets, Guerrero knew many useful places around Poseidon. Owen followed him like a puppy, or an apprentice, though uneasy that this young man was so casual about breaking rules whenever they proved inconvenient. On the other hand, Owen was afraid and lonely, and he decided that even a bad option was better than no option.

With distorted nostalgia, he told Guerrero about Barrel Arbor, despite the other young man's plain lack of interest. Finally, Guerrero said, "You're a strange one, Owen Hardy. How can you be here, and how can you have done and seen all the things you say, and still be such a babe?"

Owen didn't know what he meant. "It's who I am. Don't you see the good in people?"

"Not usually. But then I don't bother to look."

Guerrero made a habit of stealing fruit from grocers, sausages from butchers, bread from bakeries or cafés. Maybe out of some misplaced sense of honor, or just concern about Owen's ineptitude, the tow-headed young man sheltered him from stealing. "You won't be any good at it," he said. "I'll let you help out in other ways."

Over the days, then weeks, and possibly months—Owen didn't keep track; he had neither pocketwatch nor calendar, and no reason to distinguish one day from another—he got to know his companion, as much as possible. Even so, Guerrero never talked about his mother or father, never mentioned his past, and—oddest of all—never even mentioned his dreams.

They spent most nights in the streets, occasionally venturing into an unoccupied house. Once they awakened a dog that came at them; Owen couldn't see the beast, but judging by the magnitude of its barks and growls, it must have been ferociously large.

One night, a man lurched down the alley where Owen and Guerrero had taken refuge behind a tavern; the man collapsed on the ground in a stupor that smelled of ale. As he snored, Guerrero moved forward furtively, nudged the man, and rolled him over, but the drunkard merely grunted and continued sleeping. Guerrero noticed a small purse hanging at his waist and snatched it, breaking the string. As he hurried out of the alley, he grabbed Owen's arm. "Come on!"

Owen tugged his arm free. "You just robbed that man!"

"I didn't hurt him." He pulled open the purse, proudly plucked out four coins. The two used the money to get their first decent meal in some time.

From that point on, Guerrero changed his tactics. Though Owen complained about it, Guerrero waited outside taverns long after midnight, in order to follow deeply intoxicated men. Even if the drunks were still conscious, they couldn't run swiftly or in a straight enough line to catch the two young men after they had grabbed the money.

Owen had tried everything else he could think of to survive, had offered to help, struggled to work. He had found no friends, no welcoming arms, no smiles. He longed for his days with Magnusson's Carnival Extravaganza or with his father in the Tick Tock Tavern; he could not forget about Francesca, even though she had hurt him.

Guerrero was all he had.

Late one night, they followed a man who tottered and limped out of a tavern, singing a song about the Seven Cities of Gold at the top of his lungs. The man was big and shaggy, with dirty clothes and a thick jacket despite the heat. Guerrero grinned. "Oh, Cabeza de Vaca! He is a familiar face among the Poseidon City taverns. His name means head of a cow!" Cabeza de Vaca did indeed have thick, blocky features and (seemingly) a thick, blocky skull.

In a hushed, husky voice, Guerrero continued, "Oh, he has quite a reputation! Cabeza de Vaca wanders the wilderness for months on end, seeking treasure. I don't think he's ever found it, but whenever he comes back into the city, he tells people his tales so that they buy him drinks. He says he's gotten close to the Seven Cities of Gold again and again." The young man changed his voice to a falsetto, flapping his hands in the air as if he were overheating with excitement. "'I could see them! The golden walls in the distance . . . I could see them, but I could never reach them.'" Guerrero snorted. "He stays in the city until people stop buying him drinks, and then wanders back out to the wilderness to do it all over again."

Owen and Guerrero followed the shaggy man around the corner. Cabeza de Vaca kept swaying, favoring his left leg. He began singing another verse, but forgot the words and repeated the first one instead.

After giving Owen a signal, Guerrero dashed forward like a shadow and Owen approached from the other side to block the man, who reeled around. Guerrero grabbed the drunkard's jacket, fumbled in his pocket and around his waist until he found the purse. He yanked it—but the purse was attached with a thin wire instead of a breakable string.

Cabeza de Vaca bellowed in angry surprise even louder than he had been bellowing out his tune. Owen dashed in to distract him so Guerrero could get away. The shaggy man swung a fist the size of a mutton roast, catching Owen's head with a glancing blow that knocked his porkpie hat askew. De Vaca was not quite as drunk as Owen and Guerrero had thought—he merely lurched and weaved because of an injured leg.

Responding to the shouts, other men boiled out of the tavern and headed down the alley to the rescue. Cabeza de Vaca grabbed Owen's arm and locked a manacle of fingers around it. Owen tried to escape, but the drunk hooked his fingers into the fabric of his sleeve and refused to let go.

De Vaca's angry friends saw what was happening and charged ahead, howling as if they had found a new sport.

Guerrero took one look at the men rushing toward them, let go of de Vaca's wired purse, and bolted. He didn't spare even a momentary glance for his friend. Owen looked after him, wide-eyed, and then was knocked to the ground.

When the other men fell upon him, they didn't ask questions, just started punching. "Guerrero!" He heard no answer, saw no rescue. "Help!"

Owen fought back, swinging his fists, as Golson had taught him. But this was no practice sparring; through training and desperation, he managed to bloody a few noses, but there were too many opponents for him.

He broke away, bolting for the main street, and reached the mouth of the alley before his attackers caught him and knocked him to the ground again. They began kicking him and cursing.

A man walked by in the well-lit street. He had a broad chest, dark brown skin, and a bald pate that gleamed in the red-coal streetlights. He stopped to regard the altercation. Self-righteous in dispensing their justice, the roughs didn't mind having an audience, but as Owen fought to defend himself, he looked up and met the stranger's eyes, desperate and pleading.

It was the man from the Underworld Bookshop—the one the manager had called Commodore.

The man hesitated, not wanting to get involved; he took one footstep in the other direction, but thought better of it. He turned back. "There now, he's had enough," he said.

"He's had enough when we say he's had enough!"

The Commodore took out a formidable nightstick. "If you don't decide he's had enough, then there'll be a lot more pummeling in the next few minutes."

Owen groaned, bleeding in the alley. He curled up, his breath hitching. His attackers scoffed at the pathetic sight, but the bald stranger and his cudgel were enough to make them realize they had entertained themselves enough. They rounded up Cabeza de Vaca, who was still indignant and cursing. Together, the group tottered off; before they had vanished down the street, they began singing together, off key, about the Seven Cities of Gold.

Owen's rescuer looked down at him, considering the young man in silence. He seemed both disappointed and curious. "Now you'll have a chance to convince me that I haven't made a mistake."

CHAPTER 20

I have stoked the fire on the big steel wheels,
Steered the airships right across the stars

The man's name was Pangloss, and he was a steamliner pilot visiting Poseidon at the end of an airship run from the alchemy mines deep in the highlands of Atlantis. As the pilot, he called himself a commodore, although Owen could not determine who had actually given him that rank. Pangloss was entirely bald, lacking even eyebrows, but he made up for the dearth of hair on his head with a fury of black beard that spread across his chin and broad chest.

Commodore Pangloss helped Owen stumble from the alley to a clean and well-lit room in an inn several blocks from the tavern. "I have no great fondness for thieves, young man, and I would have walked by, assuming you were getting exactly what you deserved. I don't know what stopped me. Maybe it was your appreciation for books." He shook his head. "But I saw a look in your eyes, something there that I don't usually see in hardened criminals."

"I'm not a hardened criminal." Owen spat blood and wiped his mouth, but he had no excuses to make. He wasn't even sure if he was telling the truth.

Commodore Pangloss said, "Not yet, perhaps, but a city like Poseidon will ruin you soon enough."

"I've got nowhere else to go." Owen felt around in his mouth; one of his teeth was loose but didn't wobble too much.

"You can share my room right now, but I head off again in two days," the Commodore said. "Get cleaned up, and then I'll hear what you have to say for yourself."

It had been so long since Owen washed under bright lights, without fear of discovery, that he had forgotten what clean felt like. After he used soapy water from a basin and scrubbed his hands and face, rinsing away the dirt as well as drying blood, he saw that his skin was now no longer the color of grime and dirt. He sat wrapped in a blanket while the Commodore sent his filthy clothes to the innkeeper for a washing.

Owen ravenously ate some poppyseed rolls and cheese that Pangloss had left on a sideboard from his lunch, then he slurped a cup of lukewarm tea that felt like happiness pouring down his throat. He would have liked to add honey, but none was offered.

As a fugitive, Owen was hesitant to speak his name or admit that he came from Barrel Arbor. By now, the Regulators had surely broadcast an arrest warrant for him, though Poseidon City had no direct newsgraph connection to Albion. How much of a reward would the Watchmaker offer for his capture and return to face justice?

Magnusson's Carnival Extravaganza had taught him that in order to earn his supper, he had to provide a show. And since he was too bruised and battered to put on a juggling performance, he settled for a story instead. Judging by his package of new books tied together in twine, the Commodore was an appreciator of tales.

Owen went on for more than an hour, and Pangloss listened without comment. Once he got started, the young man lost track of which details he should be hiding, and so he told it all, even about Francesca, and his time with Guerrero . . . and how his supposed friend had run, abandoning him to be beaten in the alley.

Somewhere in the stories, tears began pouring down Owen's cheeks, although he couldn't say exactly which part had triggered them.

At the end, the Commodore said only, "I knew from my first glance at you in the bookshop that you didn't belong here."

"I prayed just to get away from Crown City," Owen said. "With the Regulators chasing me and alarms all across the city, I looked at the cargo steamer ready to depart and thought of everything I had heard of Poseidon, the Seven Cities of Gold, the wonders of Atlantis. I knew everything would be better there. . . . I didn't know it was all a lie."

"Aye," said Pangloss. "And everyone here has heard about the perfection of the Watchmaker's Stability and the Clockwork Angels, that nothing ever goes wrong—everything has its place, and every place has its thing. It's nice to have colorful stories that you can cling to like a blanket on a chilly evening." His lips curved upward, though they remained overshadowed by his beard. "I can tell you that few people in Atlantis would want to be locked into the rigid schedules imposed by the Watchmaker, nor would we want uniformed Regulators inspecting every frivolous thing we might do. Even if we make unwise decisions, they're ours to make, not someone else's."

Owen hunched over, pulled his blanket close, and groaned. Pangloss took pity on him. "You grew up in the Stability—I suppose you can't be blamed for who you are. I didn't originally come from here, but got . . . derailed from my own world. Nevertheless, I've made a good enough life for myself—mainly, I stay away from Poseidon as much as possible. A place like this will eat away at you soon enough."

"Where else do you go?" Owen imagined that any place had to be better than the dark and dirty streets of the city.

"Aboard my steamliner, of course." The Commodore smiled. "She's a magnificent airship—flies free through the night and then alights on the rails and take us into each station along the mining route." He heaved a sigh and spoke as if he were talking about a lover. "Not one of those lovely, bloated caravans that travels across Albion. She's just a cargo liner—but she's my ship regardless."

Pangloss scratched his voluminous beard as if searching for a lost keepsake hidden among the strands, and he fell silent, pondering. Owen could see that the Commodore was a man who liked to consider his words before saying something he could not retract. "Rest up, eat up, and get yourself well, Owen Hardy from Barrel Arbor. I could use an assistant to help me stoke the fires and guide my steamliner. Ride with me for a while."

The Commodore's airship consisted of the locomotive dirigible and seven bulky cargo cars, each kept buoyant by tightly sewn canvas bags that swelled with hot steam piped in from the main boiler. The cargo cars were scuffed and dented, but clean. On his regular run, Pangloss hauled shipments of redfire opals, chalcedony, red coal, reactive ferrocerium, and kegs of rare alchemical powders excavated from the mountains. After delivering his cargo to Poseidon, he returned to the mountains with foodstuffs, clothing, tools, and equipment.

The main engine car also served as the Commodore's traveling home. The pilot's cabin smelled of oranges from the oil with which he polished the wooden furnishings. Owen stood before the controls that guided the airship when it was aloft and looked at the magnetic alignment compass that steered the steamliner back down to the rails for a landing.

The locomotive's alchemical engine reminded him of a giant pet mastiff, powerful and growling but loyal to its owner. Also like a large mastiff, it needed to be fed regularly. Pangloss and Owen worked together, shoveling red coal and dumping barrels of sweet-smelling distillate of naphtha. The reaction was triggered by a catalyst of coldfire—premixed, packaged, and sold to

Poseidon by the alchemist-priests of Crown City.

With Owen at his side learning the tasks, Commodore Pangloss spent two days loading his cargo cars with necessities for the mining villages on the steamliner route. Owen did additional chores like sweeping, scrubbing, and painting the cargo cars; he followed the Commodore around the warehouses and supply shops. He never caught a glimpse of Guerrero.

His muscles still ached from the beating. The bruises on his body—now plainly visible because he kept his skin clean—had turned alarming shades of purple and yellow, like something the carny clowns might have painted on themselves. Seeing Owen's battered condition, some of the rough station yardworkers let out guttural chuckles, assuming Commodore Pangloss beat his apprentice. Offended by their attitude, Pangloss shook his nightstick at them, which only reinforced their assumptions.

Late one afternoon, when they were finally ready to set off, Owen's excitement built like the pressure inside the steam boiler. He looked away from the cluttered city and thought about the mysterious continent, all the unexplored places inland. Somewhere in those mountains and deserts lay the legendary Seven Cities of Gold. Though gold itself had been devalued in Crown City, thanks to the Watchmaker's alchemy, it could still purchase goods in Atlantis. Yet the wonder and mystery were the real treasure. . . .

They stoked the engines and sealed the boiler, turned the valves so that the pressure built up, filled the conduits, and inflated the zeppelin bags of the cars. The coldfire sparkled brighter in the containment chamber. The locomotive shuddered; the big steel wheels began to turn and spark, reminding Owen of the tiny flame sprites that Tomio had created as an alchemical trick for his birthday. So long ago . . .

The steamliner awakened and began to move forward. The parallel tracks that extended into the hills glowed a phosphorescent blue as the levitating train accelerated.

The Commodore stood on the pilot deck gazing through the front windows, intent on the rails ahead. Mountain silhouettes bit off the horizon, which was bathed in deepening colors of sunset.

"Go stoke the engines some more, Mr. Hardy," the Commodore said. "We need to get up our steam, inflate all the sacks. We're about to fly!"

Owen ran to add more red coal and reactive powders to the exothermic chamber. The locomotive engine puffed, growled, and bellowed like an animal declaring its territory. He ran back up to the piloting window and stood beside Pangloss as they hurtled along the rails.

The silver lines in front of them abruptly disappeared as the tracks ended.

When the accelerating steamliner reached the end of the line, it leaped into the air as gracefully as Francesca. Instead of sprouting spring-loaded angel wings, though, the steamliner lifted off the ground and soared into the sky.

Commodore Pangloss stroked his beard as he stared ahead with a proud paternal smile. "Have you ever been on a steamliner before, Mr. Hardy?"

Owen took a moment to find his voice. "Yes, and no. Never like this." He caught his breath. "Never anything like this."

They continued ahead as night wrapped around them, smooth and quiet. The Commodore showed him how to find their course with the liquid-crystal compass, how to check the way the wind blew, how to keep them aligned on the proper vector so they could find the destination rails again when it came time to land.

Owen steered the airship right across the stars, and they flew by night into the mountains.

CHAPTER 21

Stories that fired my imagination

Traveling aboard the steamliner with Commodore Pangloss, Owen rested, recovered, and remembered who he was. His bruises and his aching bones healed. His spirit awakened from its slumber.

Although his broken heart still felt heavy in his chest, he was able to wrap up his thoughts of Francesca and lock them away. The memories were there, like cargo weighing down a boat, but at least they were out of sight. On rare nights, he woke up thinking he had heard her laughter, but it was just the noise of the steamliner traveling along.

Eventually, he would be able to view his memories of her from a new perspective, as if they were pristine chronotypes, and he would remember the fond parts more easily than his disappointment. He imagined what he might have said differently, alternative choices he could have made, and how Francesca might have responded. If there were many other possible worlds, much like this one but different, perhaps in one of them another version of him had done everything right. . . .

The Commodore's route took them from one mining town to another, servicing populations increasingly distant from Poseidon. The steamliner stopped at industrial stations, smelters, open-pit mines, salt caverns, and dry lakebeds scabbed with valuable chemicals; they exchanged their supplies, filled the cargo cars, and returned to Poseidon City to unload, whereupon they set off again as soon as possible. Pangloss smiled to see how hard Owen worked. "With your assistance, Mr. Hardy, I can spend even less time in the city."

On other runs, they traveled deep into the mountains to redcoal excavation mines in isolated canyons, where expansive grottos had been hollowed out as workers chipped away to recover sardelian, cinnabar, and aventurine, and even rarer inclusions of diamonds.

Seeing the wealth of strange substances loaded aboard at each stop, Owen could not help but think of Tomio and his alchemical library of powders, liquids, and metals that combined in unusual and miraculous ways. While they worked together, Commodore Pangloss explained about the materials, which were so precious to the Watchmaker back in Albion, schooling Owen in geology, chemistry, alchemy, and even economics, for every resource was an engine that drove part of society's machinery.

The airship flew over the rugged, primitive terrain and followed the course indicated by their main dreamline compass, which guided them to the next set of destination rails. By now Owen knew that each mining town had its own character: some were dirty and smoky, others rowdy and boisterous. After his experiences in Poseidon, he had no great desire to explore taverns or rough streets, and whenever they stayed over in frontier inns, he never strayed far from the Commodore.

During their weeks and months together, Owen became very close to Pangloss. Like Guerrero, the airship pilot seemed especially reluctant to tell his personal story, and the few tidbits he did reveal were cast in such a way as to be intentionally uninteresting.

He mentioned only that he came from another place, a world that was the same but different, known to only a few and inaccessible to most. Owen didn't know what he meant, which was exactly as the Commodore intended.

"Why do you grow your beard so big and unruly?" he asked one morning as they flew across an open blue sky with a mountain range in the distance.

The Commodore narrowed his dark brown eyes. "You may as well ask why I shave my head so smooth." He ran his fingers over his dark scalp.

"Why do you shave your head so smooth?"

"Some things should not be asked."

For Owen, the best times were those quiet hours with the Commodore aboard the steamliner, alone in the sky. In an expansive cabinet that covered an entire wall of the living chamber, Pangloss kept a personal library of books. It included an impressive collection he had purchased from the Underworld Bookshop, and Courier was pleased to find special "imported" items for him. To Owen, it seemed enough words to last a lifetime, and the Commodore looked forward to acquiring more.

When Owen first poked through the library, he was disappointed to find that it lacked large volumes with lavish illustrations, such as the ones his mother had kept. He hoped for another edition of the Crown City retrospective, such as he had seen in the bookshop display window, but he found no picture books at all. Due to space constraints aboard the steamliner, Pangloss preferred compact editions, portable volumes with extremely tiny print (he sometimes needed a large magnifier to decipher the sentences).

Even without lavish chronotype plates, the books contained much of value, and Pangloss convinced him to read the words, to think about the philosophy, the history of the world(s), the underpinnings of natural science, the basic principles of hydraulics, the speculations of alchemy. As he pondered the texts, Owen created his own pictures in his mind, and they were better, sharper, and brighter pictures than the chronotypes he remembered.

After reading essays, Owen would discuss the ideas with Pangloss, who was glad to listen to alternative opinions. No one had ever asked Owen what he thought before; no one had ever encouraged him to think. Everything has its place, and every place has its thing. He remembered the hypnotic pronouncements of the Clockwork Angels—*Ignorance is well and truly blessed*—but he didn't believe that anymore. Ignorance had caused him a great deal of trouble. If he had been given the correct information, he would not have made so many mistakes; he would not have undertaken this arduous journey in the first place.

Then again, he never would have become who he was.

All is for the best.

The steamliner traveled one route after another, heading to different frontier towns. Owen experienced surprising climate changes, observed strange plants and animals, encountered odd customs, ate new foods. Though it went far beyond any wild adventure he had ever imagined, this was now his daily life. There was constant traveling, interrupted by occasional destinations.

He worked his way through the books in the steamliner's library. Many of the volumes were printed with letter-symbols unlike any language he had ever seen, so he ignored those (at least until such time as he could learn other written languages).

On a high shelf, Owen discovered a ragged, well-thumbed book with a spine so weathered that he couldn't read the letters. He took it down and opened the cover to the title page. *An Account of My Adventures, Travels, and Discoveries Across Albion, Atlantis, and Beyond.* The subject itself fascinated him, and he glanced down at the name of the author.

Hanneke Lakota.

His mother's name!

For so many years in his wandering imagination, he had fancied her exploring the world, pretending that she had not died of a fever but had slipped away from humdrum Barrel Arbor to exotic countries, intriguing cultures, breathtaking sights. In his heart, though, he had always known the hard truth that she was really buried in the Barrel Arbor cemetery, that his father had given her a peaceful grave on a grassy hillside on the edge of town. Owen remembered, despite trying his best to forget, his mother lying covered in blankets, her hair matted with sweat, his father on his knees by the bedside while the boy, Owen, was hustled off to stay with neighbors. . . .

He turned the page, looked at the first paragraph of the book. "The best place to start an adventure is with a quiet, perfect life . . . and someone who realizes that it can't possibly be enough. To most people, a quiet village might be a fine place to live, but I wanted to see the world, all of it. And so I did."

His eyes went wide, his vision blurred with tears. He took the volume to Pangloss, who stood at the control station, checking the pressure gauges of the coldfire engine. "Commodore . . . this book."

The bearded man looked at him, recognized the volume. "Ah yes, a remarkable story. She was quite an explorer, renowned, influential—and not just in her own world. Her works have trickled elsewhere, even to here, stories to inspire the imagination."

"This is my mother's name!"

"Is that so? And in her world"—he tapped the worn cover of the book—"she went out and followed her imagination. In this world, your mother stayed in a small village, got married, had a son. Now you are doing the exploring . . . while in other worlds, there are undoubtedly other Owen Hardys who never found the nerve to leave home."

Owen took the book back and curled up in a corner, poring over the words, page after page, all the way to the end of the story. Then he started over again from the beginning.

As they reached Endoline, the most isolated mining town deep in the mountains, beyond which lay only uncharted wilderness, the steamliner alighted on the rails and drew to a stop in the austere station. On each such run, they would spend the night before turning around with a full cargo load and heading back to Poseidon City. The rails ended here, and the airship portion of the steamliner could travel only a certain distance past the pivot. Beyond Endoline, travel and commerce stopped, and no one showed any inclination to extend the route.

The nearby cliffs held a rich vein of redfire opals, sparkling ruby-colored power sources that burned hot and smelled like iron. A tragic conflagration in the tunnels had recently killed ten miners, causing a shutdown of the works (and driving up the price of redfire opals across Atlantis). Now, the work had begun again, and Endoline had a load to sell Commodore Pangloss in exchange for much-needed supplies.

Thanks to their isolation, the people had to be self-sufficient for the most part. They piped in water from streams and used their own redfire opals to power the town. Hunters combed the mountains and returned with plentiful game; each household maintained a terraced garden of vegetables and herbs. The people had money, but little opportunity to spend it on comforts and desirable goods. When the steamliner pulled into the station for unloading, the villagers gleaned every possible useful item from the cargo cars; alas, because their town was the end of the line, the crates had already been picked over.

Owen ate an over-salted dinner with Pangloss in the town's tavern; each of them enjoyed a thick, gamey antelope steak and tasted a potent distilled local liquor that made Owen dizzy after only a single glass. The Commodore imbibed sparingly, having sampled the liquor before.

At a nearby table, three redfire opal miners were playing a game with cards and chips. They sang aloud, joining one another in a chorus about the Seven Cities of Gold, which piqued Owen's interest. It was the same song Cabeza de Vaca had sung in the alley in Poseidon.

In recent days, Owen had been thinking a great deal about the Seven Cities because in the travels of his other-mother, *she* had come upon the sparkling metropolis of golden buildings, an energetic civilization. The people there had welcomed her as an ambassador, feted her with amazing performances and lavish feasts; she had visited each of the Seven Cities on top of a vast mesa and stayed there for months before continuing her travels.

The legends in the storybook from his real mother had always fascinated him, and now the descriptions in the travelogue sparked his desire to see them even more.

When the song finished, he called over to their table. "Do you know where to find Cíbola—the Seven Cities? Have you ever been there?"

The men just laughed. "No one goes out there. The Seven Cities are a dream, not for any man to find."

Owen puffed up his chest. "And what if I'm not just any man?" His answer brought another round of raucous laughter, and he added, "I don't believe in the impossible. It doesn't exist."

Pangloss gave him a paternal smile. "The boy has been reading a lot. He stokes his imagination as much as he stokes the big wheels of the locomotive."

The people of Endoline obviously knew Pangloss well. One of the men joked, "You and your books, Commodore!"

Owen felt his thoughts swirl, possibly because of the surprisingly intoxicating drink. He lifted his chin. "We've heard of Cíbola from as far away as Albion. If there are so many stories, the Seven Cities must exist—or at least they used to."

"Oh, they're out there, lad," said one of the miners, "lost in the

Redrock Desert beyond the mountains. People have searched for them, but no one ever returns."

"Maybe because it's a utopia and nobody wants to leave," Owen said.

Warming himself by the glowing redfire opal blaze in the hearth, a lean and rangy man with a wispy beard set his pipe aside. "Sometimes I go hunting far to the west of the mines, and I see things out there—petroglyphs, giant carvings in the slickrock, arches and hoodoos that must have been created by powerful alchemy. It's a sight that could drive a normal person mad."

Owen replied, echoing his previous statement but not intending to be funny, "And who's to say I'm a *normal* person?"

Commodore Pangloss took him by the arm. "You've had enough to drink, Mr. Hardy, and enough conversation. Let's get a good night's sleep before we head back down the line at dawn."

Owen let himself be led with an unsettling wobbly gait back to the inn. But his sleep was restless.

Next morning, the steamliner departed from Endoline, and Owen traveled again, day by day, on the route back to Poseidon. He became increasingly fixated on thoughts of finding the Seven Cities. He reread his other-mother's adventures among the people in the legendary golden cities, tasted the food in her descriptions, heard the music she evoked with her words. The longing to see it for himself became like a sliver in his skin that he could not pluck out.

As a young man in Barrel Arbor, he had dreamed of Crown City and the Clockwork Angels, Poseidon, Atlantis, and the Seven Cities of Gold. The stories had fired his imagination.

But over the course of his adventures, those stories had been tarnished by reality. The vibrant chronotype images had taken his young, optimistic mind to imaginary lands, but the truth he saw with his own eyes was very different. He had begun to lose hope.

Crown City had not been what he expected. And the Angels, for all their synchronized beauty and grace, had been unsettling. The Watchmaker's city was not perfect, with or without the Anarchist, and Owen did not feel that the joy and pain he received were what he deserved. The carnies had been a bright spot that darkened to disappointment; what he'd thought was true love had turned out to be an illusion.

His string of broken dreams was like a sequence of derailed steamliner cars strewn across the landscape. Fleeing Crown City in disgrace, he had turned his optimistic sights instead to fabled Poseidon City, which was also quite different from what he had anticipated, and proved a devastating disappointment. His treasure chest of hopes and visions was nearly empty. None of the other stories had measured up to his optimistic expectations.

But was it possible that *all* those stories were untrue? He refused to believe it. He now had read his other-mother's descriptions. Surely at least one of the beautiful legends was based in fact.

Here in Atlantis, his life was no longer part of the Watchmaker's intricate clockwork society, nor was he trapped on a rigid rail, like the steamliners, going only to specified destinations back and forth, never straying beyond the pivot distance. He could follow his dreams now. He could see for himself.

Finding the Seven Cities was his last hope of rekindling the sense of wonder he had as a child. Cíbola had to be real.

As the steamliner traveled its routes, Owen scoured the Commodore's library for any other records of the Seven Cities, but found only offhand and contradictory references. Pangloss watched his fascination become an obsession, and he indulged Owen.

Three weeks later, after the steamliner had run its course to all the destinations and then back into the mountains to far-flung Endoline, Owen was eager to go back to the tavern.

Feeling wistful but determined, he spoke to the Commodore as the airships coasted in on the rails, braking toward the mining town. "Sir, I've appreciated my time with you more than I can say.

But now that we're here, I . . . there's something I have to do. I'm going to find the Seven Cities."

Pangloss wiped his hands down his unruly beard, and answered with a grave nod. "I knew you'd make that decision soon, Mr. Hardy. It is impossible to hide restlessness aboard a small steamliner car."

Owen swallowed hard. "If I find the cities, I might not be coming back."

"If you don't find them, you might not be coming back either. But you know how to find me, if you do."

The two men entered the tavern. Very little had changed there: the same miners were playing the same game, again singing their song about the Seven Cities. The rangy hunter was still by the glowing redfire opal hearth, and Owen approached him. "I'm going to the Seven Cities of Gold. What clues can you give me? Please, tell me what you've seen."

The card players chuckled. The innkeeper scoffed good-naturedly. "Heard that one before."

But Commodore Pangloss nodded, and the tavern patrons realized Owen was serious.

"Head west and keep walking," the hunter said. "After the mountains, you'll enter the Redrock Desert, and your feet will take you where few people have ever been. Canyons and basins, towering mesas rising out of the desert like tree stumps. They say you'll find paradise on top, if you can climb there."

"Who says that?" Owen asked.

"*They* do." The hunter took another deep puff of his pipe. "According to the legend, there is a lake between the sun and the moon, a sparkling white expanse just below a mesa. Cíbola is on top of that mesa. All seven cities." He puffed on his pipe again. "But I wouldn't go there."

Commodore Pangloss had deep sadness etched on his face that even his huge beard couldn't hide. "I won't talk you out of it, Mr.

Hardy." He let out a long sigh. "I owe you wages—I'll help you buy the equipment you need."

Owen felt feverish with his desire to see and explore the place, but he hadn't thought about the practical aspect. What supplies and equipment did a person need for such an expedition? He might have wandered off into the wilderness entirely unprepared. It would have been worse than trying to live on the streets of Poseidon, and he'd have no Guerrero to help him. With a chill, he imagined his desiccated corpse picked clean by vultures somewhere out in a forgotten wash, with no one even to stand over him and say a benediction that "All is for the best."

The following day, Pangloss did not depart on schedule, but instead spent hours with Owen, helping him purchase packaged food, water containers, rope, a knife, packets of fire-starting powder. "These supplies don't cover half of what I owe you, Mr. Hardy. Would you like the rest now in coins?"

Owen had lived with Pangloss for months, and he felt *he* owed the Commodore for all the man had done. "You can keep the wages, sir. You've done so much for me."

"And you've done plenty for me, too, young man. Do you know how long it's been since I've had a friend who was so optimistic? Someone who can see the colors of dreams?"

Owen flushed, and he felt a lump in his throat. "I always thought that was a disadvantage."

"Not for everyone. I will keep your wages for you, in trust—because I expect you to come back."

"Yes, sir." Owen considered the long journey he was about to undertake, the many nights he would spend alone out in the desert. "I have a favor to ask. . . . Do you think I might borrow the book—the one my mother wrote?"

"She wasn't your real mother, Mr. Hardy."

"But she might have been."

He smiled. "Then the book is yours."

When they had made all the necessary preparations and were just finding excuses not to part ways, they stood by the steamliner in awkward conversation. Owen tucked the travelogue by Hanneke Lakota in his pack, shuffled his feet, and made ready to go.

Holding up a finger, the Commodore climbed into the locomotive cabin and came back out with a small device similar to the one on the piloting deck. "I have a spare," he said. "Carry this dreamline compass. It will tell you where you are, help you follow the world's field lines." He pointed to a satellite watchface connected to the gears and the drifting magnetic needle of the main compass. "And this second dial shows you where you *should* be. Only you can set that."

Tears sprang to Owen's eyes as he accepted the dreamline compass. He embraced Pangloss, thanking him for everything and promising to return safely. Someday. Even the Commodore's brown eyes were wet. "I thought you were too much of a dreamer at first, Mr. Hardy, but I've gotten to enjoy the way you think big."

After all he had been through, Owen was amazed he still had some of the dreamer about him. Pangloss had given him a job, friendship, a library of knowledge, and a place to heal. And now, finding the Seven Cities would restore Owen's heart.

He thanked Pangloss again, and as the Commodore climbed aboard to feed red coal into the great hungry engine, Owen headed in the other direction, leaving Endoline behind.

On my way at last. He entered the wilderness of mountains.

CHAPTER 22

Seven Cities of Gold
Glowing in my dreams, like hallucinations,
Glitter in the sun like a revelation

A man could lose his past in a country like this—and that was exactly what Owen wanted. Parts of his past, anyway. Heading toward the west and out of the mountains, he followed his dreams and ran from his nightmares. He chose his own path and consulted the dreamline compass sparingly.

During his quiet life in Albion, he had never considered that there might be places without roads or steamliner rails, or that anyone would want to go there. The Watchmaker imposed a safety net—or maybe it was just a *net*—of civilization upon the landscape.

Now Owen walked over wooded hills, fighting his way through underbrush to reach the top of a ridge for no particular reason other than because he wanted to, and the view was worth all the effort. From the fringes of the mountain range, he looked down toward the drier western slope and the diminishing foothills that petered out into an expansive desert beyond.

The hunter in the tavern had given him guidance on which berries, mushrooms, leaves, and roots he could eat. And he warned

Owen—very wisely, now that he thought about it—to live off the land while in the forested hills so that he could save his packed food supplies for the austere desert.

Even though he was alone and in uncharted places—dependent on himself without any Watchmaker, carnies, or airship pilot to help—Owen felt refreshed. He slept well enough on the soft underbrush beneath the comforting embrace of branches. It was better than a cold, dank alley in Poseidon.

The vegetation became sparser, more scrub brush and mesquite, the trees stunted, the rocks prominent; the wide open sky seemed a more infinite blue. As he walked into the Redrock Desert, he discovered something cleansing about the landscape. He had more time to think than ever before in his life, but most of the time—as if he still followed Francesca's advice—he thought of nothing at all. The utter silence made him wonder if he'd gone deaf, until it was broken by the occasional caw of a crow.

He had no ticking clocks, no schedule, and no plan. The time he experienced was marked only by the rise and set of the sun, not by an hour hand that pointed to an arbitrary number on a clockface. He set his dreamline compass, marking a route back to Endoline, should he ever want to return there; the second needle on the compass, the one that indicated where he *should* be, wavered in random directions.

Owen chose a path that led him to interesting rock formations and followed the golden glow that he saw each afternoon at sunset. Cíbola was out there. Somewhere. He left footprints where there had never been footprints before.

High up on sheer, inaccessible canyon walls, exotic figures and towering pictographs had been scribed by members of some long-lost civilization. He craned his neck, staring at the messages and wondering if they had been meant for him. The language was as incomprehensible as the alchemical symbols he had seen in Tomio's reference books.

Owen wondered if the inhabitants of the Seven Cities were truly lost, if they had skipped over to some adjacent world, as the bookshop owner had suggested . . . or if they had just decided to hide.

But he had read his other-mother's stories, and he knew what lay out there. He imagined that the people of Cíbola had formed their own paradise far from the mines and the mountains, far from Poseidon City, from Albion and the Watchmaker. A perfect society where happy people did what they wanted, fulfilled themselves—not caring that the rest of the world had forgotten them. If he ever found the tall mesa and the Seven Cities, he would have to convince the people he was a worthy addition to their utopia. He could entertain them by juggling; he could even tend their apple orchards, should they have any.

He came upon majestic arches like windows to a new world. Lumpy obelisks and hoodoos reminded him of distorted mushrooms or playful shapes like hunched trolls. He remembered when he would look up at the clouds and point out shapes to Lavinia. With no one beside him now, all the imaginary shapes were his own.

He continued across the uneven wasteland, and his feet grew sore from walking. Roads and well-traveled paths had their advantages! He had to pick his way across stones washed down from the mountainsides in flash floods. He slogged through uneven sand, climbed rilles of sharp black rock, and followed runoff washes.

The Redrock Desert became a grim eternity of spiny cacti and Joshua trees. The only creatures he saw were lizards, scorpions, a rattlesnake. But he continued to walk, sure he would stumble upon the Seven Cities.

The nights grew cold and lasted longer than he remembered nights were supposed to last. After sunset, all the warmth drained out of the air, leaving the ground brittle and cold. He had always thought deserts were hot, dry places, but Pangloss had insisted he carry a blanket in his pack. Owen shivered and wrapped it around himself.

He scrounged scraps of mesquite wood, used a pinch of exo-thermic powder from his pack, and the alchemical reaction burst into a hot flame that ignited the wood. He huddled, trying to read by firelight, paging through the chronicle of his other-mother's life. She had had such wonderful adventures, but he wondered if they had always felt that way to her. The campfire warmed him for a while, but the dry and airy wood burned so quickly that his fire collapsed into embers before he could gather more branches.

Each morning, he woke to aching cold. He drank most of his water before he realized he had seen no fresh pools in some time. Somewhere out there, if he came upon the sparkling white lake between the sun and the moon and the great mesa that held the Seven Cities, he would have all he could wish for. For now, though, as he wandered down the canyon washes each morning, he found seeps of water covered with a diamond skin of ice, with which he tried to fill his water sack; more often his attempts resulted in sandy mud instead of fresh water.

Off in the distance, through wavering air that rippled up from the flat ground, he saw golden structures like sparkling clocktow-ers that dwarfed any architecture he had seen in Crown City. The mirage glittered in the sun, like a revelation, but as he kept walking it seemed as far away as the constellations he studied every night. When he finally arrived, the golden clocktowers were merely rock formations, weathered and uninhabited.

His water was gone, and his food disappeared the day after. When he fell to his knees, rocks bit into his skin. He dug into the pebbly dirt, hoping to uncover moisture, but he found only sand and rocks, no matter how deep he dug.

He kept plodding, but saw little now. He faced the very real possibility that he could lose his life in a country like this. Thinking of the books in the Commodore's library, he relived his adventures and wrote his story in his mind. But he had no friends, no audi-ence, and no one would ever read the tale of his life. . . .

Imagining that his carnival friends were there, even Francesca, he picked up rocks from the ground and juggled them, but he fumbled and dropped the rocks. When he turned to see if Francesca was cheering or jeering, her image had vanished.

Finally, he saw an imposing mesa ahead that seemed to rise out of an expansive white lake, like a plain of glittering diamonds. By the way it sparkled and glowed in the pounding daylight, Owen knew that this must be the lake between the sun and the moon. Refusing to believe it was a mirage, he ran to it, though his feet were bleeding, his throat was parched. At last, when he came to the crumbling shore of the blessed spring, he dropped to his knees, and plunged his hands into . . . nothing more than powder, bitter salt left by a prehistoric sea. He wept then, and his salt tears were just as bitter.

Across the lake, though, the sheer cliffs of the isolated mesa rose up like an island in the sky. As the sunlight slanted down, he glimpsed golden reflections on top, rectangular shapes, unnatural sculptures. Cíbola had to be up there . . . if only he could climb that high. With bleeding fingers, he managed to set the second dial on his dreamline compass, since he now had an anchor point.

He trudged across the dry saltpan. Occasional pools seeped through the crystalline powder, and in desperation he scooped the water into his mouth, but it tasted foul and slippery, saturated with chemicals that made him retch. His lips burned, his skin was raw, his eyes so dry and gritty that he was sunblind.

He reached the base of the mesa and picked his way through the fallen rocks until he discovered an actual path, a steep way that relied on a crack in the cliff and narrow connecting ledges. He worked his way up. When he found hand- and footholds chiseled into the slickrock, he knew that this was where he was supposed to be. He could juggle, and he had walked a tightrope; even without Francesca's encouragement, he could climb a rock wall.

The Seven Cities of Gold were up there. This must be some

sort of test, to prove to the people there that he deserved to be among them. His other-mother had done this herself. . . .

He pulled himself higher, using hands, feet, elbows, knees. He reached a dead end, then found a tiny ledge no wider than his hand. He grasped it, thinking of the windowsills and the façade of the ministry building by which he had escaped the mob in Chronos Square. He could do this. He pressed his weary body flat against the cliff and worked his way over to the next ledge.

He zigzagged from one crack to another, always climbing, giving no thought to how he would ever get back down. Once he reached Cíbola on top of the mesa, the people would welcome him. After the tribulations he had undergone to get here, he belonged with them.

When he finally hauled himself over the lip of the mesa to a wide expanse of brittle brown grass that was open to the sky, he did see a city: clusters of tan adobe buildings, some of them two stories tall with open windows like the empty eye sockets of a skull. The legendary city was not much larger than Barrel Arbor—silent, abandoned. He saw no people at all.

He staggered toward his long-awaited treasure, disbelieving, even delirious. Cíbola was already extinct. The truth had been forgotten, leaving only a few wisps of memory and exaggerated stories. Whatever the reasons, the people here had died out, or departed . . . maybe because of chaos and anarchy, maybe because of too many rigid rules.

This was a city for ghosts; the buildings were now no more than palaces for rodents. Not gold, but fool's gold. *Time to put all this foolishness behind you.* He heard no conversation or laughter, only the wind whistling through open doors. There was nothing else.

CHAPTER 23

All the journeys
Of this great adventure
It didn't always feel that way

As Owen sat alone in the abandoned city, he could not measure the vast difference between his imagination and reality—couldn't even bear to try. Hungry, parched, and lost, he crawled into the nearest building, leaned against a wall, and wept until he fell asleep.

All his journeys, all his adventures, all his dreams had led him from one place to another, but the stories had betrayed him, and people had deceived him. Maybe the Watchmaker was trying to teach him a lesson, to demonstrate that he should have stayed exactly where he was, played his part like a tiny cog in the great machine. Everything had its place, and every place had its thing.

And now here he was in the middle of the vast redrock wasteland in a haunted city inhabited by unrealistic dreams. . . .

When he awoke, cool and unexpectedly refreshed, he found that a glimmer of optimism had survived even this disappointment. He drew a deep breath, felt the reassuring weight of the walls around him, and reminded himself that he was *here*, regardless. He decided to explore.

The well-built wood-and-adobe structures remained solid, although several roofs had collapsed under the weight of time and gravity. Even though Cíbola was not a paradise filled with welcoming people, even though the buildings were not constructed of precious metals and sparkling gems, he could still sense a majesty as he explored.

The empty city held a different kind of treasure, one he needed far more than he needed gold. In a courtyard that had been untouched for countless years, he found a cistern full of cool rainwater. Owen drank his fill and felt much stronger.

Combing through the abandoned buildings, he found no secret stashes of gold, no magical treasures, nor did he uncover any hints as to why these people had vanished. He felt foolish for his desire to keep chasing silly dreams.

Clay-brick granaries were mostly empty, but he found a still-sealed one filled with dried corn; it was difficult to chew, but nourishing nevertheless; later, he could cook it for better eating. In plots between their buildings, the vanished people of Cíbola had planted gardens and fields, long since gone to seed, but Owen found a wealth of wild onions, carrots, even the dried, drooping head of a tall sunflower. After days of stumbling through the desert, this was fabulous bounty.

He could live here, for a while.

Over the next several days, Owen regained his strength alone in Cíbola. From the high mesa, he could look out across the breathtaking expanse of the Redrock Desert. As the sun rose each morning, he saw the hazy purple line of mountains and was amazed at how far he had come in his wanderings—and how far he would have to journey if he ever decided to return to civilization.

The solitude embraced him, seeped into him. As far as he knew, he had the entire mesa to himself; he was the Watchmaker of this island in the sky, and it meant more to him than all of Albion.

He thought of nothing. Later, as days passed, he thought of

Francesca enough that the memory no longer hurt. He slowly came to the conclusion that he had viewed her through the halo effect of his own fantasies. He had been foolish as much as she had been hurtful. Sometimes, he even wished he had kept the old, dried rose.

And he had made the halo mistake before. Even with all this time to ponder, he could barely recall Lavinia, yet at one time he'd been convinced she was his true love. He never wanted to be so deceived again. He hoped he had gained wisdom from his youthful mistakes. But given the chance, would he fall in love with illusions all over again? He was Owen Hardy from Barrel Arbor; he was who he was.

Just because he wanted to, Owen found smooth stones of just the right size and spent hours juggling. Apples would have been better, but he made do. Keeping his mind clear, he roamed from building to building, or strolled along the edge of the mesa while he kept the juggling rocks looping through the air in various patterns, like the artificial planets in the Crown City Orrery.

For himself and no one else, he climbed to the adobe rooftops and walked precariously across the thin support logs, either juggling or with arms extended for balance, like the most skilled tightrope-walker. He read the journal of his other-mother so many times that he memorized entire sections. This empty city was not at all like the Seven Cities of Gold that she had explored.

But he still had six more cities to find. . . .

He eventually grew determined enough to set off again across the open, mysterious terrain. He followed an overgrown path that might once have been a sweeping highway that connected the sparkling ancient civilization. It took him along the edge of the mesa, then another road extended across spotty grasslands . . . to another empty, dusty city. He found flecks of yellow paint on a sheltered adobe wall, hinting that the whole building might once have been a brilliant goldenrod color, but it was now faded.

Still, he held out hope. He wandered for weeks, traveling

haunted paths across miles, following in the footsteps of a lost civilization. He discovered two more of the legendary cities—little more than villages, actually—across the fertile top of the mesa. Each one had a few supplies, crops long gone to seed, stored grain. He lost track of time, not only the hours, but days and weeks, maybe even months.

From the season, he knew that back in Barrel Arbor, his father would be preparing for winter, pressing the rest of the cider, storing apples in the root cellar. If Owen had been home, he would have helped his father trim the branches on the trees, rake the golden leaves around the cottage. Though he hadn't realized it while he was there, Owen did enjoy that work . . . as well as planting new trees in the spring, tending the trees all summer, savoring a fresh-baked apple pie.

The best way to appreciate a thing, he realized, was to be gone from it a long time.

One night, snow fell across the mesa, and winter settled in. The nights were crystal and cold in the dry desert air, but when the sun came out and painted the sky a deep, distant blue, the snow melted. Owen had everything he needed, even for winter. His traveling clothes were worn but well made. All those empty homes were available for shelter; he had wood for fire, and enough food and water to get by.

He enjoyed the company of silence and contemplation in one place. Feeling loneliness like a healing ache, he let himself miss Commodore Pangloss and the carnies, and even his time spent with Guerrero. And Francesca.

Soon enough he grew restless, wanting to explore, remembering his original dreams. Back in Barrel Arbor, he had wanted to see the whole world, and so much of it remained to be seen.

So he set off again.

One cluster of empty buildings, and another, and another, all of them abandoned, nearly forgotten . . . but because he was there, he awakened those cities into existence by *seeing them*, remembering them, and making them real again.

Five cities found. Then six. Each discovery was like blowing out a candle, and he knew in his heart that there was no magical utopia there on the sprawling mesa, like the one his other-mother had described in her travelogue, but he kept looking anyway. His optimism kept the search alive—and the search kept *him* alive.

In the heart of winter, he finally found the last of the seven cities. It was on the far northern edge of the mesa, a long point that looked out upon a deep canyon and a lovely green river far below. The adobe buildings here were neat and intact, as if someone had swept them, added fresh paint, and closed all the doors and windows before vanishing from history.

Two tall stone monoliths guarded the city, narrow sentinels erected for some unknown reason. With the sun going down and the cold deepening in the air, Owen stood in the last city. He felt sad for finding it, as if the walking and searching had worn down not just the soles of his boots, but also his hopes and dreams. There was no gold here, and no people. Just empty buildings, far away from anything.

As the sun slipped down to the horizon, it fell between the cleverly built and positioned towers of rock. Sandwiched there, focused as if the pillars were a funnel, the ruddy sunset light fanned out from between the rocks and played across the ancient structures.

The dusty walls of the adobe buildings were transmuted into gold. An amazing light pooled across the ground, swept up like a wizard's broad paintbrush to varnish all the buildings in a beautiful yellow glow more pure than the Watchmaker's private reserve of honey. The city itself seemed to shimmer and throb.

Owen couldn't breathe; it was the most incredible sight he had ever seen. He just stared, as if he had been transported into a treasure vault. Faced with such a sight, even the Clockwork Angels would have been wonderstruck.

Time stood still for him. The astronomical masterpiece lasted an eternity and was over in an instant. The sinking sun fell out of alignment, and the gold faded, leaving the empty city with common tan walls again.

Owen felt as if he had been given an incalculable gift, an ethereal reward after so many tribulations. He realized that if he hadn't seen so much else, gathered so many points of comparison, he would not have appreciated the full extent of its majesty.

After his many months of solitude, Owen had learned how to measure other things, too. The treasure of this city of gold would have been so much more valuable if only he had someone to share it with.

That was when he finally knew he had to rejoin the rest of the world.

Over the next few days, he made his way back to the first empty city and refilled his packs with all the food and water he could carry, locked the return course to Endoline on his dreamline compass, and set off for the hazy mountains.

He had learned much from his first trip through the desert, and this time he consumed his supplies more wisely. He rested in canyon shadows during the heat of the day and wasted no opportunity to replenish his water.

And he survived, tougher, wiser, more confident, resilient—but at his core he was still Owen Hardy, an optimistic dreamer from Barrel Arbor.

When he reached the mining town of Endoline, he walked into the tavern and stood before the people there, much to their surprise and disbelief. The rangy hunter who had given him advice saw Owen's darkened skin, his lean, toughened body, and the look in his eyes.

"No one ever comes back from out there," he said.

"I did," Owen answered. The muscles in his cheeks and mouth felt strange—and he realized he was smiling.

They treated him as a hero. The miners and the innkeeper bought him food and offered him glasses of the oily intoxicating liquor, although he contented himself with drinking great quantities of water. He slept in a soft bed and, to his surprise, found it no more comfortable than the hard ground under the starry desert sky.

They asked for his stories, and he told parts of the journey, explained the things he had seen, the wilderness he had wandered. But he didn't tell it all.

What they most wanted to know was whether he had found the Seven Cities of Gold. Owen had reflected a great deal on his arduous trek back, however. He remembered the bright songs they had sung about the legend, the treasures, the gold, and the glory. For so long, his own beautiful dreams had sustained him, inspired by the images in the book his mother had shown him, and by the alternative account his other-mother had written about her travels. Without those stories to fire his imagination, would he ever have done . . . anything?

He had been out there himself and found his answers. He had reached the lake between the sun and the moon, he had climbed the tall mesa—and he had found the truth. With a single explanation, Owen could erase those marvelous legends, turn them to dust. He would be a killer of dreams.

Yes, he had experienced deep disappointment upon finding only adobe huts instead of solid-gold buildings, but he also recalled how powerful those dreams had been. They had given him a sense of wonder. The Seven Cities did exist, but only for those who could see them—and they were not what anyone expected. The treasure was the *hope* of finding them, not the cities themselves, a hope of what remained to be seen.

Perhaps in another one of the many possible worlds, the buildings really were made of gold instead of clay. How could he know for sure? His other-mother had certainly found them.

Unwilling to shoulder the burden of quashing everyone else's imaginations, he answered only, "The Redrock Desert is vast, and I explored many wonderful places, but I never found the Cíbola of legend." He gave a mysterious smile. "The Seven Cities must still be out there somewhere."

Two days later, the Commodore's cargo steamliner arrived on its regular route, delivering supplies and picking up a fresh load of redfire opals. When Pangloss saw Owen approach his locomotive with a large grin, his mouth dropped open and his voluminous beard bristled like the fur on a startled cat. He bounded forward to sweep the young man into an enthusiastic embrace. "Mr. Hardy, you're back! You survived."

Owen laughed. "That much is obvious."

Pangloss mopped his dark scalp, trying to recover from his shock. "Will you join me again on the steamliner? I never realized how much I appreciated your help." He wrapped a beefy arm around Owen's shoulder and squeezed him so hard Owen thought bones would break. "You've been away so long I was beginning to develop a jaded view of the world again."

Owen smiled. "We can't have that, Commodore. I'll ride with you for a while, but once we get to Poseidon City, I might go elsewhere, work aboard a cargo steamer for a while and see other shores . . . maybe even head toward Albion."

Pangloss laughed. "You have changed! I thought you'd never go back to your quiet and uninteresting village."

"I didn't say that was where I'd go." He thought of the carnival traveling around the countryside. Maybe he would be brave enough to go there. "I haven't made up my mind yet."

The following day as the steamliner took off again, Pangloss let him stoke the alchemical furnace, just like old times. Owen took the controls and steered the airship, accelerating as they rolled down the rails and leaped aloft. Clanging the passage bell, he guided the cargo train eastward out of the mountains, toward the motley, festering city of Poseidon.

This time, Owen did not fear anything about the city. With Commodore Pangloss at his side, he was respectable. After unloading the redfire opals, chalcedony, aventurine, cinnabar, and sardelian, the Commodore insisted on paying him his overdue wages (far more than Owen expected).

"I can help you get a position aboard a cargo steamer," Pangloss said.

All of the steamer captains knew Pangloss, and the Commodore put in a good word. Owen was pleased to learn that the next ship due to leave port was the same one he had taken to Atlantis, with Captain Lochs at the helm. The steamer captain had never questioned Owen's desperate claims, had never dreamed that the young man was escaping arrest from the Regulators.

Lochs formally shook Owen's hand, saw how much the young man had changed. "Your special task is finished then, young man?"

"Not finished," he said as he boarded the cargo steamer, "but I'm ready to move on."

"I'll be happy to have you aboard. You did good work last time," the captain said. "Provided you can keep from getting seasick."

Owen hefted the coins Pangloss had paid him, then he gave them all to Captain Lochs, much to the man's surprise. "This is to repay the money you gave me when I arrived in Poseidon . . . and to pay for my first passage. I—" He paused, then forced himself to confess. "I wasn't really on a mission for the Watchmaker."

Lochs raised his gray eyebrows. "Oh? And how can you be so sure?"

Owen didn't have an answer for that.

CHAPTER 24

All I know is that sometimes you have to be wary
Of a miracle too good to be true

Either the seas were calmer, or Owen himself was calmer, more stable, more grounded. This time the passage of the cargo steamer was less grueling than his first miserable experience. Owen was no longer running, no longer hiding, and he felt good about being here.

Under sunny skies, the waves were calm, and the steamer puffed exuberant pillars of white smoke into the air, carrying its load of precious gems, valuable minerals, and alchemical supplies across the Western Sea. Owen was glad to be aboard the ship, sailing on the open sea. He thought he might like this life for a while, and the captain seemed happy enough to have him.

Although he kept quiet about the debacle in Chronos Square and why the Regulators had been chasing him, he had plenty of other stories to tell. In the evenings, he ate dinner with Captain Lochs on the bridge deck, looking out at the brooding waves and talking of his adventures. The lonely captain quietly absorbed every part of every tale.

Owen described bucolic Barrel Arbor with a wistful nostalgia, aware that he was painting a picture through a tinted fog of memories instead of what he actually remembered. He talked about his days with the carnival, but spoke quickly so as to dodge the heartbreak of what Francesca had said to him. *I would never let myself be trapped like that.* And Owen hadn't been trapped, either. He thought of the marvels he'd experienced since leaving the carnival. If he'd stayed with Francesca, he would never have gone to Atlantis and lived on the streets of Poseidon City. He would not have learned to steer an airship across the sky, nor would he have seen the redfire opal mines. He would not have lived in the Seven Cities of Gold— the king, and only living member, of a lost civilization.

If he were given the chance to live it all again, he wondered if he would fall in love with Francesca. He was a different person now.

Captain Lochs seemed to understand that the young man refused to tell part of his story. As he listened, he ate fish from his plate, nodded in appreciation toward Owen. "You can serve aboard this ship, young man, but you may find that it isn't what you expect, after all. I used to think a sea captain's life was filled with adventure." He dabbed his mouth with a napkin. "Now, it does take me from Crown City to Atlantis and back . . . and back again, and forth, and back. I'm content here on my ship, and I'm glad you've done the adventuring, so that I don't have to."

The next day, clouds gathered like a congealing smoke pudding. Owen went out on deck to breathe the brisk air, hoping to keep seasickness at bay. Other than a twinge of queasiness, his constitution seemed better able to handle an unsteady world. Two other crewmembers had set up a chess board, playing the game as the steamer swayed in a slow-motion waltz.

Owen asked for his list of chores, but Captain Lochs told him there would be plenty of time. "You did pay for your passage this time, Mr. Hardy. We don't usually put paying passengers to work."

Owen smiled, thanked him, and helped the sailors anyway. "It's the best way for me to learn the ropes." He wanted to keep busy, not just because it made him feel worthwhile; he didn't want to think too much about where he was going. He hadn't decided yet whether he should go back to Barrel Arbor, live somewhere else in Albion, or just keep sailing. For much of his life, he had tried to convince himself that Barrel Arbor was the place where he belonged—home, peace, a daily routine with family and neighbors. Everyone else was content with that life; why couldn't he be? He thought of the Tick Tock Tavern, imagined himself raising a pint of hard cider (or maybe he would even try a cup of honey mead); he would listen to Mr. Paquette read the daily printout from the newsgraph, hear him give reports of far-off places. He and his father would wind all the clocks in the house every night, and Owen would tend the orchard, pick the apples, live his life. . . .

As he thought of the people in Barrel Arbor, he wondered what Mr. Oliveira would have done if given the opportunity for such adventures. Or Mr. and Mrs. Paquette, or Mr. Huang. Wanting nothing exotic and strange, they would probably have stayed home with their plain lives.

And they would never have seen the outpouring of molten-gold sunlight across the walls of an empty city, or the constellations from the deck of a flying steamliner, or even the hypnotic Clockwork Angels in Chronos Square.

He remembered a plump, orange cat that had frequented the Paquettes' newsgraph offices. The lazy cat curled up in any patch of sun, sleeping away the day, content with its sluggish dreams. Everything had its place, and every place had its thing.

Pondering such a mundane life—a dream that was far less pleasant than imagining the Seven Cities of Gold—he looked up to the sky. Against the brooding gray backdrop of clouds, he spotted the white balloon sack of a small wooden-hulled airship that was drifting on the winds.

Owen watched the tiny airship and wondered what could possibly be out here—they were still two days' journey from the coast of Albion, and the flying craft would be far from the pivot of any steamliner track. He went to the bridge deck to ask Captain Lochs, but they peered in vain, unable to find any sign of the mysterious airship.

That night, a storm unleashed itself upon the sea, bearing down with the sharp teeth of a hurricane. Waves crashed against the hull, tossing loose objects around the cabins. In the hold, several ropes snapped, spilling crates of rocky minerals into unruly heaps. Fortunately, none of the dangerous reactive substances mixed. On deck, heavy tarpaulins flapped about in the wind and downpour; sailors struggled to lash them down before crates of supplies were drenched.

Though he wasn't on duty, Owen made his way from his cabin to the bridge deck. As he braved the outer stairs, he was too unnerved by the storm to feel queasy. Captain Lochs stood at the wheel, struggling to keep the cargo steamer on course.

To verify their heading, Owen withdrew the dreamline compass Pangloss had given him. The needle spun, as if confused about which way to go; the secondary dial that showed where Owen should be also wobbled with seasick indecision.

"I've never seen a storm like this," Captain Lochs said through clenched teeth. "The winds and the currents have taken us off course."

"So where are we?" Owen had to raise his voice against the drumbeat of rain on the windows.

"Unknown, but once we have clear skies I'll be able to navigate to Albion. Right now, I'm just trying to keep the steamer afloat."

A huge wave crashed against the bow, and the engines groaned and thrummed. The vessel tilted severely, as if teetering on the edge of a cliff, before it swung back again.

The two chess-playing crewmembers burst into the bridge house, looking bedraggled. "Captain, we can't take this much longer. We're being battered!"

"The storm has got to let up soon," Owen said.

"Does it?" asked one of the men. "The Watchmaker's Almanac doesn't apply out here on the open sea."

"The weather-alchemists can't help us now," said the other.

Captain Lochs tried to see through the sheet of water that flooded the windowpanes. "Look at that! I thought I spotted something!"

Owen stared into the storm, saw only the night and driving rain—and then a ghostly light appeared like a beacon off the starboard side. "What's over there?" he said. "Is there anything this far out on the charts?"

"The charts are no good here, Mr. Hardy," Captain Lochs said. "We know little about what's off the route between Crown City and Poseidon."

"Is the light beckoning us to safety?" Owen asked. "Like an . . . Angel?"

He imagined one of the heavenly clockwork figures glowing in the middle of the storm, extending her hand, spreading her wings as if to swoop toward their ship and rescue them.

A sweeping wave washed over the bow, sending cargo crates overboard. Owen was thrown to the deck, and the two chess players clung onto anything they could find. The light shone out again.

The captain's face went pale. "We'll have to chance it. That light means someone else is out here—like a miracle, right when we need one."

Owen didn't question it, but the miracle seemed too good to be true. Lochs turned the wheel, setting course for the tantalizing beacon. Maybe it was an island or some other ship, perhaps a manifestation of light.

Or maybe it was just a trick of the eye.

Regardless, it was possible safety, and Captain Lochs drove the cargo steamer forward, squeezing every last measure of power from his engines. As the glowing beacon grew brighter, his eyes lit up with hope. Salvation was at hand.

Hoping to see some unexpected safe harbor where they could take shelter, Owen peered through the driving rain. The cargo steamer was still some distance from the tempting light, but as he looked beyond the bow, a curl of foam appeared—unexpected breakers roaring against an unseen shore.

These were not safe and sheltered waters at all! "Reefs, Captain!" he yelled. "We're about to—"

The force of the engines and the heavy waves drove the cargo steamer aground with an awful sound. He felt a shudder as reefs ripped open the hull like a fisherman gutting a trout.

Everyone on the bridge went flying, slammed against the bulkheads. Captain Lochs's head split open, and he fell limp, bleeding onto the deck. Still at full steam, the engines kept pushing the vessel up onto the saw-toothed reefs. On the engine deck, the main steam boiler burst open with a roar.

Above all the noise, Owen thought he heard an impossible chorus of cheers in the distance.

As the storm continued to slash and shove, the steamer flooded and began to sink. The crewmembers ran out on deck, shouting at one another. Life preservers went overboard but were washed away in the snarling spittle of breakers. Owen watched brave, or simply foolish, sailors jump overboard, only to be swept away into the gray cauldron of the sea or battered to death against the rocks.

Owen hauled Captain Lochs out into the open, struggling to save him; the man was limp and bleeding profusely from his split skull. "Help!" Owen yelled, but the winds snatched his cry away. He found a life preserver, snagged it, and wrestled the captain's arms through the hole.

A large wave swept up and over the bow. Owen held on with

one hand, gripped Captain Lochs with the other, but the force of the rushing water swept the unconscious man off the ship and into the sea. Owen grabbed for the rope and yelled in dismay, but no one heard him. The backwash knocked the life preserver free of the captain's limp arms, and the old man was gone.

Owen huddled in a sheltered pocket against the wall. He wrapped a shredded length of rope around his chest, securing himself to the deck. He would not voluntarily slide into the teeth of an icy grave.

He could make out voices, shouts, and cheers from below. When he dragged himself to the deck rail, he discerned human shapes, people in strange costumes, oil slickers and hoods, thick gloves. They were tied together by ropes and moved in a human chain across the reefs, holding onto poles to anchor themselves. They were working their way toward the wrecked ship.

"Help!" Owen waved to them. "Help, save us!"

The strange people below looked up, but they seemed less intent on rescuing any survivors than on grabbing crates of cargo. Their backs were stooped with the weight of the treasure they bore; they staggered away across the spray-slick rocks. He called again to the rescuers.

Owen saw two of his struggling shipmates crawl up onto the reefs. One broken sailor raised a beseeching hand for help. A few strangers ran forward and then, to Owen's horror, clubbed the sailors and kicked the bodies out into the water, where the foam became tinged with red.

Another wave washed over the rail as the ship settled on the rocky reef. Owen spluttered, shook the salt water from his eyes. He hid there and watched the strangers scuttling over the tilted deck, ducking into the cargo hold, hurrying away with kegs and boxes of valuables.

He saw no one else from the cargo steamer, and he guessed he might be the only survivor—at least until these murderous strangers killed him. He kept hold of the rope that prevented him from washing overboard, and he scrambled about the flotsam on the deck, trying to find a weapon so he could at least defend himself.

A cargo crate had smashed open on deck, spilling chunks of rocks and minerals from Atlantis. Owen found a heavy rock large enough to batter an attacker. From his days with Commodore Pangloss, he even identified what it was. Dreamstone.

As he watched the predatory strangers pick their way across the deck, close to finding him, he kept an eye out for large waves. He clutched the heavy dreamstone, raised it—and a wave slammed down on the deck like a vengeful hand, driving Owen up against the sidewall with a heavy blow to the head. Unconsciousness was blacker than the storm.

CHAPTER 25

The days were dark and the nights were bright

When Owen awakened, he was very much surprised to find himself still alive—which should have been no surprise; otherwise he wouldn't have awakened in the first place.

He found himself lying on a mattress stuffed with rags, rather than in a pool of blood on spray-washed reefs. Someone had wrapped a woolen blanket around him. Maybe the storm, the deceptive beckoning light, the cargo steamer running aground, the deaths of Captain Lochs and his crew were all just a dream . . . a horrible one.

So many of his other dreams had proved false, but this one, he feared, was real.

He was in a cluttered cabin with the window open to let in fresh, cool air; the room had an undertone of damp saltiness. He touched his head and discovered bandages bound around a sore spot. His left arm was also wrapped tight; he didn't even remember getting a gash there. He sat up in the bed and groaned. This was a strange sort of hospital.

"I thought you'd wake up sooner," said a stern female voice. He saw a big-hipped, middle-aged woman whose dark hair was laced with strands of gray. She wore a black dress wrapped in a magenta shawl and scarf, both adorned with bangles. "I made some fish broth for you to regain your strength, but it's cold now."

"Sorry, I didn't know anyone was waiting for me to wake up," Owen said.

He remembered the shadowy figures that had roped themselves together in the storm, ransacking the wrecked steamer and staggering away with heavy loads on their backs. Barbarians, pirates . . . they clubbed to death the sailors who had washed overboard, even though they begged for rescue. He felt a thrill of fear, wondering if this woman would kill him now, even though she must have had ample opportunity to do so already.

"Who are you?" His voice was raspy, his throat raw. He remembered how much he had shouted during the hurricane, for all the good it had done.

"I'm Xandrina," she said. "Not that I expect you to remember it. And you are Owen Hardy from Barrel Arbor."

He was baffled that she knew his name. Unless some other sailors from the cargo steamer had survived after all? How long had he been unconscious? "And who are *you*? *Plural?*" he asked. "Your people? I saw them on the reefs. That light that lured us in . . ."

"We're the Free People of the Sea," Xandrina said with an undertone of pride. "Misfits and outlaws, treasure-seekers—anyone who doesn't want to be tied down."

"You wrecked our ship!"

"That's why some people call us the Wreckers."

The Wreckers! He recoiled in the bed, and the sharp movement set off a clamor of pain inside his skull. She bent over to feed him lukewarm, salty soup with lumps of fish. The flavor was so strong he gagged, but his body asserted itself, and he ate the rest of the bowl. By now he had concluded that his injuries were minor. He didn't understand why the Wreckers hadn't clubbed him to death and dumped him into the sea, like the others.

"How do you know who I am? And why did you save me?" Owen would not have had to ask that of many people; helping someone in need was a perfectly normal thing that needed no explanation. But these people had showed no measure of mercy.

Xandrina adjusted her improbably colorful scarf and looked down at him. "We know who you are. He already told us. He told us to save you." She left the small cabin, as if she had finished her job and had no intention of giving him any more of her time. "You're supposed to recover so you can be useful."

Though confused, Owen slept again, and when he woke, he felt alive enough to ease himself out of bed and walk on unsteady legs across the unsteady floor. He opened the door of the small room.

Stepping into the open air, Owen found himself on an island of ruined ships—countless hulls lashed together in an uneven cluster of floating wrecks.

He recognized the form of one particular vessel: another cargo steamer from Albion. It was lashed to an adjacent wooden sailing ship, whose masts stood up like winter trees without leaves. The spreading conglomeration of wrecks drifted along on the open sea. Each time the Wreckers destroyed a ship, Owen realized, they took the hulk and add it to their growing "country."

Hundreds of people had taken refuge here, squatting in available cabins or claiming territory on the uneven decks. Laundry dried on clotheslines strung from rails to masts. On the drab gray metal and weathered brown wood, the Wreckers had done their best to add color with banners and pennants, ribbons that fluttered in the breeze. A man played an exotic-sounding instrument that reminded Owen of a clarinet.

A small boat pulled up to the edge of the conglomerate raft, carrying a net full of fish. Men and women stood on the outermost hulls, trailing fishing lines into the water. They all wore colorful clothes with bold geometrical lines or random patterns.

On the other side of the clustered vessels, Owen saw a small, tethered airship, an inflated dirigible sack connected to the wooden hull of a boat. This must be what he had seen from the deck of the cargo steamer—a scout for the Wreckers. It must have spied on them, hoping for a storm so the Wreckers could seize the opportunity and lure them onto the reefs. Shading his eyes, Owen looked into the distance to see the foamy line of breakers.

His wounded head pounded, and he touched the bandage, felt a spot of fresh blood. Xandrina bustled up to him. "About time you decided to stretch your legs. You've missed midday meal already, but I could find you some cold scraps. I'm supposed to take care of you—he paid me two diamonds for the work, but I didn't know you were going to be so difficult."

"I don't have a pocketwatch," he said, looking around. "So this . . . all of you are the Wreckers?"

"The Free People of the Sea," she corrected.

"You're pirates. You killed Captain Lochs—he was a good man."

She made no apology. "We're hunters, and we hunt ships. The Watchmaker's trade with Atlantis keeps us in diamonds and treasure. After what we pulled off that cargo steamer of yours, our raft is so heavy it's riding a full handspan lower in the water!" She chuckled, but he could think only of how many crewmembers had died when the ship crashed on the reefs.

Wreckers leaped from one deck to the next across the floating hulls. Men and women danced to raucous music that had no melody Owen could discern. All the men sported beards and wore stylish daggers at their hips; their shirts were loose, their pantaloons tight. They were a loud and physical people, chuckling boisterously, punching one another, slapping shoulders, giving playful shoves. The laughter sounded both jovial and derisive.

Their wild unruliness reminded him of the carnies, but only in the most superficial way.

Xandrina brought him food and insisted that it was the last time. "You'll have to find your place and take care of yourself from now on. That's what freedom is all about."

"I'd rather find my way back home," he said. *Anywhere but here.*

She sniffed. "If you made your own home, you wouldn't have to find it elsewhere. Here among the Free People of the Sea, it's every person for himself."

Xandrina didn't wait for him to finish his cold meal; she left him on business of her own. As he ate, several scuffles broke out nearby, but he couldn't determine if they were simple horseplay or genuine feuds. During one altercation, a portly man with a tight head scarf was knocked overboard; though he flailed in the water, choking and sputtering, no one tried to help him. The man managed to pull himself back aboard, stalked up to the laughing man who had pushed him overboard, and punched his rival full in the face. The man spat blood, reeled backward, and both men went their own ways, grumbling.

When Owen wandered the deck, no one seemed interested in asking who he was. They glanced at him, then dismissed him, wanting no friendship or conversation; they probably saw him as another mouth to feed, someone who would take a share of the spoils the next time they ransacked an unsuspecting ship.

Owen did not feel comfortable at all here. The Wreckers might have thought themselves free, but they were deadly, lawless. His head hurt, and his heart was heavy. He still did not understand why these people had rescued him at all.

He told us to save you.

"You travel a very random course, Owen Hardy of Barrel Arbor." Owen turned to face a man with a familiar haughty expression, lifting his chin and raising his significant eyebrows. He stroked his pointed beard, and Owen stared at the alchemical tattoo on one hand, the burned scar on the other. "Without the Watchmaker's own destiny calculator, I would never have known how to intercept you!"

Owen stared and shuddered. The last time he had seen those eyes, above a breathing mask, the man had been setting a detonator, trying to destroy Chronos Square. "What are you doing here?"

"The Wreckers are my kindred spirits," the Anarchist said. "That much should be obvious."

Owen realized he *hated* this man and the flippant turmoil he caused, mayhem for no purpose other than mayhem itself. The Anarchist had intended to wipe out thousands of people, the Watchmaker, the coldfire nexus, the Clockwork Angels, the carnies . . . and Francesca. Worse, Owen had taken the fall for his crimes; he'd been forced to abandon any hope of rejoining his friends, his surrogate family.

The Anarchist gestured around the motley collection of wrecked ships, exuding pride. "When I told them my great mission, they saw the potential, and they've embraced it wholeheartedly. Now they seize every opportunity to sink cargo ships and prevent vital alchemical materials from reaching Crown City. We cut off the Watchmaker's supply. I want to deprive that evil man of everything he needs so that his own coldfire grows dim! As for the Wreckers"—he shrugged his narrow shoulders—"well, they're just happy to plunder the ships."

Owen was at a loss for words. "*You* told them to save me? You knew I was on that ship."

"Our life journeys intersect often, my good friend, usually by design," the Anarchist said. "I've mapped out all the branchpoints, tracked what you would do." His eyes sparkled. "Until we break the stranglehold of the Watchmaker, nothing is random, no matter how much you think it might be. And I understand how important you are, Owen Hardy."

"I'm not important to anybody!"

"Which is exactly why you are so necessary." When the Anarchist smiled, the pointed ends of his mustache jabbed upward like two sharp rapiers. "I am the Mysterious Angel, the Watchmaker's greatest nightmare. And you are the lynchpin—exactly what we need to destroy the Stability."

CHAPTER 26

All the highlights of that headlong flight,
Holding on with all my might

By the next day, Owen's injuries had stopped bleeding, though the ache was still there. He did not feel any safer among the Wreckers, nor any more welcome. Even the Anarchist left him alone, knowing his prisoner could go nowhere. Owen slept in the recovery cabin where he had awakened. No one gave him other instructions, no one seemed to care.

The hodgepodge raft drifted far from the treacherous reefs; with large engines and powerful screws attached to the mismatched hulls, the Wreckers could propel their island wherever they wished.

The following morning, the Anarchist met him on the decks of the raft city. He strode forward wearing a bright, sharp-edged smile, and his dark eyes glittered like sunlight off chips of obsidian. "A lovely morning. Today, we continue your education." He put his arm around Owen in an unwanted gesture of comradeship. "Soon we'll begin our real work, my good friend."

With distaste, Owen squirmed out of the man's embrace and spun to face him. "You're a stranger, a *dangerous* stranger—not some long-awaited friend. I don't want to be here, and I certainly don't want any of your 'education.'"

The Anarchist chuckled. "I would never force you." His pointed mustache drooped. "But any truly free man should not be afraid to listen to other ideas. Are you afraid?"

"Not afraid," Owen corrected. "Just not interested."

With a jaunty stride, the Anarchist climbed over the edge of one deck and dropped onto another captured ship. Against his better judgment, Owen followed the man. He still did not understand why he was here or what his place among the Wreckers was meant to be. How was he a . . . lynchpin?

"You've been brainwashed by the Watchmaker. There's nothing dark and evil about anarchy. The word simply means a society without a defined leader. People making their own decisions, leading their own lives. We don't need a dictator to rule every second of every day."

Owen didn't believe him. "And what are you known for? Disruptions and deadly explosions. You and the Watchmaker are two extremes." He hurried along, but the other man didn't seem to care whether or not Owen kept up with his pace.

"And you have experienced two extremes. You've had your eyes opened."

At the edge of the conglomeration raft, the Anarchist stopped to watch the scout airship inflate its main canvas balloon and two outrider levitation sacks; he paid no attention to Owen, who stood beside him. The scout pilot tugged on her patchwork jacket and fingerless gloves before stoking the engines so she could take off. Two pairs of round wheels stabilized the scoutship on the deck, rocking back and forth as the balloons inflated, and a blocky cold-fire engine sent steam exhaust chugging through nozzles.

Though the air vessel operated on the same principle as Commodore Pangloss's steamliner, its pilot had a different mission. She would drift high among the clouds, scanning the expanse of ocean for other victims. On deck, a helper detached mooring lines, and the scout airship lifted off and flew away, with a triangular rudder sail dangling below.

The Anarchist followed his gaze. "Airships usually can't travel this far out to sea, but the pilot uses this giant raft as a base, a place to take off and land. She doesn't need rails or a pivot point."

"What if she gets lost?" Owen asked. "If she flies beyond her range, won't she crash into the sea?"

He shrugged. "A life without risk is a life without . . . *life*. She loves to fly free up in the sky, and we all benefit from her efforts. Otherwise we'd have to find our prey some other way." He gestured Owen to follow him. "But we would still manage—the Free People of the Sea are good hunters."

The Anarchist took him toward a skeletal scaffolding tower built on the deck of a salvaged cargo steamer. Suspended from the framework was a dazzling blue-white alchemical globe, like a captive star. The beacon was dim and quiescent now, but with the addition of concentrated fuel Owen guessed the dazzling light would be intense enough to pierce any storm.

And signal false salvation to any unsuspecting sailors.

The Wreckers must have maneuvered their cluster-raft into position on the far side of the reefs, then lit their tantalizing beacon to draw Captain Lochs onto the jagged rocks.

The Anarchist wrapped his tattooed hand around a slat on the skeletal crane structure. "As a farm boy, you climbed apple trees. I know you climbed ropes, buildings." Smiling, he seized one of the rungs, swung himself up, and reached back down with his burned hand. "Come on—you need to see this."

Owen chose to resist. "I can see just fine from here."

"You can see fine from the top of the tower, too." Rather than offering further assistance or encouragement, he continued to climb, assuming Owen would follow.

The young man heaved an annoyed sigh and scrambled up after

him. He was not afraid of the height, and even with his bandaged arm the climb was no more difficult than ascending the pole to Francesca's trapeze platform.

At the top of the tower, the Anarchist stood free, extending his arms to embrace the open sky and the brisk breezes. "Can you feel it, Owen Hardy? No safety net, no harness, just the wind and freedom!"

Owen wrapped his arm around one of the high bars to stabilize himself. Back in Barrel Arbor, he would have felt nervous to be so high. Now, having walked tightropes, both willingly and by accident, he felt confident in his balance and his grip—but the Anarchist seemed more dangerous than a fall from any height.

"Why don't you smile? Feel it, in here." The stranger pounded the center of his chest. "You're free now. You should rejoice."

"Rejoice?" Owen couldn't believe the man's attitude. "I'm miserable! I watched innocent people from my ship *die* just so these thieves could rob them! I'm lost. I have no place to go."

"No encumbrances. The purest definition of freedom!" the Anarchist said. "You just needed a nudge, and all was for the best." His grin seemed snide. "I chose you long ago in Barrel Arbor, watched your sleepwalking life, and I sensed there was a spark in you that needed to be fanned into bright flames."

"You . . . watched me?"

"It was easy to slink around your village. No one saw me because they had long since forgotten how to look for anything out of the ordinary. Why do you think your sweet, vapid Lavinia failed to join you that night under the stars? She was such a creature of habit it was easy for me to slip a potent sleeping draught into the cup of warm milk she drank every night before she went to bed."

Owen stared at him, wide-eyed at the revelation. The Anarchist gave a flippant wave to trivialize what he had done. "It was probably unnecessary. I very much doubt she would have been bold enough to join you anyway—even such a tiny straying from the rules seemed beyond her abilities. On the other hand, she might not have had the imagination to disagree once you told her what to do. So, I needed to make certain. I had to give you your complete freedom." He grinned. "If Lavinia had come out after all, you wouldn't have had the incentive to leave, and you wouldn't have had . . . all this!"

Owen couldn't stop himself. "I hate you!"

"Yes, it's good to feel something, isn't it? Think about where you are. What do you lack now? You have no responsibilities, no obligations, no expectations. No anchors dragging you down! I gave that to you." He seemed to expect applause.

Owen couldn't believe what he was hearing. "You gave it to me? You *did* it to me." He couldn't articulate all the pain and heart-break, the tribulations, everything he had endured since leaving his village. "You wrecked my life just like these people wreck ships."

The Anarchist remained smug and unsympathetic. "Oh? And having lived such an adventure, do you regret it? Would you give it all up? There's world enough out there and time." He gestured to the open sea. "The Watchmaker imprisons time. We have to free it and free ourselves."

His dark eyes became distant and unfocused, and he absently toyed with the stickpin at his collar. "I destroyed the Alchemy College, and that was just the beginning. Once we get back to Albion, you and I can continue the campaign of disruption. It'll be like shaking a sound sleeper awake. Difficult, yes, but tough times demand tough hearts."

Owen shrank away. "I'm not your apprentice! Being reckless is not the same as being free. You're insane."

The Anarchist looked at him with withering disappointment. "Insane . . . That's what the philosopher-professors and analysts said about me back at the college, when they stripped me of my robes and banished me. I told them the Watchmaker himself had sent me secret messages, had egged me on so that I could be his successor one day, but they assumed something was wrong with me. They said I suffered from malignant narcissism."

His anger cut the air like a sword blade. "They tried to understand me, analyze me. They assumed that once they found the malfunction in my mental clockwork, they could *repair* it. I had nothing but contempt for the ordinariness of their minds."

He leaned back, held onto the tower with one hand, and recklessly swayed out over the open drop to the deck below. "The Watchmaker never defended me, never admitted his role. Only later did I realize that he *wanted* me to fail! Oh, but he wasn't prepared for what he created."

Laughing, he swung himself around again. Owen hoped he might slip and fall to his death, thereby saving hundreds, *thousands* of lives from his violence. With one quick shove, Owen could send him plunging off the tower. . . .

He was horrified at himself for the very thought.

But the Anarchist's grip was firm. He seemed to be testing Owen. Giving the young man a look that was a strange combination of satisfaction and disappointment, he pulled himself back to a stable position. "Analysts, doctors, philosophers. I baffled their orderly diagnoses. They didn't comprehend my mind or my heart, but the one sure thing is that they will never forget me."

Owen's head pounded, and not just from his injury. "And now you're the leader of the Wreckers? I thought you said the very definition of anarchy means to live without leaders."

The man chuckled at Owen's clumsy trap. "These people need my guidance, but it's only a step. They're more interested in themselves and their treasure. They're driven by simple greed, not ideology, but I can work with that. You, my good friend, are a much more important piece in the game. The true revolution has to come from simple, everyday people like you. Not from grand pronouncements, but a quiet and building roar from a small crowd whisper. And you'll be the first one. You'll be a hero."

"I'm nobody's hero," Owen said, "especially not yours."

He looked across the water and saw the scout airship returning. Knotted steam spilled out in a vapor trail, and Owen could tell that the pilot had pumped up her engines to the highest capacity, racing headlong back to the floating island. Faintly through the open air, he could hear a clanging bell.

"I suppose she's found another ship to wreck," Owen said bitterly. "More innocent victims."

"That's a different sort of alarm. Something interesting is about to happen." He sounded disturbed, and then hungry. "We should climb back down."

By the time they worked their way to the deck, the scout airship had landed, wheels bouncing on the deck. Tied by a single mooring rope, with its levitation sacks still inflated, the vessel bobbed haphazardly. As the pilot jumped out, waving her gloved hands, her face was filled with concern, even panic. "They're coming—a full force! To arms!"

"Who's coming?" Owen asked.

The Anarchist's significant eyebrows drew together, and his expression was grim and determined. "The Watchmaker, of course."

The first airships appeared on the horizon: big war dirigibles larger than the majestic steamliners that carried cargo and passengers throughout Albion; each of these was emblazoned with a bold honeybee, poised to sting. A force of armored battleship steamers cruised across the waters, belching so much white smoke and vapor that it looked like a fog bank rolling toward the Wreckers' raft city.

"It seems we've been found." The Anarchist stood with his hands on his narrow hips; he raised his voice to all the scurrying people: "Embrace the opportunity! Draw your swords and prepare to fight! You are the Free People of the Sea!"

The Wreckers yelled to one another, scrambled to their quarters or rushed below decks to arm themselves with swords and cutlasses. Owen spotted his "nurse" Xandrina taking up a long butcher knife and standing firm; she had tied her bright magenta scarf in place. The scoutship pilot in her patchwork jacket tapped a long cudgel against her gloved palm—just like the ones the Wreckers had used to club his shipmates to death on the storm-washed reefs. . . .

The Anarchist shouted orders. Sometimes the Wreckers listened; other times they cursed at him and did whatever they liked. A few "free people" detached individual floating boats and drifted away to escape the imminent battle.

The Watchmaker's war dirigibles closed in overhead like dark thunderheads, and blue-uniformed Regulator soldiers dropped down from dangling rope ladders. The battleship steamers surrounded the raft island and dispatched their squads as well.

The Free People of the Sea held up their blades, shouting in defiance.

Coming aboard the hodgepodge raft, the Watchmaker's forces moved in perfect ranks, shoulder to shoulder, one wave after another. They carried long-barreled single-shot rifles, and once the weapons were packed and loaded with lead shot, the Blue Watch soldiers actuated a propulsive spark. The rifles fired a deadly barrage into the mobs of Wreckers who rushed forward, bowling them over in a wave of bloodshed.

Owen couldn't imagine how or why the Watchmaker, after more than a century of Stability, had any cause to manufacture such deadly weapons or to drill his elite Regulators for such a murderous attack. Yet, they performed like components of the most intricate machine.

People screamed and fell, bleeding. A few pellets ricocheted around the shacks and mast, and Owen ducked as a ball struck the wooden wall next to his head. Instead of using lead shot, the Watchmaker's rifles fired bullets of gold.

In response, the wild Wreckers ran forward in complete chaos. After the first Regulators fired their rifles, the vanguard stepped aside to reload, while the second line lowered their barrels and opened fire. The Wreckers fell upon them with flailing swords.

Breathing heavily, the Anarchist rushed up to Owen. His hair was disheveled, his face flushed, his cheek smudged—but he looked excited rather than frightened. The long sword he carried was much more imposing than the one Tomio had used at the carnival. He pressed the hilt into Owen's hand. "Take this and fight!"

Owen didn't intend to hack or stab anyone, but before he could argue, the Anarchist had dashed off, leaving him with the sword.

More blue-uniformed soldiers disembarked from the battleship steamers, swarming in perfect precision across the decks with a resonant thunder of marching feet. By contrast, the chaotic Wreckers charged into the neat and ordered ranks, slashing, stabbing, and clubbing while well-practiced Regulators stepped back to reload their rifles.

Owen sought shelter as the waves of battle came toward him. Despite his sword, he had no intention of fighting to defend these murderous pirates. They had wrecked his ship, caused the deaths of Captain Lochs and all the sailors aboard. Was that how they bought their "freedom"? Owen wanted no part of it!

He saw his reluctant benefactor Xandrina stumping forward with her butcher knife, her scarf torn loose and her hair flying free. She wore a bloodthirsty expression. Two Regulator soldiers gunned her down, and she collapsed on the deck.

From the other side of the conjoined hulls, the Anarchist emerged carrying pots filled with chemical mixtures. He hurled them, smashing the pots among the Regulator soldiers; once liberated and exposed to the air, the chemical mixtures burst into silvery white heat. Explosions scattered the Watchmaker's organized ranks like dry leaves in the wind.

A new squad of red-uniformed Regulators marched in from Owen's left, having disembarked from a war dirigible overhead. One of the Anarchist's bombs exploded nearby, and Owen had to duck and run, swept along by the tides of battle.

As another explosive pot tumbled through the air, the scout-ship pilot ran forward, waving her cudgel, too impatient to wait for the bomb to do its work. She swung her stick at one of the Watchmaker's uniformed soldiers, just as the bomb exploded between them, killing both.

Owen felt sick.

A special black-uniformed contingent came over from the lead battleship steamer; each Black Guard wore a red sash with a gold honeybee insignia. They closed ranks, protecting and escorting an old man who moved stiffly, formally.

For some reason, the old man with the special black guard pointed a stiff arm at *him* and shouted in a tantalizing voice, "What do you lack now, Owen Hardy?" Then he laughed.

A cold prickle skittered down his back. He had heard that call before—from the strange pedlar who had given him the horrific book, *Before the Stability*. Though he was not dressed in pedlar clothes and stovepipe hat, Owen realized this was the same old man, but different . . . undisguised.

Owen held up his sword in surrender. "You're the pedlar!"

"I am many things. I keep an organized list."

The Black Watch marched toward Owen, closing in. He had nowhere to run, wasn't sure he even wanted to run, because he certainly wasn't safe among the Wreckers either. The old man called to him again. "The principle is proved. You belong with me!"

Oblivious to the mayhem going on around him, the old man marched across the decks as if he were immortal. And maybe he was. Owen finally realized that this was the Watchmaker himself!

Assuming victory, the Regulator soldiers closed in, but the Anarchist surprised them by launching one of his bombs into the air. The huge eruption ignited one of the war dirigibles, and the flaming airship careened off to crash into the ocean. The Watchmaker didn't even flinch at the disaster.

"Owen Hardy, by now the need for perfect order is obvious.

You've seen the dangerous alternative. Let me cut to the chase—you must choose Stability. Step back into line. I have watched you, and now I'll use you. A simple, normal man to be my example. Your numerous mistakes will discourage anyone else from dreaming about leaving their preordained life. As my representative, you will save the Stability. Thanks to you, no one else will ever be tempted by such foolishness again."

The Anarchist dispatched more bombs that released clouds of acrid red fumes to form a smokescreen. Through the scarlet mist, wild Wreckers charged forward with their swords and caught the organized Regulator soldiers by surprise. The Watchmaker dispatched his elite Black Watch to join the battle.

Sure of his victory, the old man turned to Owen. "Wait here, and I will take care of the evil Anarchist. All is for the best." He marched after his guards, leaving the young man by himself, as if he didn't imagine for a moment that anyone would question his instructions.

Owen stared at the rigid forces of the Watchmaker clashing with the Anarchist and his frenetic Wreckers. He threw down his sword. He didn't like either alternative.

While the battle continued to rage, he ran to the lone scout airship.

CHAPTER 27

Belief has failed me now
Life goes from bad to worse
No philosophy consoles me
In a clockwork universe

Disgusted with the extremes of both sides, Owen scrambled aboard the tethered scout airship. Only one haphazardly tied guy-line held it to the decks of the Wreckers' raft. The female pilot had been killed in an explosion, and no one watched the drifting vessel now.

The Watchmaker and the Anarchist had demanded that he choose between them, but Owen Hardy from Barrel Arbor—a mere assistant manager of an apple orchard, who had traveled so much, endured so much, *seen* so much since his modest beginnings—chose not to decide. *That* was the choice he made. That was his free will.

He had discarded the sword, so he tugged and yanked at the mooring rope until he worked the knot loose. The levitation sacks were already inflated, the low-capacity boiler was still up to pressure, and the scoutship drifted free.

The war dirigibles were anchored in the sky overhead, and more uniformed reinforcements joined the Watchmaker's soldiers on the decks below. Additional Wreckers fled the besieged raft island in their own small boats.

Owen handled the controls easily, thankful for all that Commodore Pangloss had taught him. At first, no one noticed his tiny airship rising up and away amidst the smoke and explosions, the rifle fire and clash of swords. He stoked the engines, powered the propeller, and turned away.

Yes, he had stolen the ship, but he felt little guilt; those were the rules of the Free People of the Sea. Under such circumstances, his friend Guerrero would not have hesitated to grab the airship and flee. In fact, Guerrero wouldn't have waited for Owen at all but would have just escaped by himself. . . .

He increased power and set a course eastward in the general direction of Albion. He had no coordinates, nor did he know how far he was from land, but if he traveled long enough in the correct direction—if his fuel lasted that long—he couldn't help but stumble upon an entire continent.

Below, the random explosions continued to roar, accompanied by gunshots that fired at regular intervals, as if timed with a stopwatch. One of the Regulator soldiers turned his rifle upward and fired at the escaping scoutship. The pressure-monitoring gauges on the pilot deck indicated a leak in the left outrigger balloon; one of the golden bullets must have pierced the coated canvas sack.

"Life goes from bad to worse," he muttered. The leak would not immediately affect his ability to fly, and he tried to gain as much distance as possible. Judging from the supply dials, the pilot carried little extra fuel. She must have burned most of her alchemical resources during the morning scout flight. Owen had only enough fuel to keep the engines stoked for a couple of hours . . . but that should be sufficient for him to get away.

Behind him, smoke from fires and explosions filled the sky like an angry storm cloud. The Watchmaker's overwhelming fleet engulfed the mishmash raft of salvaged ships. Regardless of the outcome, Owen was sure their conflict would not end with a single battle. Too much order and too much chaos—it was like a swinging pendulum. Extreme order provoked a need for extreme freedom, and vice versa.

After the scoutship finally drifted to relative safety and silence, he heard the whisper of breezes far above the restless ocean. At last, he had a moment to catch his breath. Owen shuddered violently with the realization of what he had just been through. A lifetime ago, he had been a naïve, starry-eyed young man counting the days until his seventeenth birthday, believing with all his heart that Lavinia was his true love. The wonders of the world were encompassed by the delightful chronotype images in his mother's picture books. He had been so optimistic. He had wanted to see so many things. But now he had seen it all, and nothing had turned out as he expected.

Worse, what he'd experienced had ruined his old life, for he could never again be content back in Barrel Arbor. He had listened to his father explain the Watchmaker's plan. He was brought up to believe, but that belief had failed him now. He had always been so optimistic, but he could not be consoled by the philosophy of Anarchy or the philosophy of Stability. He felt as adrift as the airship.

But even though his life had tossed him about, battered him and disappointed him, he still wanted to live. Despite grieving for what he had lost, he could still survive. Somewhere in the world, he might find what he was searching for. All dreams couldn't be illusions. He would find a measure of love and laughter, and he would give of himself in return. He just needed to discover the right place, the right people. Somewhere. *That* was something he could believe in. He wouldn't let optimism abandon him entirely.

He took time to assess the scoutship's cabin, which was cluttered with keepsakes, clothing, scraps of food, knives, and toys: all sorts of flotsam and jetsam stolen from unsuspecting ships ruined

on the reefs. As he dug around in the paraphernalia, he found, to his surprise, a large sack stuffed with glittering diamonds, hypnotic redfire opals, and dreamstones—enough treasure to buy all of Barrel Arbor.

In his pocket, he found the old dreamline compass, but the main needle was broken and gave only the vaguest approximation of north. The smaller needle, however, the one that indicated where Owen was *supposed* to be, pointed in a steady, firm direction.

He flew onward as night fell, using the last gasps of alchemical power to keep the boiler up to pressure, hoping to sail just a little farther. He filled the intake chamber with the last of the powdery fuel, which glowed but quickly burned out. The coldfire dimmed and died.

The bullet hole in the airsack had taken its toll, and the levitating balloon deflated even as the steam engine ran out. Owen used every last trick he remembered to keep the scoutship aloft, but it wasn't enough. The vessel descended toward the open darkling sea. He held on, fearing a crash as disastrous as when Captain Lochs's ship had run aground on the reefs. With no pretensions of gentleness, the wooden-hulled airship landed in the water, throwing Owen to the deck. The steam boiler gasped and coughed; it would have exploded had there been any pressure left. The deflated air sacks collapsed like a smothering blanket over the top of the vessel.

Owen scrambled among the debris strewn about from the impact (though the mess looked no more disorganized than before), grabbing one of the pilot's long knives, which he used to saw through the ropes that connected the air sacks to the hull. He succeeded in cutting away the heavy canvas and cast it overboard, and at last he could see where he was.

Under the open sky, Owen looked at the stars as his boat drifted along.

CHAPTER 28

All that you can do is wish them well

He drifted for days in the battered hull of the crashed airship. He ate the food stored aboard; he caught water from a brief but enthusiastic rain squall, which quenched his thirst but also made his clothes wet and uncomfortable.

With no maps, he had no idea how far away the coast of Albion might be. He didn't know what time it was, didn't even know the date or the day of the week. Most surprising was that it didn't matter to him.

He spent a gray day in a thickening mist that smothered the view, but there was nothing to see anyway. The fog reminded him of the fog around his own life. The Redrock Desert wasn't the only place with mirages. . . .

His daydreams had made him ripe for the picking, and both the Anarchist and the Watchmaker wanted to pluck him for themselves. He had made his own decisions—or so he thought—but, reflecting on how his life had proceeded, and unraveled, he wondered how much of it had been his free will and how much had been subtle manipulations. Watchmaker and Anarchist had set him in motion like a windup toy. On that first night, if the Anarchist had not drugged Lavinia, would she have come out to meet him at midnight? And if she had done that one small daring thing, would Owen have contented himself with that faint taste of excitement? He would always wonder.

With his ruthless Regulators, the Watchmaker had caused him grief, inflicted hardships, made certain that Owen's innocent choice to leave his village resulted in as much misery as possible. That was his intent? To punish a single honeybee that decided to stray from the hexagonal lines? If the Watchmaker had simply let Owen see the marvelous sights of the big city, have his little adventure, the young man would probably have gone home to Barrel Arbor and settled down, happy enough to tell his stories in the Tick Tock Tavern.

Instead, the two men had caught him in their own trap, played a tug of war with him. Because he was so innocent and optimistic, they had fought over him, broken and humiliated him—all to *prove a point*. He was glad to be quit of both of them.

Eventually, he heard a growling sound in the distance, a rumbling roar that could have been curling waves striking a beach, or maybe just another bank of deadly reefs. He tried to discern anything through the mist; unable to change course, he hoped his fragile ship would not be smashed against the rocks.

Eventually, as the sound of breakers grew louder, the folds of mist parted to reveal the gray line of a slumbering shore, a pebbly beach and sandy cliffs—not jagged reefs that would tear his boat to pieces.

Owen stood up in the drifting airship, strained to see any fishing boats, shore settlements, or tidepool harvesters, but he saw only an uninhabited expanse. At least it was land . . . surely, the coast of Albion.

When the unguided boat drew close to the unknown shore, Owen decided to slide overboard and swim the rest of the way.

He took only the satchel of diamonds and watch jewels—which would be useful for buying food, clothes, lodging—and slid into the cold water. He swam to the rocky beach and eventually climbed out on solid land, dripping, shivering. He was no longer adrift, but he couldn't say he was saved.

He trudged past clumps of sad-looking seaweed and picked his way up the crumbling sandy slope to the top of the headlands. His clothes were crusted with salt. The air was damp and chill, but he warmed himself by walking at a brisk pace over untracked grasslands. He was sure that if he kept going he would stumble upon an isolated village somewhere, a place he could buy food, clothes, and a place to rest.

Farther inland, he found a rutted road, which made his heart lighter. He would have been more pleased to see steamliner tracks, but a road had to lead *somewhere*, or else why would anyone make it?

The fog remained his persistent companion as he followed the track over the moors. He came upon a wide field that had been trampled, the grass and heather matted, many footprints and wheel indentations in the soft ground. It looked as if some army had gathered here—he wanted nothing to do with armies. Or maybe, he thought with a spark of optimism that still managed to stay alight, it was a festival. . . .

He stopped to listen and heard only the air, not a bird call, not even a rustle of leaves or grass, despite a faint breeze. Then the sound of paper fluttering in the wind broke the stillness, a crumpled sheet blowing aimlessly. It danced across the top of a puddle and nudged up against a hummock of grass: a colorful but wadded broadsheet. Owen trotted after it, but the capricious wind sent the paper skittering away, and he caught it just a second after it came to rest on a muddy puddle.

He yanked the paper out of the water, shook brown drops from it, and opened the crumpled sheet. The printing was familiar to him, since he had posted many such broadsheets himself. Even so, Owen held the paper without comprehension, as if he were more blind than the haberdasher in Crown City.

The Magnusson Carnival Extravaganza
Final Show of the Season

He looked around the trampled meadow, imagining echoes of the crowds, the carny barkers, the clowns, the raucous music, the creaking rides, and the laughing children.

He followed the fresh wheel ruts and a large bootprint pressed into the muddy side of the path. Despite his hunger and exhaustion, he increased his speed as the road widened, leading him through spotty trees to an intersection with another rutted road that extended to equally unknown country in another direction.

Near the intersection stood three well-kept houses with whitewashed walls, open shutters, oak trees in the yard. A beefy woman worked in the front, bending over a wash basket, extracting wet clothes and flapping them out, humming to herself. She clipped the clothes onto a rope strung from the oak tree to the house, hanging them out to dry, though to what effect, Owen didn't know because the day remained cloudy and dreary. Obviously, she was an optimist herself.

He hurried forward, calling out, but his throat was dry and the words were reluctant to come. She heard him nevertheless and looked up in surprise. He held up the wrinkled broadsheet advertising the carnival. "Were they here?" he finally managed to say as he came up to her.

She eyed him up and down, concerned more about his disheveled appearance than what a stranger might be doing on the road. "The carnival? You're too late. They played yesterday, headed off this morning." She smiled. "You look as if you could use some hot soup. And a bath. I could warm up the stove, heat some broth and some water—"

Owen's stomach growled, but he knew he couldn't stay. "They left this morning?"

She jerked her head toward the crossroads, indicating the perpendicular track. "They headed off that way. Carnival season is over."

He made sure to thank her before he hurried onto the road. He knew how slowly the loaded carnival caravan traveled as they made their way to the next destination. When Owen thought to look behind him toward the cluster of houses, he had already left them far behind. His feet knew where they were going.

The mist and clouds dissipated, leaving a patchy blue sky. Climbing a swell, he heard noises ahead and topped the rise to look down into a comfortable tree-lined valley.

And he saw the carnival.

Owen stared at the colorful pavilions, the game booths, the sleeping tents, the steam wagons, and the components of the Ferris wheel.

A brusque voice made him snap his head around. "Halt! Who goes there?"

A wiry man stepped out of the trees and came toward him brandishing a narrow sword. Owen's mouth fell open. "Tomio!"

The other man dropped his sword and ran to sweep Owen into a hearty embrace. "It's Owenhardy from Barrel Arbor, returned to us at last! Now, there's a trick better than any I've ever performed." He stood back, looked at the young man's bedraggled form. "You're a frightful mess. You shouldn't let Francesca see you like this." Before Owen could say anything, Tomio grabbed his arm and hauled him toward the main carny camp. "We've got a visitor!"

The carnies turned to see who the stranger might be. Owen's stomach knotted, but he couldn't turn down the help. And he was brave enough to face anything, even Francesca. After all he had done and seen, he realized that *this* was what had made him happiest.

Louisa the bearded lady was the first to rush to him. "There's our dear boy back among us, where he belongs. Get this lad some food and some clothes!" Louisa tugged on his hair. "He could use a haircut too. And a shave—and probably a good night's sleep."

"First things first." César Magnusson came forward, propping hands on hips and regarding him. Magnusson wore no polished top hat, and his short dark hair was slicked back. But the ringmaster looked different without a mustache on his face; the extravagant handlebar had been one of his most distinctive features.

Owen looked at the man strangely. "What happened to your mustache?"

Magnusson brushed the comment aside with a laugh. "I just didn't apply it this morning. No need to keep up the charade, now that we're off season."

Owen realized something else that had been right in front of him all along. The ringmaster had loosened the buttons on the vest, no longer hiding the swell of breasts beneath the shirt. "You're a woman!"

"Always have been. Real name is Cassandra, not César. It's just a haircut, a false mustache, and a name. The carnival has to keep up appearances."

Tomio flexed his sword. "My mother is good at her own illusions."

"Mother?" Owen asked.

"I have to maintain the disguise because some obscure ruling in the Annals of Law forbids women from owning circuses." Magnusson rolled her eyes. "A slow day in the lawmaker's offices, that was. Even my great-grandmother can't explain it. The Watchmaker has too many silly rules."

Then, as if field lines had begun to thrum through the ground, Owen felt a presence nearby, heard a quick silence among the carnies. He turned to see Francesca coming toward him, her black hair long and lush, her face as beautiful as ever, her lips quirked in a private smile. "About time you came back, Owenhardy. How long did you expect me to wait for you?"

"You were . . . *waiting* for me?" Owen's heart did flips more complicated than any trapeze act Francesca had ever performed. "But you laughed at me. You turned me down and made it clear you wanted nothing further to do with me. You said you wouldn't be trapped."

She shook her head with a sincere sigh. "Oh, Owen, you have such an imagination, such a good heart, and I love that part of you. But you took me by surprise. I wasn't laughing at *you*—just at the suggestion that I'd be content to stay forever in a small town. Can you imagine me settling in Barrel Arbor? To be honest, I never dreamed that you, yourself, could be content with that anymore."

When Owen swayed on his feet, it had little to do with weariness or hunger. He had given no thought to how *she* might have heard his proposal. Not trapped by marrying him, but trapped in one small place. When he looked at Francesca now, compared her to the bland and quiet Lavinia, he could not imagine this amazing and energetic woman as the mousy wife of an assistant apple orchard manager.

Francesca stepped closer. "You ran off without giving me a chance to suggest that you stay among us. Then I might have given your proposal a different answer."

Owen had trouble finding words. "You would want that?"

As her answer, she kissed him.

------◆◆◆------

The Magnusson Extravaganza was heading toward a place where they often spent the winter. During carnival season, they traveled their Watchmaker-approved route around Albion, and afterward, they retreated far from the Watchmaker's territory to an off-season home where they relaxed and enjoyed one another's company.

Owen could barely remember the wide-eyed young man who had left Barrel Arbor, who had become an adult upon reaching his seventeenth birthday, and then had become a man after continuing his journey. Finally, over the course of it all, he had become an *individual* by getting to know himself as well as the world and by making his own choices.

On a hill outside of the carny camp, he found a stunted old apple tree, part of some long-forgotten orchard that was now overgrown and wild. He sat down to think, because he knew that was what he had to do.

Francesca walked toward him through the grass, intent, as if she was crossing a tightrope. Owen didn't say anything to her, and they sat together, staring at the clouds. She pointed. "That one looks like a horse."

He was startled. "Yes, it does." But he looked at her instead of at the clouds. "You see it."

"Of course." Finally, she said, "I'm sorry I laughed and broke your heart. I didn't understand."

"It wasn't just you—I've been tricked every step of the way," Owen said, though he heard her voice echo in his head. *I'd never let myself be trapped like that!* "From the stories in my mother's books that made me want to run away and see Crown City, to the spiteful people in Poseidon, the empty Seven Cities of Gold, and the Wreckers who killed so many good sailors without a measure of mercy. But I kept searching and hoping that at least one of those dreams would be what I expected."

He shook his head. "Worst of all, the Anarchist tricked me away from home with the intent of making me his pawn. And the Watchmaker with his schemes—they tried to make me part of a plan that I have no interest in."

Francesca reached out to stroke his arm. "Thank your stars you're not like them."

His nostrils flared as he thought of how much pain they had caused him. "I wish I could convince them to stop scheming."

She pushed a strand of hair out of his eyes. It was much longer now than the last time she had seen him. "You can't change the Watchmaker. You can't change the Anarchist. You'll never agree with their reasons, so why bother asking them why? Maybe they'll change someday, maybe they won't. You can't do anything for them—just keep on going and wish them well."

"But what should I do about it?" Owen said.

She leaned back against the trunk of the tree. "Remember those pig farmers in Ashkelon, when you tried to defend me? You can't fix everyone. Turn your back and walk away. If you hold a grudge too long, it'll eat you up like a poison inside."

"So I should just forget about what happened?"

Her eyes sparkled. "You don't have to forget everything, but you're not responsible for it all either."

He thought about that as they contemplated the clouds.

------◆◆------

He decided not to go back to Crown City or Barrel Arbor or Poseidon or Cíbola . . . or any place about which he had preconceptions or misconceptions. He would travel with the carnival, but he would make his own life. He hoped Francesca would have him, but he would accept his life either way.

Wish me well.

He went to the bright red booth of the gypsy fortune teller and wound the key on the side, watched as the clockwork mechanism animated her. He had missed their conversations. The faint blue glow of quintessence filled her biological head, and she opened her rheumy eyes. "It is good to see you again, Owenhardy."

"Were you sleeping?"

"I was dreaming of other timelines. The others are interesting as well."

Owen was sure Commodore Pangloss would have liked to talk with the gypsy fortune teller. "And do you think all those places have the Watchmaker?"

"Every place has something like my father."

He looked at the ancient crone who had been kept alive far, far beyond the point when her body should have failed like a piece of broken machinery. "Your father is the Watchmaker?"

"My father *became* the Watchmaker, and I became this." The mechanisms in her artificial body moved her arms and raised her gloved hands, although her head remained anchored in place. "He was trying to save me, but I have lived long enough to come to my own realizations." She wore a wan smile. "That's what makes me such a good fortune teller."

Owen leaned closer. The key was winding down, and the fortune teller's mechanisms moved more slowly. "And what's my fortune?"

The mechanical hands moved back and forth, pushing aside her tarot deck. Instead, she picked up a card on which words had been printed, a special fortune. "I always knew your destiny, Owenhardy, but I could not tell you until you were ready to hear it."

"What is it?" he said.

She dropped the card into a slot. Owen pulled it out and read the words, which remained cryptic to him. *Tend your garden.*

The clockwork fortune teller wound down without explaining further.

EPILOGUE

A garden to nurture and protect

Rather than just sitting by the fire and boring the grandchildren with stories, as I have done for so long, I've decided to write my memoirs—for all to read (or ignore). Everything I am and everything I've done deserves to be remembered, even if only by a few people who might care—like the boy, Alain.

When I see the sparkle in my grandson's brown eyes, I recognize the thrill of imagination, a longing to go off and find adventures of his own. Maybe he won't stay with the carnival after all, but will set off to find his own life, explore the world, or maybe even some of the other worlds, as my other-mother did.

I have given him my earnest blessing to do whatever it is that makes him happy. As I have learned for myself, there are dangers in encouraging too many dreams, but there are rewards as well. Who am I to choose for some other person? I love Alain and respect him, and I wish him well.

I know that all is for the best—because I made it so for myself. Sometimes stories are all we have, even if they don't always fall into lockstep with memories, or facts. A long time ago, I was pleased and surprised to learn that even my father, in his later years, spent every night at the Tick Tock Tavern telling listeners about my adventures. I know he never understood what drove me away from a seemingly perfect life in Barrel Arbor, but in the end I think he was proud of his son, nevertheless. . . .

When I publish the book, I think I'll make a point of sending copies across the Western Sea to Atlantis. It's been too long since I visited Poseidon City. Given the right alignment of time and place, I'll ask Mrs. Courier (or just Courier) to carry it on her shelves in the Underworld Bookshop. Maybe it will be shelved beside my other-mother's travelogue.

Old Commodore Pangloss will get an inscribed copy; that goes without saying. Maybe other steamliner captains on long and tedious journeys will also be amused by my ramblings (both my rambling feet and my rambling pen).

I've seen and done many things. I know that I have plenty to tell, but the question remains whether I have anything to *say*.

———— ✦◆✦ ————

A weathered stone figure stands at the edge of my garden, a statue of an angel. It cannot capture the beauty of the Clockwork Angels, but that is no fault of the sculptor's. The angel's wings are spread, but she is made of stone and will never fly.

There's a practicality to tending a large garden, especially with such an extended (and hungry) family, which includes all the carnies. They work up a good appetite as they practice their acts and perform the myriad chores on the estate during the off-season. The strongman has to build up his muscles, the knife thrower practices his aim, and the clowns rehearse and rehearse so that their bumbling pratfalls occur with effortless perfection. Even the roustabouts have to haul heavy equipment, stake the tents, maintain the components of the Ferris wheel and the other rides.

Everything has its place, and every place has its thing.

The harvest feeds them all, but the purpose of gardening isn't just to provide food. Beauty is its own reward, and I am quite proud of my flowers, too, especially the gladiolas. Tall spikes of blossoms, a name derived from *gladius*, or sword. A fitting name, although I would never engage in a flower duel with old Tomio; he could still outmaneuver me, I think.

Each fall, I dig the bulbs and store them in a cool, dry root cellar for the winter, and I plant them again in spring. I love watching the green shoots push like daggers through the soil. Family members indulge me, respect what I choose to do, and applaud the results.

I can mix and match the colors—yellow, crimson, peach, scarlet-fringed white, pink. The bees pollinate as they wish, while I have my own cross-pollinating schemes. Maybe there's a bit of the Watchmaker in me after all . . . but I let the bees make their own hives wherever they like, and harvesting the wild honey is like a treasure hunt for gold. A life without risk is a life without *life*. The Anarchist wasn't wrong about everything.

In Crown City—safely far away—the Watchmaker maintains his Stability, believing he is doing the best for his people. I don't know what ever became of the Anarchist; perhaps his inner pools of poison ate his heart away. Maybe he died in an ill-conceived explosion. Maybe he came to his senses. Or maybe he still fights the Watchmaker in a constant tug of war between chaos and order. The pendulum swings.

I don't think about it anymore; I have my garden to tend. I have to finish writing my own story, and I turn the page. I measure my life differently.

As the gladiolas grow in their rows, I see the colorful spikes of flowers anxious to show off their blossoms to the world. They reach for the sky, but remain anchored to the ground . . . as a good dreamer should be. I cut several of the most appealing stalks and head back toward the house. It'll make a beautiful bouquet for the dinner table.

Across our sprawling family estate, which I purchased using the accidental bounty of jewels from the Wreckers' scoutship, rows of colorful practice pavilions have been set up in the bright day. At the game booths, carnies are adding a touch-up of paint, getting ready for the season. With a thump and a puff of colored smoke, another explosion comes from Tomio's cottage—but it is a small, not-unusual explosion, so nobody pays much attention.

Our sons and daughters are practicing their team moves on the trapeze, a much more complex and breathtaking act than when Francesca performed alone. Laughing, they move together like clockwork gears, but they improvise as well. *Goofing off.* Some of the grandchildren are being trained to participate in the act, but for them, it's mostly just play. Other than nurturing and protecting them, the greatest reward we can give is to let them be children. When it comes time, they can choose what they want to do.

My Francesca is still beautiful, although she insists she's no longer limber enough to perform her high-wire and trapeze act. She has happily turned over those responsibilities to our oldest daughter, who is now training our granddaughter, Keziah. The young woman springs up on the rope, preparing for a complicated, dangerous, joyous trick. Knowing that we are all watching her, she performs with such grace under pressure that my heart skips a beat. Leaping high, Keziah spins a somersault in the air then pulls the cord, and her spring-loaded angel wings pop out. She glides to the ground and stumbles in an awkward landing. But this is just practice, just *play*, and we applaud anyway.

With a flourish (and a twinge in my back), I offer the beautiful gladiolas to my beloved Francesca, and she turns to smile at me. I find it unsettling that she has applied the extravagant handlebar mustache, just to get into character. The black jacket fits her nicely, but she will have to tie down her breasts to hide them once the carnival heads off again on its route. To me, the saddest part is that, upon assuming the role of César Magnusson after her mother retired, Francesca had to chop off her beautiful black locks. Nothing could diminish her beauty in my eyes, not even a mustache, but when I see her face I can't believe that her striking femininity isn't obvious to everyone else, despite the close-cropped hair. Most people take comfort in their illusions and they see what they want to see.

Keziah bounds toward the trapeze pole, ready to try again, although she has trouble latching down the springs on her mechanical angel wings. Her cousins giggle at her contortions.

"Are you sure they've practiced enough?" I ask.

"Carnival season starts in a week, so they've practiced enough,"

Francesca says. "We have to keep to a schedule, at least for some part of the year."

In two days, the carnival caravan will leave our estate, far up the coast, and spend the season performing for village after village, ultimately reaching Crown City. They'll play to large crowds, even in Chronos Square before the Clockwork Angels. They enjoy living in the limelight.

But I never liked to be the center of attention—the part I enjoyed most was being among the carnies. During the years I traveled with the Magnusson Extravaganza, I made a point of returning to Barrel Arbor so I could visit my father, while he was still alive. He was lonely but had fallen into a comfortable routine without me. At first, he was confused that I didn't intend to stay, but he shrugged and accepted. "It's not ours to understand."

Lavinia found someone else, married, had a family, had a life that fit her definition of happiness. I didn't notice her in the crowds at any of our Barrel Arbor shows, but I never imagined her as a lover of carnivals. I wonder if she even remembered me.

This season, I've decided to stay home on the quiet estate. Time to retire. With a few months of solitude, like my time out in the Seven Cities of Gold, I am going to write my book and relive all the journeys of that great adventure. Each moment is its own memory. If I don't write it, no one will.

The seasons pass, I get older, and the hours tick away. I never did replace the pocketwatch that was stolen from me in Poseidon City. I never felt I needed one again. Here, the days are bright, and the nights are dark.

Francesca takes the bouquet of gladiolas, gives me a kiss—which tickles because of the false mustache—and I return to the garden, where a large and beautiful sundial tells me everything I need to know about time, and this garden has taught me all I needed to know about measuring my life. The shadow of the gnomon slowly tracks across the face of the sundial, letting me know that it is always *now*.

Engraved on the stone pedestal is a verse I have taken to heart, something I heard in my own adventures:

The sun comes up, the sun goes down.
Then there's all the time in between.
Hope is what remains to be seen.

Before the ancient clockwork fortune teller wound down for the last time, she told me, "Measure your life not by schedules or riches. The treasure of a life is a measure of love and respect."

Love and respect, love and respect—I have been carrying those words around with me for years. Some people want fabulous wealth, some want great power, some (like me) wanted amazing adventures and to see the wonders of the universe. Some, like the Watchmaker and the Anarchist, want to change the world (though in opposite ways).

But if you scrape away the gold paint, the ornate façade, or just the covering of dirt, everybody wants to be loved and respected. And neither is any good without the other. Love without respect can be as cold as pity; respect without love can be as grim as fear.

It took me a long time to understand, but fortunately through blind luck, and years, and my wonderful family and friends, I realized that love and respect are the greatest gifts we can receive, the greatest legacy we can leave behind. It's an elegy we'd like to hear with our own ears, "You were loved and respected."

If even one person could say that about me, I'd consider it a worthy achievement. If I can multiply that many times—by living each day with the kind of integrity and generosity that earns respect and love—that is true success, by my definition, at least. The measure of a life.

I think of what I've done. I think of my friends, my family, the satisfaction of the carnival and the sheer small pleasure of my garden. "Are you content?" the fortune teller had once asked me.

"Are you happy with what you did, what you are doing, and what you are going to do?"

A complex question and too weighty for a young boy from Barrel Arbor to answer properly. But after traveling, observing, living, and learning, I know that I can boil the answer down to one word.

Yes.

I look around me at the rows of exuberant gladiolas, the haphazard green beans, tomatoes, and corn, even the dozen apple trees I have made into my own new orchard. I planted my seeds, nourished them with my optimism, and tended my garden. I'll harvest what I deserve, and all is for the best.

It is a fine garden.

CLOCKWORK ANGELS

THE ALBUM

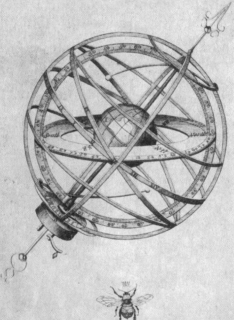

In a world lit only by fire
Long train of flares under piercing stars
I stand watching the steamliners roll by

The caravan thunders onward
To the distant dream of the city
The caravan carries me onward
On my way at last
On my way at last

I can't stop thinking big
I can't stop thinking big

On a road lit only by fire
Going where I want, instead of where I should
I peer out at the passing shadows
Carried through the night into the city
Where a young man has a chance of making good
A chance to break from the past
The caravan thunders onward
Stars winking through the canvas hood
On my way at last

In a world where I feel so small
I can't stop thinking big

I was brought up to believe
The universe has a plan
We are only human
It's not ours to understand

The universe has a plan
All is for the best
Some will be rewarded
And the devil take the rest

All is for the best
Believe in what we're told
Blind men in the market
Buying what we're sold
Believe in what we're told
Until our final breath
While our loving Watchmaker
Loves us all to death

In a world of cut and thrust
I was always taught to trust
In a world where all must fail
Heaven's justice will prevail

The joy and pain that we receive
Each comes with its own cost
The price of what we're winning
Is the same as what we've lost

Until our final breath
The joy and pain that we receive
Must be what we deserve
I was brought up to believe

High above the city square
Globes of light float in mid-air
Higher still, against the night
Clockwork angels bathed in light

You promise every treasure, to the foolish and the wise
Goddesses of mystery, spirits in disguise
Every pleasure, we bow and close our eyes
Clockwork angels, promise every prize

Clockwork angels, spread their arms and sing
Synchronized and graceful, they move like living things
Goddesses of Light, of Sea and Sky and Land
Clockwork angels, the people raise their hands—As if to fly

All around the city square
Power shimmers in the air
People gazing up with love
To those angels high above

Celestial machinery—move through your commands
Goddesses of mystery, so delicate and so grand
Moved to worship, we bow and close our eyes
Clockwork angels, promise every prize

"Lean not upon your own understanding*
Ignorance is well and truly blessed
Trust in perfect love, and perfect planning
Everything will turn out for the best"

Stars aglow like scattered sparks
Span the sky in clockwork arcs
Hint at more than we can see
Spiritual machinery

* Proverbs 3:5 [and In-N-Out milkshake!]

"What do you lack?"

IV › THE ANARCHIST

Will there be world enough and time for me to sing that song?
A voice so silent for so long
For all those years I had to get along, they told me I was wrong
I never wanted to belong—I was so strong

I lack their smiles and their diamonds; I lack their happiness and love
I envy them for all those things, I never got my fair share of

The lenses inside of me that paint the world black
The pools of poison, the scarlet mist, that spill over into rage
The things I've always been denied
An early promise that somehow died
A missing part of me that grows around me like a cage

In all your science of the mind, seeking blind through flesh and bone
Find the blood inside this stone
What I know, I've never shown; what I feel, I've always known
I plan my vengeance on my own—and I was always alone

Oh—They tried to get me
Oh—They'll never forget me

Under the gaze of the angels
A spectacle like he's never seen
Spinning lights and faces
Demon music and gypsy queens

The glint of iron wheels
Bodies spin in a clockwork dance
The smell of flint and steel
A wheel of fate, a game of chance

How I prayed just to get away
To carry me anywhere
Sometimes the angels punish us
By answering our prayers

A face of naked evil
Turns the young boy's blood to ice
Deadly confrontation
Such a dangerous device

Shout to warn the crowd
Accusations ringing loud
A ticking box, in the hand of the innocent
The angry crowd moves toward him with bad intent

What did I see?
Fool that I was
A goddess, with wings on her heels
All my illusions
Projected on her
The ideal, that I wanted to see

What did I know?
Fool that I was
Little by little, I learned
My friends were dismayed
To see me betrayed
But they knew they could never tell me

What did I care?
Fool that I was
Little by little, I burned
Maybe sometimes
There might be a flaw
But how pretty the picture was back then

What did I do?
Fool that I was
To profit from youthful mistakes?
It's shameful to tell
How often I fell
In love with illusions again

So shameful to tell
Just how often I fell
In love with illusions again

A goddess with wings on her heels . . .

A man can lose his past, in a country like this
Wandering aimless
Parched and nameless
A man could lose his way, in a country like this
Canyons and cactus
Endless and trackless
Searching through a grim eternity
Sculptured by a prehistoric sea

Seven Cities of Gold
Stories that fired my imagination
Seven Cities of Gold
A splendid mirage in this desolation
Seven Cities of Gold
Glowing in my dreams, like hallucinations
Glitter in the sun like a revelation
Distant as a comet or a constellation

A man can lose himself, in a country like this
Rewrite the story
Recapture the glory
A man could lose his life, in a country like this
Sunblind and friendless
Frozen and endless

The nights grow longer, the farther I go
Wake to aching cold, and a deep Sahara of snow

That gleam in the distance could be heaven's gate
A long-awaited treasure at the end of my cruel fate

The breakers roar on an unseen shore
In the teeth of a hurricane
We struggle in vain
A hellish night—a ghostly light
Appears through the driving rain
Salvation in a human chain

All I know is that sometimes you have to be wary
Of a miracle too good to be true
All I know is that sometimes the truth is contrary
Everything in life you thought you knew
All I know is that sometimes you have to be wary
'Cause sometimes the target is you

Driven aground, with that awful sound
Drowned by the cheer from ashore
We wonder what for
The people swarm through the darkling storm
Gather everything they can score
'Til their backs won't bear any more

The breakers roar on an unseen shore
In the teeth of an icy grave
The human chain leaves a bloody stain
Washed away in the pounding waves

All I know is that memory can be too much to carry
Striking down like a bolt from the blue

All the journeys
Of this great adventure
It didn't always feel that way
I wouldn't trade them
Because I made them
The best I could
And that's enough to say

Some days were dark
I wish that I could live it all again
Some nights were bright
I wish that I could live it all again

All the highlights of that headlong flight
Holding on with all my might
To what I felt back then
I wish that I could live it all again

I have stoked the fire on the big steel wheels
Steered the airships right across the stars
I learned to fight, I learned to love and learned to feel
Oh, I wish that I could live it all again

All the treasures
The gold and glory
It didn't always feel that way
I don't regret it
I never forget it
I wouldn't trade tomorrow for today

I learned to fight and learned to love and learned to steal
I wish that I could live it all again

"What do you lack?"

X ⟜ BU2B2

I was brought up to believe
Belief has failed me now
The bright glow of optimism
Abandoned me somehow.

Belief has failed me now
Life goes from bad to worse
No philosophy consoles me
In a clockwork universe

Life goes from bad to worse
I still choose to live
Find a measure of love and laughter
And another measure to give

I still choose to live
And give, even while I grieve
Though the balance tilts against me
I was brought up to believe

All that you can do is wish them well
All that you can do is wish them well

Spirits turned bitter by the poison of envy
Always angry and dissatisfied
Even the lost ones, the frightened and mean ones
Even the ones with a devil inside

Thank your stars you're not that way
Turn your back and walk away
Don't even pause and ask them why
Turn around and say goodbye

People who judge without a measure of mercy
All the victims who will never learn
Even the lost ones, you can only give up on
Even the ones who make you burn

The ones who've done you wrong
The ones who pretended to be so strong
The grudges you've held for so long
It's not worth singing that same sad song

Even though you're going through hell
Just keep on going
Let the demons dwell

Just wish them well

In this one of many possible worlds, all for the best, or some
    bizarre test?
It is what it is—and whatever
Time is still the infinite jest

The arrow flies when you dream, the hours tick away—the cells
    tick away
The Watchmaker keeps to his schemes
The hours tick away—they tick away

The measure of a life is a measure of love and respect
So hard to earn, so easily burned
In the fullness of time
A garden to nurture and protect

In the rise and the set of the sun
'Til the stars go spinning—spinning 'round the night
It is what it is—and forever
Each moment a memory in flight

The arrow flies while you breathe, the hours tick away—the cells
    tick away
The Watchmaker has time up his sleeve
The hours tick away—they tick away

The treasure of a life is a measure of love and respect
The way you live, the gifts that you give
In the fullness of time
It's the only return that you expect

The future disappears into memory
With only a moment between
Forever dwells in that moment
Hope is what remains to be seen

AFTERWORD

by Neil Peart

H ere is a photograph I took of Kevin on the day he and I began
seriously discussing the novelization of *Clockwork Angels*. It
was August 17, 2010, and the setting was Mount Evans, Colorado.
At 14,265 feet, Mount Evans is one of Colorado's "fourteeners"—
summits higher than 14,000 feet. Kevin lives in Colorado, and has
climbed all fifty-four fourteeners, often with a recorder in his
hand—while he hikes, he dictates chapters for upcoming novels.
At that time I was on tour with Rush, with a day off between two
shows at Red Rocks near Denver, so Kevin invited me to join him
on one of the "tamer" fourteeners.

For something like twenty years, Kevin and I had discussed working on a project together that would marry music, lyrics, and prose fiction. The right idea and timing eluded us for a long time, but at last, both converged perfectly. It is as though that occasion had to wait until both of us were truly *ready*, as mature artists and—perhaps—as mature human beings, too.

I had started working on the lyrics in late 2009, and in early 2010 the band recorded the first two songs for the album, "Caravan" and "BU2B." Several of the others were written by then, and I had the lyrics fairly well mapped out. I described to Kevin the basic skeleton of the plot and characters, and he had many wonderful ideas for expanding both. Kevin has unparalleled world-building and story-building skills, and he brought both fully to bear on this project. We started "framing" this alternate world, building its foundation, its infrastructure. We had to reinforce and develop my sketchy ideas on how alchemy might fit into the steampunk scenario—"the future as seen from the past," from, say, the late nineteenth century, as imagined by Jules Verne and H.G. Wells. What came to be known as the steampunk genre was partly pioneered by Kevin in his early fantasy writings—when, as he says, "We didn't know there was a 'thing' to be part of."

Steampunk is also sometimes described as "the future as it *ought* to have been," for it often portrays a romantic and even utopian "alternative future." I wanted that quality in this world—for it not to be a dystopia—and I believe that despite the Watchmaker's oppressive rule, Albion is rather a *nice* place. And who wouldn't want to visit Crown City and see the Clockwork Angels? (And breathe that heady colored smoke?)

On the story-building side, right away Kevin recognized the basic symbolic themes of the Watchmaker and the Anarchist—extreme order versus extreme freedom—which I had not consciously noted. Together we developed their characters and interactions, bridging my necessarily "brisk" plot points in the songs with connective

tissue and richer details. Over
the next eighteen months, we
continued to share ideas and
suggestions—sometimes many
times a day, and each of our
"flights" would spark the other.

As my thirty-eight years with
Rush will attest, I very much
enjoy collaboration with like-
minded artists. Working up this
story with Kevin was one of the
easiest, yet most satisfying projects I have ever shared—easiest,
because we almost always simply agreed with each other's additions
to the story, and most satisfying because I am so proud of the result.

The same applies to the contributions by Hugh Syme, whose
art has glorified every piece of work bearing the band's name, or
my name, since 1975. From the very conception of the *Clockwork
Angels* story, Hugh shared the "vision," and between us we developed the wonderful illustrations he created, and which enrich this
story so much. As always, if I could imagine it, he could picture it.

Voltaire's *Candide* (1759) was an early model for the story arc: a
philosophical satire about a naïve, optimistic youth whose upbring-
ing ("I was brought up to believe") does not prepare him for the
harrowing adventures that bring him to grief, disillusionment, and
despair. Finally, Candide finds peace and wisdom on a farm near
Constantinople, working in his garden.

First reading *Candide* in my twenties, I was amazed to discover that Voltaire was a philosopher with a sense of humor—the
only one I know of even now, apart from Nietzsche (occasionally). Right from the beginning of *Candide*, the tale is woven with
a needle of irony dipped in acid—sometimes only just keeping
its clever head above sarcasm—and within a couple of pages you

encounter a laugh-out-loud farcical scene being observed, where the "sage Dr. Pangloss" is in the woods, "giving a lecture in experimental philosophy" to a chambermaid, "a little brown wench, very pretty and very tractable."

Voltaire's story about Candide was delivered with a light-hearted, impish wit that, three centuries later, would inform John Barth's picaresque play on the story, *The Sot-Weed Factor*—another little influence on the plot for *Clockwork Angels*.

The character of the Anarchist, perhaps a classic "screen villain," was partly inspired by Joseph Conrad's *The Secret Agent*, and by a character in Michael Ondaatje's *In the Skin of a Lion*—two very different takes on anarchists, who can be either idealists who believe that humans don't need leaders, or brutish, murderous sociopaths. (Obviously those polarities resonate in our own timeline.) The carnival setting is drawn from Robertson Davies's *World of Wonders* and the fine Beat-era novel by Herbert Gold, *The Man Who Was Not With It*.

The fascinating history of Spanish exploration in what is now the American Southwest was largely driven by an enduring legend of the Seven Cities of Gold. The setting was irresistible to me, and to Kevin, because we have both traveled widely, on wheels and on foot, in the Western deserts of Utah, Arizona, New Mexico, and California. (Though I was not dictating books along the way.) Echoes are plain in the arches and other redrock formations of Southern Utah, the "Island in the Sky" in Canyonlands National Park, Acoma "Sky City" and the abandoned pueblos in New Mexico.

In contrast, the idea for the Wreckers came from another "Far West"—Cornwall, in England—drawn from some of Daphne du Maurier's stories of that region, both fictional and historical. Years ago I read *Jamaica Inn* and others set in the eighteenth and nineteenth centuries in that part of the world, and was appalled to think that people not only plundered wrecked ships without a care for rescuing survivors, but were so cold-blooded as to lure them to their dooms with false lights.

Two songs that were late additions to the album, "Halo Effect" and "Headlong Flight," had their own stories. During our hike up Mount Evans, Kevin and I also talked about our own youths, and the kind of naïve illusions that had colored our histories. That became "Halo Effect." In late 2011, my longtime friend and drum teacher, Freddie Gruber, passed away at age eighty-four. Near the end, he would rally briefly and entertain his friends and students gathered around with tales from his adventurous life—Manhattan in the forties, Vegas in the fifties, Los Angeles in the sixties and seventies and up to that day. Then he would shake his head and say, "I had quite a ride. I wish I could do it all again."

I felt inspired to echo that lament in the song "Headlong Flight"—although I had never felt that way myself. To the contrary, as much as I appreciate and enjoy my life now, I remain glad I don't have to do it all again.

That dichotomy is reflected in the ending of *Candide*. Dr. Pangloss continues to hold forth with his Spinoza-based "all is for the best in this best of all possible worlds," which Voltaire has been gleefully skewering throughout the novel. (I felt the same about Schopenhauer's evil pronouncement that informs what Owen Hardy was "brought up to believe": "Whatever happens to us must be what we deserve, for it could not happen if we did not deserve it." *Outrageous!*)

In the final scene of *Candide*, the title character displays his impatience with philosophy and reveals the pragmatic wisdom he has attained. "Pangloss sometimes would say to Candide, 'All events are linked together in the best of all possible worlds; for, after all, had you not been kicked out of a magnificent castle for love of Miss Cunégonde, had you not been put into the Inquisition, had you not traveled across America on foot, had you not stabbed the Baron with your sword, had you not lost all your sheep from the fine country of El Dorado, then you wouldn't be here eating preserved citrons and pistachio nuts.'

'Excellently observed,' answered Candide; 'but we must cultivate our garden.'"

Kevin and I had great fun coming up with names for the places and characters. Watchmaking components gave us Barrel Arbor, the Winding Pinion River, Crown City and its circular boulevards (Crown Wheel, Balance Wheel, and Center Wheel), and the Regulators. Albion is an ancient name for England, while Poseidon was the legendary capital of Atlantis. Cíbola was one of the Spanish names for the Seven Cities.

In 1527, a Spanish expedition of 600 men set out from present-day Florida to occupy the New World. In a land without maps, they were immediately lost, and the force was steadily depleted by starvation, thirst, disease, exposure, a hurricane, and being enslaved by the natives (ironic foreshadowing). The expedition's treasurer was Álvar Núñez Cabeza de Vaca (meaning "cow's head," it actually was a noble entitlement, not an insult), and he ended up as the leader of only four survivors who made it to Mexico City, after many harrowing adventures. Another unlikely survivor was an African slave, Esteban, and he and Cabeza de Vaca were the first to spread tales of the Seven

Cities of Gold. Their stories would lure many another adventurer.

The Anarchist's stage name among the carnies, "D'Angelo Misterioso," was modeled after a bit of rock trivia: George Harrison's contractually necessary pseudonym on the Cream song "Badge," which he co-wrote and played guitar on, was "L'Angelo Misterioso."

At first Kevin and I were building the story around a character referred to only as "Our Hero," but we needed a real name—so I suggested we use those initials: Owen Hardy. (Owen from one of my daughter Olivia's picture books, and Hardy because the village of Barrel Arbor has a Thomas Hardy air of bucolic quaintness.)

Kevin wanted Owen's first love to have a kind of "vanilla" flavor, so I suggested the near anagram of Lavinia. With the omnipotence of the world-builder, I was determined to make this society entirely mixed in racial characteristics, from skin colors to names, so together Kevin and I made her family the Paquettes (a fallen woman in *Candide* is named Pacquette), and introduced Oliveira, Huang, Tomio, Francesca, Guerrero (Spanish for "warrior"), and so on. Owen's mother is named Hanneke Lakota, which, like his brown skin, suggests that he might have Native American blood.

Kevin also had fun weaving in many references to Rush lyrics, and though they will not disrupt the reading experience for those who don't get them, they may entertain those who do. (Perhaps one day we'll have a contest to see how many of them people can find.)

All of those details built up over several drafts, with special attention brought to specific scenes in between. And still notes were exchanged in rapid-fire volleys. Kevin writes extraordinarily fast, often working on a few projects at the same time, but he is able to bring complete focus to any story because while he writes it, he *lives* it. Sometimes, while he was hiding away in a cabin in the Colorado mountains and working on the story, he would end a note with something like, "Now I have to go do terrible things to Owen in Poseidon City."

In mid-May 2012, Kevin sent me what we considered to be the final draft of *Clockwork Angels: The Novel*. I had the typescript printed and bound, and took it with me to a cabin among the redwoods in Big Sur. Sunlight filtered down through the big trees, Steller's jays visited my porch railing, the Big Sur River murmured in its rocky bed, and woodsmoke from the neighboring campground perfumed the air.

What a delight it was to read our story that way, freshly immersed in it after several somewhat scattershot previous readings, and truly *feeling* it—Anton Hardy's sorrow over his lost wife, and Owen's attempts to find his way—find *himself*—through the tribulations that mold him into a strong and righteous man. In response to suggestions from his sharp-eyed editor (and wife) Rebecca Moesta, a few trusted "test readers," and myself, Kevin had added many little touches of detail and humor—like the antics of the three clowns imitating their fellow carnies. (No prizes for guessing who those three characters are modeled after!) He also further developed some of his marvelous "inventions," like the clockwork Orrery, the "Imaginarium," and the Destiny Calculator, that I already considered astonishing, while weaving additional splendid details into scenes like the performance of the Clockwork Angels.

After finishing that final read, and pouring myself a celebratory beverage to toast the big trees, the jays, the river, and the book, I wrote to Kevin:

"Bleary-eyed, but triumphant, I have just finished a pleasurable day of lying around my cabin in the redwoods and reading the book. Though I had been facing the task as something of a 'duty,' it turned out to be a very pleasurable experience."

After a bit of "technical talk" about various details and improvements, I concluded:

"The entire end section, from the Wreckers out, felt like an emotional climax, not just a dramatic one.

"I am so glad we made this happen."

ACKNOWLEDGMENTS

Many people helped us create this story, the world, the characters, and the words that convey it all.

Special thanks go to Geddy Lee, Alex Lifeson, Hugh Syme, Pegi Cecconi, Bob Farmer; Rebecca Moesta, Louis Moesta, Deb Ray, Steven Savile; Jennifer Knoch, Jack David, David Caron, Erin Creasey, Sarah Dunn, and Crissy Boylan at ECW; and John Grace at Brilliance Audio.